# A Piece of Paradise

Other books in the
**Randy Lassiter & Leslie Carlisle Mystery Series**

*An Undercurrent of Murder*

*A Nasty Way to Die*

# A Piece of Paradise

A Randy Lassiter & Leslie Carlisle Mystery

Joe David Rice

Copyright © 2022 by Joe David Rice.

All rights reserved. No part of this book may be reproduced in any form, except for brief passages quoted within reviews, without the express written consent of the author:

> Joe David Rice
> joedavidrice@yahoo.com

The characters and events portrayed in this book are fictitious. Any similarity to real persons, living or dead, is coincidental and not intended by the author.

Grateful acknowledgement is made to The Pennsylvania State University Press for permission to publish excerpts from Ivelaw Lloyd Griffith's *Drugs and Security in the Caribbean: Sovereignty Under Siege.* Copyright 1997 by The Pennsylvania State University Press.

ISBN (paperback): 978-1-7362391-4-8
ISBN (ebook): 978-1-7362391-5-5

Cover and book design: H. K. Stewart

Printed in the United States of America

This book is printed on archival-quality paper that meets requirements of the American National Standard for Information Sciences, Permanence of Paper, Printed Library Materials, ANSI Z39.48-1984.

To my sister **Robbi Rice Dietrich**
for her love, support, and encouragement

# ~ ONE ~

All ten toes were in heaven. I'd never felt finer, softer sand in my life.

"Those palms will be perfect." Leslie, my bride of two weeks, pointed up the empty beach to a small grove she'd discovered the previous afternoon. Nestled between the surf and the long, steep dune that paralleled the shore, the tall, stately trees looked like a picture-perfect oasis.

"I still think we're an hour early."

She wrapped a tanned arm around my waist and pulled me close. "I suspect we can put any extra time to good use."

It was about 6:15 in the morning. I'm not normally very active at such an absurd hour, but I'm not normally honeymooning on Eleuthera. Months ago, my fiancée had suggested we combine our wedding holiday with her assignment from *Southern Living* to photograph the Out Islands of the Bahamas. Of course, she had failed to mention the obligatory sunrise shot as we planned the trip. Or that I'd often be toting 30 pounds of camera gear as we went from one scenic location to the next.

We'd met a year earlier when another photography job for the magazine had sent her deep into the Ozark Mountains of north-central Arkansas to capture the fall foliage. I'd been on a multi-day backpacking trip with my annoying brother-in-law, and we'd encountered the lovely Ms. Carlisle on a remote wilderness trail along the Buffalo National River. Our chance meeting soon evolved into something very special.

As we neared the palms, Leslie steered me away from the water's edge. "Can't have any footprints in this photograph." She stood on her tiptoes and kissed my cheek. "Once I get the shot, we'll frolic on the beach to your heart's content."

When we arrived at the cluster of trees, I leaned her camera bag against one of the rough, towering trunks and extended the legs of the tripod and locked them in position, more or less accomplishing my unspecified duties as a photographer's assistant. Leslie spent a quarter of an hour moving from spot to spot, visualizing her options. During our time on the islands, I'd often taken secret pleasure in watching her work, always captivated by her creativity and enthusiasm.

"This is the place," she eventually pronounced, standing behind two of the graceful palms. "If the clouds will cooperate."

While she situated the tripod and searched through her gear for the proper lens, I stared at the relentless surf, realizing the only thing between Africa and me was 4,000 miles of open Atlantic. One after another, the waves broke over the reef, then swept up the shore before sinking into the spongy pink grains of the deserted beach. We were a long way from Little Rock.

"Come here, Randy." Leslie reached for my hand. "Tell me what you think."

I crouched behind her tripod and peered through the viewfinder. She'd arranged her top-of-the-line Nikon for a vertical shot, using the broad fronds and curving trunks of the palms to frame the composition. A lone coconut lay on its side in the untrammeled sand, halfway to the surf. All she needed was for the sun to lift behind a promising bank of low clouds on the eastern horizon.

"You've done your part," I said. "If Mother Nature helps out, this has potential for a cover shot." If she didn't get the photograph today, we'd try again tomorrow. Or the next day.

I stepped back from her camera and plopped against the base of the dune, wriggling into the cool sand. Leslie did the same, draping an arm across my bare chest. She nibbled on my ear and tousled my hair.

"This isn't such bad duty, is it?" She leaned in for a kiss.

Before our lips met, an airplane screamed overhead, missing the top branches of the palms by mere feet. Something crashed through the limbs and slammed into the ground near Leslie's camera bag as the roaring plane dropped even closer to shore, skimming over the beach.

"Good God!" Leslie bolted upright. "What's going on?"

We watched, spellbound, as package after package tumbled to earth before the twin-engine aircraft, its lights off, lifted and banked out of sight within seconds.

My pulse was still racing when two figures appeared less than 100 yards down the shore. Dashing through the sand, they each bent and lifted one of the bundles before darting back into the brush. In the dim morning light, I couldn't discern what they'd retrieved. But I felt sure the long, slender silhouettes hanging from their torsos weren't walking sticks.

"This doesn't look good," I whispered, feeling the hair rise on my neck. "Keep still. When I move, come with me. We'll have to be quick."

In moments, the pair reappeared and hauled away another load. As they vanished, I leaped to my feet and grabbed the camera bag and tripod. Leslie followed and collapsed beside me in the jumbled shadows of the grove. The men returned to the beach. Jogging through the thick sand, they stopped 50 yards away and each recovered a bag resembling an undersized pillow. They headed away from us at a trot.

"We've got to hide." I shoved the tripod into Leslie's hands. "This dune is our best chance."

I clambered up the steep ridge of sand with the camera bag while Leslie scrambled after me. She took cover behind an ancient agave and I fell in place at her back, every nerve on edge. I peeked through the sharp, fleshy leaves. The men came into view once more and made a beeline for our grove. Stopping a few yards short of the palms, they again collected a pair of the mysterious packages, dashed down the beach, and soon turned and vanished into the undergrowth.

9

My green trunks and Leslie's khaki shorts blended in with the foliage, but her neon yellow bikini top might as well have been a beacon. Or maybe twin beacons. She must have reached the same conclusion; she slipped it off and stuffed it into her camera bag.

"Are we in the middle of a drug drop?" Leslie asked with a whisper.

"That's my guess. Let's pray they don't see us."

"I thought Jonah said the island is crime-free."

"Maybe he's never been on the beach at sunrise."

Moments later the pair reappeared. Heads down and advancing one stride at a time, they searched the sandy beach, drawing closer with every step.

They were near enough now that I feared they could hear the pounding of my heart. One of them kicked at the coconut Leslie had planned to include in her photo, muttering, "Goddamn it, mon, there was supposed to be another."

His partner changed course and studied the waves as they broke along the shore. "Most likely landed in the water," he said. "No use wasting our time there."

Tall, handsome and looking to be in their mid-twenties, they had the delightful accent of the locals. Somehow, the shotguns hanging from their shoulders ruined the effect.

The one nearest the surf glanced at his watch. "Time to haul ass, mon. Derek's expecting us."

"Let me check under these trees."

The second young man strode through the palms, pausing as he passed not 20 feet below us. A sweaty white undershirt and red, low-riding shorts did little to conceal a muscular build. My eyes were drawn to a stylish gold medallion swinging from his neck, its heavy chain gleaming against his ebony skin. But a faded New York Yankees baseball cap kept his face in the shadows.

Leslie's grip on my knee tightened. She must have noticed the same thing that I'd seen. Our footprints seemed to be everywhere—and they led up the dune to an agave that now struck me as entirely inadequate for a hideout. But he wasn't hunting for tracks. His gaze lingered across the sand for what felt like minutes before he turned and joined his accomplice. "Okay," he said. "Let's go."

The men hurried away and were soon out of sight. Leslie sighed and then nudged me with her elbow. "Look what we missed." She stared to the east.

A tropical aurora borealis hung on the horizon, painting the sky with a kaleidoscope of colors.

"Now there's a money shot if I've ever seen one."

# ~ TWO ~

We had arrived on Eleuthera at noon on Monday, November 3. Leslie had discovered and reserved our beach house over the internet, dealing with its owner, a retired Miami policeman who'd bought his own piece of paradise. Scores of vacation properties were available online, and Leslie had spent hours sorting through the lodging options. She rented our cottage, named Barracuda Bay, following an exchange of e-mails.

"The rates are reasonable, the place is on an isolated beach located in the middle of the island, and the reviews are superb," she'd told me weeks earlier after completing the arrangements. "Plus, he has a sense of humor and he replies promptly—and his messages aren't full of typos." My bride is a stickler for accuracy.

We met the proprietor and her punctual penpal, Jonah Jefferson, after landing at the Governor's Harbor Airport. Eleuthera was the third and final stop on our Bahamian tour. We'd spent the two previous weeks on Andros and Cat Island. Serving as my wife's assistant was a welcome change of pace from my usual job of running Lassiter & Associates, an up-and-coming advertising agency in Little Rock. No clients to coddle. No deadlines to meet. No pitches to make. No personnel matters to mediate. And, as Leslie had reminded me on more than one occasion, the perks weren't bad either.

She had chartered a private plane for the quick flight from Cat Island to Eleuthera. Occupying an uncomfortable rear seat, I'd been staring over the wing, transfixed by the indescribable hues of the waters, when our pilot pointed toward the shore.

"Want to see a local curiosity?" he shouted over the roar of the engine.

Leslie, who'd pulled rank and claimed the co-pilot's chair, nodded and then removed her camera from a bag. The plane dipped sharply before leveling off at about 500 feet. In less than a minute the pilot banked hard to the right, almost standing the aircraft on its wingtip.

"There's a reminder of the wild days," he said.

Directly below, resting on the sunken sands between a pair of enormous coral heads, was what appeared to be the skeletal remains of a DC-3. Leslie aimed her camera and the motor drive fired a burst of shots as waves washed over the rusting tip of the plane's tail.

"It crashed in the mid '90s," our guide said. "The smugglers got away, but left a planeload of a certain prohibited product from South America. Nowadays, snorkelers and divers love the wreck."

As we neared Governor's Harbor, Leslie replaced the memory card in her camera. So far, she'd filled half a dozen, collecting hundreds of images of wild orchids, smiling kids, hand-built monasteries, pristine beaches, and piles of conch shells. But she still hadn't captured the perfect sunrise.

\* \* \*

"You won't have any trouble recognizing me," Jonah had written Leslie. "I'll be the bald white guy."

Fifty or so people milled about in the crowded terminal at the Governor's Harbor Airport. About half were locals, dark-skinned descendants of nineteenth-century slaves. Loud, sunburned tourists made up most of the rest. Several sported Club Med caps or shirts, and three or four of the young women wore their hair in dreadlocks. The place sounded like a mini-UN with French, German, Spanish, and English conversations surrounding me. Strange, I thought. Everybody here has an accent but us.

Jonah was right about the head, but his skin hadn't been white in years. It was about as dark and leathery as a football. Piercing blue eyes squinted from beneath his animated, bushy eyebrows. Dressed for comfort, he wore a pair of scruffy leather sandals, black gym shorts, and a matching tank top. A shade less than six feet, he had the grip and body of a serious weightlifter.

"Welcome to Eleuthera!"

After a quick round of introductions, Jonah grabbed most of our bags with one hand and led us to the beet red Jeep Wrangler included in the package deal. The top lowered, it looked like a perfect vehicle for the balmy November weather.

"My house is near your cottage," he said, sliding into the driver's seat. "I'll leave the vehicle with you and walk home once we get there."

After covering his bald pate with a Miami Dolphins cap, he drove us a few miles in the direction of Governor's Harbor before turning east at a small but handsome sign: Barracuda Bay – Private Drive. We bounced down a potholed and unpaved road before topping a short rise. "There's your home for the next week." He pointed to an attractive enough bungalow to the right.

But our eyes skipped to the pink crescent-shaped beach and beyond that to the Atlantic's cerulean blue water spotted with reefs. The scene was postcard perfect, as if it'd been arranged by the Bahamas Tourist Bureau.

When we parked at the base of the porch, Leslie stepped from the Jeep and turned to face the water. "Jonah," she said, "your website's photo gallery doesn't do this place justice."

"Maybe you can help me with it," he said with a wink. He carried an armload of luggage from the Jeep and placed it on the porch. "I live 200 yards to the south," he said and pointed to a narrow track running in front of the cottage. "If you'd like, come by about six for cocktails."

"That sounds great." Leslie answered for us. "We'll see you then."

"My little soirées are always real informal. I'll be in my trunks." Jonah gave us a casual salute and began the short hike to his home.

We spent our first afternoon in the community of Governor's Harbor, eating a late lunch of conch fritters before wandering along the quiet streets for a couple of hours. Leslie took notes of places she'd like to photograph. The two-story government Administration Building, pink as a flamingo, made the list as did the harbor itself, especially once she learned that the weekly mail boat would arrive the next day. We bought an island map, groceries, beverages, and other supplies before returning for our first trip to the empty beach in front of our cottage. After an hour of playing in the waves, we dressed and walked to Jonah's house, a modern and striking structure featuring lots of glass and concrete. Perched at the end of a dune and overlooking the ocean, it wouldn't have been out of place in *Architectural Digest*. The pension plan for Florida's men in blue must be pretty good, I thought.

He met us on the deck, a fat cigar in one hand and a half-full martini glass in the other. But he didn't wear trunks, at least not by my definition. His lavender bathing suit was as skimpy as the bottom half of a woman's bikini—and every bit as tight. As he turned to pour Leslie a Margarita, I caught her ogling his firm, narrow butt. She shrugged and shot me an impish smile. After Jonah tossed me a beer, he nodded toward a trio of sling chairs facing the Atlantic.

"Have a seat. And I'm sorry about the beer, Randy. Kalik is the local brew and it's about all I can get."

As Leslie and I sank into our seats, our host appeared with a tray of appetizers. He was right about the beer, but the snacks were tasty. That is, if you could ignore the pungent fumes wafting up from the citronella candles surrounding the deck. I wondered which was worse—the aroma or the insects.

"This bread is incredible," Leslie said.

"Homemade," said Jonah. "One of my hobbies."

I grabbed another canapé before forcing a swallow of the beer. I'd grown accustomed to an IPA from a favorite craft brewer back home and this beverage was a poor substitute.

"Tell me again what brings Arkansas newlyweds to Eleuthera. And where is Arkansas anyway? Somewhere around Texas or Colorado?"

"Your geography is halfway right," I said. "We're between Dallas and Memphis."

"As I mentioned in my e-mails, *Southern Living* magazine has sent me here." Leslie took another long sip of her drink. "With an assignment to produce a photo-essay on The Out Islands of the Bahamas. We're combining it with our honeymoon."

After a hearty "Congratulations," Jonah turned his gaze turned to me.

"I'm in the advertising business," I said. "But right now, I'm an indentured servant for the lady." I thought it sounded witty, but Leslie rolled her eyes.

Jonah gave us a quick tour of the house. Compact but comfortable, it could have been a gallery in Nassau. Bright Bahamian folk art, watercolors for the most part, hung from the walls of nearly every room. The one exception was a small office that doubled as his shrine to the Miami Dolphins. An unbelievable clutter of Dolphin paraphernalia—clocks, posters, mugs, stuffed toys, and pennants—filled the space. Like sacred objects, a collection of autographed footballs, each housed in its own acrylic display case, filled a cabinet. "You could say I'm a fanatic," he said. His computer system even had a screensaver with an official Dolphin mascot swimming from one side of the monitor to the other.

Our next stop on the tour was across the yard at what Jonah called his shed. In addition to sheltering his old Ford pickup truck and a riding lawn mower, it held a spacious workshop with enough tools to stock a small hardware store. Half a dozen birdhouses, some quite elaborate, sat in various stages of completion on his workbench. "I've become something of an avian architect," he said, pointing to several impressive examples—all apparently occupied—as we walked back to the house. "Helps keep the bugs under control." I swatted another mosquito and decided the citronella candles weren't so bad.

After adjourning to the deck, our host regaled us with stories of island life and gave Leslie more than a few intriguing suggestions for promising photo locations—and even offered to guide us to a handful of his secret spots. I found myself liking the man, Speedos or not.

We learned that Jonah had lived on Eleuthera for the better part of a decade. He'd retired on a partial disability from the Miami Police Department following 20 years of service. That pension, combined with an inheritance from a favorite aunt and proceeds from the sale of a pair of lucrative real estate investments in southern Florida, had allowed him to buy five acres of prime Bahamian beachfront property from a distressed seller.

"And I love this small, remote island," he said. "Wonderful people, incredible snorkeling, and perfect weather." He took a pull from his cigar and then exhaled a nasty cloud of smoke over the railing. "Aside from the occasional hurricane, that is."

"That's a primary reason the magazine sent me here," said Leslie. "Eleuthera, in many ways, represents another era."

"And here's the best part, especially for an ex-cop." Jonah arched his thick eyebrows and waggled the cigar at Leslie. "Crime doesn't exist."

## ~ THREE ~

Leslie and I remained hidden behind the agave for a full hour after the armed men left the beach. Waiting and watching from its patchy shade, we slapped at voracious no see 'ems feasting on our bare legs, arms, and shoulders as the sun slowly lifted above the Atlantic. Wind whistled through the tall, thin casuarina pines clinging to the top of the dune and, overhead, the occasional gull glided past, its dark, shiny eyes searching the shore. Hurling themselves against the beach, frothy blue-green waves attacked the sand with a relentless rhythm, one after another after another. In the nearby brush, clumsy land crabs startled us every few minutes rattling through the dried leaves. But we saw no other humans.

"To use an apt phrase, I'd say the coast is clear."

Leslie stood and stretched with a groan. "My editor won't believe this story. That is, if I ever see her again."

Clutching the tripod and camera bag, I scrambled down the loose sand into the grove to search for the mysterious object that had crashed through the trees, bringing our photo-shoot to an unexpected halt. Leslie slipped on her bikini top, over my protests, and joined in the hunt.

I'd decided to give up when she kicked aside a downed palm frond. "Bingo."

A white cloth bag filled a shallow crater in the sand. We studied it from a distance, as if it were an unexploded bomb.

Leslie edged a step closer, leaned forward, and shook her head. "Something tells me this won't make very good bread."

Squatting beside her, I stared unbelievingly at a bright yellow label: Robin Hood White All-Purpose Flour—10 lbs. A portrait of Robin, in a stylish green cap and wearing a devilish grin, stared back at me. I slipped my hands under the sack and removed it from the sand.

"Please don't tell me that you're thinking about bringing that to our cottage." Arms crossed over her chest, Leslie gave me a look far removed from the devoted and loving gaze of a new bride.

I shrugged. "I thought we might hide it in the bushes. Let things blow over. We'll see if it's still here in a day or two."

"And then what?" She shook her head. "I'm not interested in a honeymoon hero."

"We'll report it to the proper authorities. Or better yet, enlist Jonah's help."

Carrying the sack to the crest of the dune, I scooped a hole in the sand at the base of the agave and placed the bag in it before shoving a layer of sand and dried leaves across the top. I marked the spot with an empty wine bottle I'd found in the brush.

"I hope you realize what you're doing—and the dangers involved." Leslie swept away our tracks with a handy frond. "My family and I've already suffered enough because of these folks."

Years earlier, long before I'd met Leslie, her older brother and sole sibling had been murdered during an armed robbery. The random target of a desperate drug addict, he was shot one evening at an ATM near his Houston neighborhood. The killer confessed, admitting he had committed the assault to support his cocaine habit. Leslie seldom spoke about the event but regularly contributed to organizations aiding victims of violent crimes.

"Perhaps," I said, "this is a chance to help even the score."

Leslie made a final swipe with the frond, flung it aside, and met my gaze. "This is not a game, Randy Lassiter," she said. "And that 'score,' as you put it, can never, ever be evened."

Leslie's lips trembled and a tear collected in her eye before it slid down her cheek. I pulled her close and wrapped my arms around her. "I'm sorry. It wasn't my intention to sound like such a jerk."

With her face buried against my chest, I could feel her gentle sobs. She sniffed and cleared her throat. "I'll be okay. I just want us to be cautious. These people can be ruthless."

"I love you," I said. "I intend to spend the rest of my life—and that's many, many years—with you."

After gathering her photography gear, we began the long walk to our cottage. Within a few minutes we passed a small gap in the dune where a faint path led into the dense underbrush. I hadn't noticed it in our hurry earlier this morning. Judging by the smear of footprints in the sand, the two commandos had used this route for their escape.

"Can you wait here for a moment?" I set the camera bag on the sand and started to follow the trail.

"What are you doing?"

"I just want to see where these tracks lead."

Leslie lowered the tripod to the ground and placed her hands on her hips. "I'm not sure that's a good idea."

"I'll be back within a minute. That's a promise."

A pair of vicious sandspurs drew blood from my bare feet before I'd gone ten yards. I limped up the dune, peeked over its top, and slipped into a thick tangle of Caribbean jungle. A heron flashed from a mango tree, sending my heart into instant palpitations with its loud, frantic exit. The twisting path led to an overgrown, rutted road heading west toward the Queen's Highway, a 100-mile strip of potholed asphalt connecting one end of Eleuthera to the other, seldom more than a mile from either shore. Tire tracks, beer cans, and cigarette butts littered the area. I'm not sure what I expected, but I didn't find it. Glancing over my shoulders, I hurried to Leslie's side.

Fifteen minutes later we climbed through another break in the sand and trudged to our cottage, rinsing our feet at the outdoor shower. As we stepped to the porch, Leslie pointed at the picnic table. "We've had a visitor." A brown paper sack sat in the middle of the table with a note taped to the top. "It's from Jonah," she said, turning to me with a delighted grin. "He left us a loaf of his homemade cinnamon-raisin bread."

* * *

Leslie and I fixed a quick breakfast—to include toasted slices of Jonah's tasty gift—before heading into Governor's Harbor. She drove. I'd yet to get the hang of staying to the left and had caused a couple of near misses on the other islands. Lucky for me, the native drivers have good reflexes and forgiving waves. Besides, sitting in the passenger seat gave me a chance to enjoy the ever-changing roadside scenery.

Leslie spent half an hour photographing the commonwealth's Administration Building. A pair of bright-eyed kids walked by cradling a catatonic iguana, and she talked them into posing, repaying them for their efforts with *Arkansas the Natural State* T-shirts I'd acquired from a friend in Little Rock. We'd already left several handfuls with previous volunteer models—children and adult—on Andros and Cat Island. I smiled, imagining the double takes they'd cause among the tourist traffic.

While Leslie got her shots, I borrowed her phone and called the office, something I'd done every three or four days to verify that Lassiter & Associates continued to operate as a moderately profitable advertising agency. My assistant assured me the doors remained open and that my absence, while noted, seemed to have had no adverse impacts on the firm's operation. "Things are going great," she said. "Don't feel rushed to return."

When a small ship appeared in the distance, a hospitable shopkeeper confirmed the mailboat's arrival. "It should be very exciting," she said with a warm, toothy smile. "Lots of activity."

Her prediction proved correct. Uniformed custom officials marched into the crowd, clipboards in hand, looking stern as the crew unloaded the boat's cargo. The dawdling pace would have driven a time-and-motion expert crazy. A pile of lumber was haphazardly stacked between a container of watermelons and cases upon cases of Kalik. Next came a pungent crate of bleating goats followed by four pallets of sacked cement. A crane positioned on the bow of the boat lowered an assortment of large boxes onto the dock, including one holding a 20-horsepower riding lawnmower, if the label was to be trusted.

A navy-blue Toyota sedan starred in the final act. The crowd grew quiet as the crane operator, responding to a cacophony of directions from the boat's crew, lifted the vehicle from the deck and swung it over the water before placing the car in the last empty spot on the pier. As soon as the tires touched down, the hubbub returned. People milled about, studied shipping labels, and then gestured for authorities who disinterestedly flipped through page after page of paperwork. Following a blast from its horn, the boat cast off and headed out of the small port.

Moving through the happy throng like she was one of the locals, Leslie took countless shots. After she'd worked the dock for an hour, I noticed her giving me an urgent nod.

I met her near the goats. "What's the matter?"

"See those two guys getting into that van?"

I glanced up in time to see the nearest one pulling the driver's door shut. "Potential models?" Splotched with rust, the white Chevrolet cargo van left the harbor followed by a trail of thick blue smoke.

She shook her head and frowned. "I can't guarantee it, but I believe they're the ones we saw on the beach this morning."

* * *

After finishing her work at the dock, Leslie spent another hour photographing gravesites at the Governor's Harbor cemetery. A block away and overlooking the sound, it reminded me of the burial grounds in New Orleans with weathered vaults placed on top of the thin soil. But the decorations of conch shells and tropical flowers brought me back to Eleuthera.

"How 'bout a late lunch?" Leslie asked. "I'll treat."

She picked a colorful eatery with a warped wooden deck cantilevered over the Caribbean. As we settled next to the curling and comforting smoke of a mosquito coil, Jimmy Buffet's *Cheeseburger in Paradise* greeted our ears. It seemed I'd heard the song a 100 times over the past two weeks. Well, maybe on a half a dozen occasions.

"What's your recommendation?" I asked our friendly waitress. She wore one of Buffet's colorful Parrothead T-shirts, tight in the wrong places.

"Conch fritters," she said. "For drinks, I'd suggest our Paradise Punch. Jimmy swears by it."

"Do you know him?" Leslie asked, shooting me a subtle wink.

"Jimmy's been several times," she said with the sincerity of a used car salesman. "But always on my day off."

We'd heard the same story at many of the bars we'd experienced in the Bahamas. And we'd sampled similar drinks, too: in every case a brilliant red, rum-based concoction topped by a miniature plastic umbrella. I managed to swallow most of the sweet, fruity punch before opting for a cold Kalik. But the fritters were tasty enough that we ordered another serving.

# ~ FOUR ~

I never imagined an alarm clock ringing at 5:30 a.m. on my honeymoon, but that's how our second morning on Eleuthera began. Just like the first. My bride still needed the requisite sunrise shot.

After slipping on my trunks, I opened the cabinet under the kitchen sink and removed a picnic hamper I'd discovered while washing dishes the previous evening. While I filled it with breakfast goodies and a red plaid tablecloth, Leslie packed her camera bag. By 6:15 we were on the deserted beach heading toward a familiar grove of palm trees.

Marching through the silky sand, our eyes darting from the dune to the sky and back, we weren't the carefree, giggling newlyweds we'd been a day earlier. I'm not sure we ever looked at the Atlantic.

The hike up the quiet and empty seashore took 15 minutes. As before, I extended the tripod and Leslie positioned her camera, composing a shot to take in the strong, graceful trunks of the palms. Yesterday's coconut had vanished, but a pair of weathered conch shells had washed ashore in its place, much to Leslie's delight. It was premature to make predictions on the "awe factor"—as Leslie called it—of the sunrise, but a line of lingering clouds on the eastern horizon put a spring in her step.

As she tended to last-minute photographic rituals, I located a spot well removed from the direction of her shot, laid the cloth over the sand, and began spreading out our breakfast. Leslie soon dropped to the sand next to me while I peeled and sliced fresh mangos.

"I assume you're going to check on your buried treasure?" she asked, her voice lacking enthusiasm.

"Let's have a quiet breakfast and enjoy the spectacle. If things remain peaceful after you get your photo, we could perhaps do a little exploratory digging."

"I'm still not sure we're doing the right thing," she said, shaking her head. "This is the kind of stuff that gets tourists in trouble. Big trouble."

I scooped yogurt into bowls and poured us each a cup of orange juice. "We've got the place to ourselves," I said. "What could go wrong?"

She bit her lip before casting an appraising eye in my direction. "Where's the coffee?"

Sometimes it's best for the help to feign deafness.

The sun seemed reluctant to rise, teasing us with brighter and brighter rays. But then, like a seasoned actor stepping onto the stage, it finally burst into view. And what an entrance, with dazzling colors arcing across the sky like slow-motion fireworks.

Crouched behind her tripod, Leslie kept the motor drive humming, changing settings and lenses with a cool and practiced efficiency. During a break in the action, she glanced at me with a smile rivaling the sunrise. "Apollo," she said, "is looking upon us with favor this morning."

I hoped the rest of the gods would be likewise inclined.

Fifteen minutes after taking the first shot, Leslie packed her gear and plopped down beside me. "If there's not a good image in that bunch, I'll turn in my light meter." After kissing me on the cheek, she reached for a slice of mango.

We took our time with breakfast. The tide was coming in, and each wave seemed to creep an inch or two higher up the beach only to sink into the sand. A few gulls glided overhead before disappearing behind the dune. Miles offshore, a freighter crawled across the Atlantic. And Leslie spotted the tip of a ray breaking the surface not 20 yards away. But neither airplanes nor beachcombers interrupted our meal.

Around 8:00 a.m. I stood, brushed the sand from my butt, and stretched. Leslie did the same and started to fill the hamper.

"Not so fast," I said. "I have plans for our picnic basket."

Carrying it to the crest of the dune, I spotted the empty wine bottle and dropped to my knees behind the agave. Like a nervous lookout, Leslie hovered above our picnic spread, glancing up and down the beach as I pushed the bottle aside and dug into the sand.

"It's here!" With trembling hands, I lifted the Robin Hood sack from the hole, shook off the grit, and slipped it into the hamper. After scurrying back down the dune and rejoining Leslie, I folded the bright tablecloth and placed it on top of the suspicious flour sack. The remainder of our breakfast went in next.

"This has not exactly been a typical honeymoon picnic, although I'm sure it'll be memorable," Leslie said as she lugged her camera bag to a shoulder. "Shall we go?"

Balancing the hamper in one hand and her tripod in the other, I fell in place beside my bride. As we trudged toward the cottage, casting wary glances at the dune, we spoke in hushed tones.

"What are we going to do with this…uh…recent acquisition?" Her eyes stared deep into mine. "Your recent acquisition."

"I thought we might take it to Jonah's first thing."

"Now?"

"He said something the other evening about being an early riser."

Leslie stopped, lowering her bag of photo gear to the sand. "You realize, of course, that we hardly know this man," she said. "More than one cop has been caught with his hand in the till."

I swung the picnic hamper and tripod to the ground next to her camera bag. "I think we can trust him," I said. "He's not hiding anything." I paused, and then added, "Remember the Speedos?"

She kicked sand at me.

* * *

After a brief stop at our cottage to drop off Leslie's photo equipment and our dirty dishes, we walked arm-in-arm down the narrow track to Jonah's house, the hamper swinging back and forth in my free hand. Jonah sat on the deck, coffee mug at the ready, studying a sheaf of papers. Spotting us, he stood and waved. Yep. The Speedos again.

"It's another perfect day in paradise," he said as we climbed the steps. "Could I offer you some coffee?"

"That would be wonderful," Leslie said, answering for both of us.

"Please sit down," he said. "I'll be right back."

After Jonah delivered our cups of the steaming beverage, he returned to his papers and waved a single sheet. "Got my weekly fax on the Dolphins this morning. The analyst thinks they'll beat Dallas Sunday."

"I hope so," said Leslie. For some reason, she's always hated the Cowboys.

"Me, too." Jonah raised his eyebrows. "I've got a couple hundred riding on Miami." He pointed to the Dolphins cap resting on his head. "This is my lucky hat. I found it on the beach earlier this summer and haven't placed a bad bet since."

After sharing the obligatory remarks about the weather, Jonah nodded at the hamper I'd placed beside the table. "Going on a picnic?"

Leslie lowered her coffee. "We just got back." She turned her gaze to me, delivering a subtle cue.

"Actually," I said, clearing my throat, "we wanted to talk to you about something."

Jonah's eyebrows notched up again.

"At dinner the other night you said Eleuthera is crime-free."

"Almost," he said, cracking a small grin. "I had a bicycle stolen five years ago."

"We think we may have witnessed a drug drop," Leslie said. "Yesterday morning."

Jonah sat upright, his elbows on the table, as he leaned forward. "Are you sure?"

"We were a mile or so up the beach at dawn," Leslie said. "I had hoped to get a classic sunrise shot from under a grove of palms."

"I know the spot," Jonah said. "It's a great place for a nap."

27

"Just before the sun rose," I said, "a twin-engine plane swung low over the beach, dropping bags onto the sand."

Jonah's jaws tightened. "Then what?"

"Two young men came out of nowhere, collected them, and disappeared over the dune."

"Damn it!" Jonah slammed a fist on the table. "I thought we were through with that crap." He shoved his chair back, stood, and marched across the deck. He stopped on the far side, his back to us, facing the Atlantic. "I can't believe it."

Moments passed. When Jonah returned to the table, his shoulders were sagging. "I should have asked this first: you weren't spotted, were you?" He slumped into his chair.

"We hid behind some bushes," Leslie said. "They didn't see us."

"Everything happened so fast," I said. "We didn't notice any markings on the plane."

"What about the men?"

"Locals," I said, "from the accents. But we never got a good look at them either. They were in the shadows, plus their shotguns distracted us."

Jonah grimaced.

"One of them even mentioned a name. Derek."

"Every other family on the island has a Derek," Jonah said. He ran a hand over his shiny pate. "I must know half a dozen myself."

"I saw a couple of guys resembling them yesterday in Governor's Harbor," Leslie said. "But I couldn't swear it was the same pair."

"Can you describe the bags?"

"We can do better than that," I said and reached for the hamper. "We have one with us."

## ~ FIVE ~

"You what?" Jonah's blue eyes were as large as the key limes growing on the tree next to his deck.

"The ground crew missed one of the bags," Leslie said. "A palm frond fell on top of it, and the guys never found it."

"We sort of…uh…hid the bag after they left," I said. "It was still there when we returned this morning." I opened the hamper.

Jonah stumbled to his feet and glanced around the yard. He then reached over and grabbed my elbow. "Let's take the hamper inside."

We followed him into the kitchen. I placed the picnic basket on the counter and removed the mysterious sack, giving it to our host. He held the bag in his hands and stared at it for a full minute before a heavy sigh shook his body.

"Drug running was an everyday occurrence when I first moved here years ago. Bales of marijuana literally washed ashore on our beaches," he said. "But a new prime minister cleaned things up. I thought—even prayed—we were done with this damn plague." He placed the bag on the counter next to the hamper.

"What do you think it contains?" Leslie asked.

Jonah opened a small drawer below the countertop and removed an ice pick. "There's one way to find out." He jabbed the tip of the shaft into a corner of the sack and then dribbled a few specks of fine white powder onto an index finger. He touched it to the end of his tongue. Eyes shut, he worked his mouth. "Cocaine," he said, shaking his head. "Pure, unadulterated coke."

"Worth how much?" I asked.

Jonah dropped the ice pick into the sink before rinsing his hands. "I'm not current on this stuff anymore. But I'd guess it would easily wholesale for a quarter of a million dollars."

"You're kidding," Leslie said.

Jonah hefted the bag with both hands. "Uncut and in this quantity," he said, "maybe even a lot more."

A fusillade of footsteps clattered across the deck and the screen door flew open.

"Jonah! Anybody home?"

A pale man, somewhere in his mid to late '50s and on the thin side, burst into the house. Wearing pressed khaki shorts with a matching shirt, black knee-high socks, lightweight hiking boots, and a pith helmet, he could have been an anemic archaeologist coming in from a dig. Two other males, somewhere in their teenage years, trailed him into the kitchen, both dressed in the more typical garb of island adolescents. One was tall and white, the other a bit shorter and black. The trio came to a stop five feet in front of us.

"Sorry, old man. I trust we're not interrupting anything." The ringleader of this unexpected delegation looked first at Jonah and then to Leslie and me before his eyes settled on the sack in Jonah's hands. The young men behind him followed his line of sight, staring at the bag of cocaine.

His neck and face growing redder by the second, Jonah finally turned and placed the bag on the countertop and scooted in front of it to block their view. It was not what one might describe as a subtle move. "Good morning, Nigel," he said. "I'm pleased you stopped by. I'd like you to meet my latest guests." Jonah swept an arm toward us. "Leslie Carlisle and Randy Lassiter."

We shook hands.

Nigel nodded at the boys. "And this is my son Gilbert and his friend Briscoe."

The sullen pair didn't move.

Looking to us, Jonah waved an open hand toward the threesome. "I've known Briscoe since he was a kid." The young black man smiled sheepishly before tilting his head and gazing down at the floor. "Nigel and Gilbert Watlington are my new neighbors. They live a couple of hundred yards down the beach. Moved here about a year ago from London."

"And what a smashing decision it was," Nigel said. "But that's another tale. I hoped, dear chap, we might borrow your fearsome lawn machine again. And some petrol. My groundsmen," he said, gesturing at the two young men, "have eaten their brekkers and are eager to get on with the mowing."

Their expressions indicated otherwise.

"Of course," Jonah said. "It's in the shed."

Nigel and crew took the hint, turned, and walked to the door.

"As you know, I ordered one several fortnights ago. The contraption arrived yesterday via the regular packet, but the bleeding authorities refused to release it," Nigel said. He appeared just short of apoplectic. "Insufficient paperwork, they claimed. What rubbish!"

While Jonah led the two young men to the shed, Nigel, Leslie, and I watched from the deck. The Englishman wiped his perspiring face with a handkerchief.

"My mate Jonah is a saint," Nigel said. "I cannot begin to tell you how many times he's saved my effing arse."

The rumbling racket of an internal combustion engine ended the conversation. Briscoe steered the riding mower through the open door of the shed, followed by Gilbert carrying a gas can. With a jaunty wave, Nigel bounced down the steps and fell in place behind the boys, saluting Jonah with a flourish as they passed.

Jonah joined us on the deck. "He's a nice enough guy," he said as Nigel marched out of view. "A bit pushy at times, though. Your basic British expat."

"His kid seems a little withdrawn," Leslie said.

"Gilbert got into some kind of serious trouble back home. Nigel had made a fortune in imports and was ready to retire. He moved himself and Gilbert to Eleuthera for a fresh start."

"I'm afraid we had the classic deer-in-the-headlights look when they barged in," I said. "What an awkward moment."

Jonah shrugged. "We can hope they didn't know what they were seeing."

"Doesn't Nigel knock?" Leslie asked.

"Knocking is not his style."

A pair of hummingbirds zipped across the deck before making a pit stop at a nearby bougainvillea.

"Here we are in paradise—and cocaine rears its ugly head again," Jonah said. "I still can't believe it."

The tiny birds lifted from the bush and disappeared into the deep blue sky.

"What should we do with that bag?" Leslie asked.

Jonah rubbed his chin for a moment as he gazed across the Atlantic. "I'm leaving for Dunmore Town at the north end of the island later this afternoon. After weeks and weeks of delay, a state-of-the-art modem for my computer has finally arrived," he said. "I think this might be a good occasion to drop in and have a quiet chat with a special contact in law enforcement and present him with your find."

"I'm ready to get rid of it," Leslie said, nodding. "I'm sure Randy agrees."

I blushed, realizing I'd been fantasizing about how a financial windfall could improve our lifestyle. No more pre-dawn photo shoots, for one thing. No more boring civic club luncheons. And no more genuflecting to annoying and unrealistic clients.

"Leslie's right," I said. "We have now placed the Robin Hood bag in your possession."

"Why don't you come by for dinner this evening?" Jonah asked. "Say around seven. We'll throw something on the grill, and I'll give you a full report on what I learn about our interesting little item."

After we said our goodbyes to Jonah and were headed back to our cottage, Leslie caught me smiling. "A penny for your thoughts," she said as she took my free hand in hers.

"I'm glad this thing is empty." I held the hamper shoulder high. "We're done with that matter."

# ~ SIX ~

The rest of the day passed far more quickly than I expected. While Jonah had plans to visit Dunmore Town on the north end of the island in his rusty Ford pickup, Leslie and I ventured in the opposite direction. She wanted to photograph an abandoned lighthouse at Eleuthera's southern tip. Or at least what remained of it. We'd been told that Hurricane Hugo and then Hurricane Floyd hadn't been easy on the relic.

Thank God our trusty little Jeep Wrangler had four-wheel drive. Relying on intuition and Jonah's vague directions, I steered us over the last six miles of alleged road, dodging downed palms, a plague of potholes, and a smashed fishing boat turned upside-down a good quarter mile from the shore. We hadn't seen any other people in hours.

When we could drive no farther, we parked and hiked several hundred yards through a jungle of sea oats to the top of a bluff and found ourselves standing on Cape Eleuthera, the island's southernmost point. Directly east, far in the distance, lay Cat Island, its northern end faintly visible across the wide expanse of open water. Below us and to the left, the surging currents of the Atlantic crashed against a craggy shore. To our right, the prettiest beach either of us had ever seen stretched far up the coast with acres upon acres of brilliant sand, massaged at regular intervals by gentle waves. The Caribbean, its aquamarine surface spotted with reefs, never looked better. I halfway expected to see a film crew for the TV series *Survivor* encamped on the shore.

The emasculated lighthouse provided the sole sign of civilization. Although no longer suitable as an aid to navigation, it held plenty of promise as a major photo op. While Leslie grabbed her gear and went to work, I did a bit of beachcombing before curling up under a palm and taking a short nap.

At midday we enjoyed a quick lunch of snacks we'd bought en route. I'd decided that my role as photographer's assistant was a pretty good gig. And my bride was beaming.

"I cannot imagine a better location," Leslie said. "This combination of rock, sand, and water is incredible. Not only that, I photographed an osprey with a huge fish in its talons!"

After our break, Leslie spent another two hours behind her camera, much of the time devoted to what was left of the lighthouse. For one set of her shots, I climbed among the ruins and posed gazing through a weather-beaten window frame, trying my best to look contemplative.

We returned to Barracuda Bay with just enough time for an enjoyable joint shower before making the short walk to Jonah's, arriving about a quarter after seven. We'd be fashionably late, I told Leslie.

After knocking on the screen door a couple of times, we called his name, and waited on the deck for a few moments before following Nigel's example and pushing the door open and walking inside. The dark house was quiet and empty.

"It appears he's not yet returned from Dunmore Town," Leslie said.

We stepped into the kitchen and flipped a light switch. Breakfast dishes were stacked in the sink along with the ice pick. An unexpectedly pleasant aroma crept into my nostrils.

Leslie discovered the source, pointing to a large mixing bowl in the middle of the counter. "He must be running real late." Bread dough drooped over the edges. She removed her rings, washed her hands, and reached for the fragrant bowl. "This is way overdue, and I don't think he'll object."

While she kneaded the yeasty mound, I checked the rest of the house. Vacant. Same for the shed. Jonah's truck was gone.

"I suspect he's had trouble with his pickup," I said, returning to the kitchen. "Maybe he had a flat tire or his battery died."

"That'd be my guess," Leslie said as she slipped on her rings. "It looked like an older model." We'd heard horror stories about getting vehicles repaired on the islands.

We sat on his deck for half an hour as dusk turned to darkness. When Jonah failed to show, Leslie wrote a note on the back of one of her business cards and stuck it in the door before we left.

A bright moon, three-quarters full, provided more than enough light for our walk back to the cottage. As we drew even with it, I grabbed Leslie's hand. "Let's check the beach."

Dark, undulating waves crashed against the pale shore, their sparkling tips flashing in the moonlight like ribbons of static electricity discharging into the cool night air. Miles away, lightning silhouetted the horizon for a moment before vanishing into the distant clouds.

"Five miles of perfect beach and it's all ours," I said. "Let's go for a swim."

"Don't sharks feed at night?"

"I'm willing to take a chance." I stripped down and trotted to the water's edge.

After a moment's hesitation, Leslie pulled off her top, stepped from her shorts, and then removed her bra and panties. "If I'm eaten by a shark, Randy Lassiter, I will never, ever forgive you." She tossed her clothing over a piece of driftwood and walked toward me. She looked like a long-legged goddess going for a moonlight bath. Leslie stopped, put a hand on her bare hip, and gave me a clever smile. "This is probably illegal."

My naked bride was correct. While a few Caribbean islands allow public nudity, Bahamian statutes prohibit it. I suspected British prudishness had something to do with it.

"Sometimes," I said, "the authorities must be ignored."

"There's a bit of scofflaw in you, isn't there? I like that."

As we waded into the gentle waves, I dropped an arm around her narrow waist and pulled her close, still stunned that such a beauty had married me.

"I know you're disappointed you didn't get to see Jonah cavorting in his bathing suit again."

Leslie doused me with a splash. "Let's just say I noticed it." She soaked me again. "But that reminds me of something."

"What's that?"

Chest-deep in the warm water, we bobbed face to face as the warm waves surged around us.

She caressed my cheek. "You've never made love to me in the ocean."

Draping her arms over my shoulders, she kissed me lightly on the lips, her breasts brushing against my chest as the swells lifted and lowered her perfect body. She wrapped her legs around my hips.

"Would you?"

\* \* \*

With Leslie's sunrise shot marked off her list, we slept late the next morning before heading north for Hatchet Bay. Leslie had heard rumors of a legendary "shark lady" and wanted to explore the possibilities. It proved to be a dead-end, but my favorite photographer more than made up for it with a visit to the picturesque straw market. Under one stand she discovered a litter of "potcakes," the local term for dogs of mix-and-match breeding. She placed an armful of wiggling puppies in an exquisite hand-woven basket and got a series of shots that even I had to admit were cute.

Early afternoon found us back at the cottage for a late lunch. After slathering on the sunscreen, we spent a delightful two hours snorkeling over and around the reefs off our beach. The sea life was stunning. I felt like I'd been plucked from land and dropped into God's personal aquarium. We saw queen angelfish, triggerfish, a pair of wary sea turtles, and even a school of spotted eagle rays. But Leslie made the discovery of the day—a six-foot reef shark—as we swam to shore. Until that moment, I'd never found myself on the wrong end of the food chain. But the toothy beast turned with a quick flip of its long tail and disappeared before I could panic.

In late afternoon, we strolled to Jonah's, arriving as Nigel and his son drove the lawn mower into the shed. While Gilbert turned and trotted in the direction of their home, his dad walked toward us like a man on a mission.

"Have you encountered Jonah, perchance?" Nigel lifted the pith helmet and wiped the sweat from his face with a monogrammed handkerchief.

"He's not home?" Leslie asked. I caught a touch of alarm in her voice.

"I assume he's away," Nigel said and pointed to the shed. "His lorry is absent."

"We haven't seen him today," I said.

"Then I shall thank him another time." Nigel shrugged and began to turn from us. "Guests are arriving shortly, if you'll excuse me. Cheerio!"

Leslie waved her hand as if addressing a teacher. "We were supposed to have met Jonah for supper last evening, but he failed to show," she said. "Do you—"

"He's quite the lecherous bloke," Nigel said, interrupting. He flashed me a conspiratorial wink. "Jonah has a girlfriend in Gregory Town. And a smashing bird she is. Dabney Attleman's her name. She owns the local frock boutique. Perhaps he passed the night at her place, although I doubt if he got much sleep. The lucky chap." He winked again before bidding us a hurried good-bye.

"Maybe he's right," I said. "Jonah could have simply forgotten about our plans."

Leslie looked skeptical. "Let's check the house."

The business card still hung from his door, and the bread dough had grown to monstrous proportions. But there was no sign of Jonah Jefferson.

We skipped an evening swim, opting instead to relax on the cottage porch with a tray of cheese and crackers along with a pitcher of fresh Margaritas and watch the nighthawks perform their twilight acrobatics high overhead. Miles offshore, a cruise ship slipped across the dusky Atlantic, lit up like an oceanic ornament.

"I'm worried," Leslie said. "I'm afraid we may have steered Jonah into some trouble."

"He can take care of himself. The man's an ex-cop, not to mention he's strong as an ox."

Leslie sighed and shook her head. "Those things may not matter to somebody desperate for a million-dollar prize."

A sudden shower sent us inside. We stood at the window, my arms wrapped around Leslie, and watched the water droplets sliding down the windowpanes. I kissed the top of her head and asked, "What would you like to do tomorrow?"

"Let's visit Gregory Town in the morning. I've never met a woman named Dabney."

# ~ SEVEN ~

While Leslie drove, I studied our map of Eleuthera. Gregory Town lay some 25 miles to the north, beyond the communities of James Cistern and Hatchet Bay, and about halfway to Dunmore Town.

As I examined the map, I noticed Spanish Wells, Palmetto Point, and Tarpum Bay. Like real southern boys, all the towns seemed to have double names. Upper Bogue. Lower Bogue. Rock Sound. Alice Town. No wonder I liked this island.

We had pulled away from our cottage soon after eight, and the trip took a full hour. With the Caribbean glistening to the left, the narrow, twisting Queen's Highway wasn't for drivers suffering from attention deficit disorder.

We made a slow pass through Gregory Town, waving at cheerful kids on bikes and craning our necks as we searched for Dabney Attleman's dress shop. No luck. We turned around and drove back into the community, stopping at the local BP station. While I filled the Wrangler's tank, Leslie went inside and asked for assistance.

"It's a block off the highway," she said a few minutes later. "We go south past the third church and then turn left. There'll be a sign in the front. 'Designs by Dabney'."

The directions were perfect. As luck would have it, the store didn't open until ten o'clock according to a small hand-lettered placard posted on the glass inside the front door. And that was island time. Eleven might be more like it.

We left the Jeep parked in front of the shop. After Leslie grabbed her camera, we set out on foot to kill an hour at least. In the first block, an elderly resident pulled us aside for an unsolicited but colorful history of his community. We learned that Gregory Town is Eleuthera's pineapple capital, and that the local folks have perfected a unique pineapple-flavored rum. Our new friend leaned close, whispering that he made the best brew on the island and offering to sell us a fifth for three dollars. When we demurred, he insisted we try a complimentary sample, reminding us that pineapple is the universal symbol for hospitality. The stuff tasted surprisingly good, even at such an early hour. After purchasing two bottles with a five-dollar bill, we continued our self-guided walking tour. Leslie stopped half a dozen times to take advantage of what she called "indigenous photo ops"—ancient church doors, pastel window boxes, and garden plots lined with conch shells.

A hot pink Volkswagen Beetle had parked next to our Wrangler by the time we entered the store a few minutes before noon. While I'm not a dress shop devotee, the place appeared prosperous with a diverse inventory fetchingly displayed. An attractive young woman who couldn't have been past her late teens stood next to a counter and folded a stack of colorful blouses. Tanned and petite with short, bleached blonde hair, she wore a minimalist white halter top over a long wrap-around skirt sporting an attractive seashell design. Fully accessorized, her outfit included gold earrings as big as silver dollars, a diamond-studded nose ring, several bracelets on each wrist, and rings on almost every finger. Even a couple of her toes were ringed. But it was a stylish rose tattoo resting on the top of her left breast that caught my eye.

"Hello," she said, looking up as we walked in. "May I help you?"

I peeked but couldn't see if a stud had pierced her tongue.

"We'd like to talk with the owner," Leslie said. "Do you know when she'll be in?"

The young woman smiled and extended her hand. "I'm the owner. Dabney Attleman."

Leslie's chin nearly dropped, but she recovered at once, shaking Dabney's hand and introducing us as Jonah Jefferson's guests.

Dabney's smile brightened. "Jonah's such a dear. He sends lots of customers my way. How's he doing?"

"We're trying to find him," I said. "One of his neighbors, an English gent named Nigel Watlington, recommended that we check with you."

"Nigel!" She wrinkled her cute nose. "He's a no-good Neanderthal, always making vulgar remarks when he thinks he can't be overheard. The slimy bastard touches me every chance he gets." Clutching a crimson blouse that almost matched her face, she lowered her head. "I'm so sorry. My manners can be atrocious."

"I don't much care for him either," Leslie said.

Dabney bit her lip and then looked up. "Did I understand correctly? You're searching for Jonah?"

"We're guests staying in his cottage, and he'd invited us over for supper night before last," I said. "When Jonah failed to show, Nigel thought he might…uh…be with you."

"That sounds like Nigel," Dabney said and rolled her eyes. "Always suggesting things." She glanced at her watch. "It's lunch time. Let's run across the street for sandwiches and you can tell me what's going on."

After hanging an embroidered *"Closed for Lunch"* note on the door, Dabney led us around the corner to a lime green concrete block building not much bigger than a garage. The attractive hand-painted sign read, **Sister Sarah's ~ Restaurant, Tavern, Grocery**. Advertising at its most basic I thought, but I suspected the message worked just fine.

The proprietor—Sarah, I assumed—stepped from behind a short, empty bar and greeted Dabney with a hug and shared a warm smile with Leslie and me. We sat at one of the four small tables along the far wall. When Dabney caught me searching for a menu, she pointed to a dusty chalkboard above a shelf stacked high with an assortment of canned goods. A hand-written list promoted "Grouper Sandwich's" as the day's special. Back in Little Rock, my copywriter would have grimaced.

"Today's special is my favorite," she said. "And her sweet potato fries are to die for."

While we waited for our orders, Dabney explained she'd that owned the shop for almost two years, buying it with her parents' help following what she called "an abbreviated stay" at the Savannah College of Art and Design. She hoped to create and produce a line of affordable tropical sportswear, with plans to hire local seamstresses who needed jobs. Jonah had introduced her to a pair of buyers from Miami who'd requested samples of her work. And she'd just turned 24. So much for my ability to gauge a woman's age.

"What's this about Jonah standing you up?" she asked after Sarah delivered our meals.

"We'd been invited to join him for dinner following his trip to Dunmore Town," I said. "The best we can tell, he didn't return that night."

"And doesn't appear to have been back since," Leslie added.

Dabney brushed a lock of hair from her narrow face. "Jonah and I have a relationship of sorts. An on-again, off-again thing. For the past few months, it's been in the off position. In fact, I haven't seen him in quite some time."

"Perhaps he decided to stay with friends on the north end of the island," Leslie said.

"That doesn't sound like Jonah. Unless he's hooked up with a new girlfriend," Dabney said. She slid a fry into her mouth and turned her gaze to me. "Which is always a possibility with men."

I started to object, but decided that finishing my sandwich might be a wiser option.

"If you liked that, you'll love Sarah's key lime pie."

We ordered three servings of the homemade pie, and my little green triangle tasted like a slice of perfection. Had I been alone, I would have licked the plate clean. Or devoured a second piece.

"You mentioned that Jonah left for Dunmore Town," Dabney said as we walked back to her shop, dodging an aggressive rooster. "Any idea why?"

"Something to do with his computer," Leslie said. "A new part, I believe."

"He would have met with Malcolm McDaniel," she said. "He's the island's self-proclaimed nerd. Pleasant enough, but a geek through and through. I'll give him a call."

As soon as we entered the store, Dabney stepped behind the counter and reached for the phone. When she replaced the receiver, her shoulders told the story. "Malcolm still has the modem. Jonah had called to make an appointment that afternoon, but never came by."

"We don't know Jonah very well," Leslie said. "But I get the impression he's pretty dependable."

"Like most men, Jonah can be aggravating, irritating, and stubborn," Dabney said. "And that's on their good days."

Leslie leaned against me and gave my butt a discreet but reassuring pat.

"But you're right," Dabney said. "Jonah is reliable. I think it must have something to do with his law enforcement background." She shrugged and shuffled through some papers on the counter. "Here's a business card, complete with my home number. Give me a call if you find out anything." She led us to the door and shook her head. "Something's not right."

# ~ EIGHT ~

As we left Gregory Town, Leslie slammed a fist onto the steering wheel. "Where could Jonah be? There must be some answers."

"First, though, another question. What did you think of Dabney?"

Moments passed. "I like her," she said at last. "She's different, but seems pretty solid to me. What's your take?"

"I have trouble picturing her and Jonah as a couple—unless they're the ultimate example of opposites attracting. They're at least a generation apart in ages."

"You're just jealous. A much older man with a sweet young thing."

I pretended not to hear her. "As for our conversation," I said, "Dabney appeared to be leveling with us. My BS detector didn't go off."

"And she seems genuinely surprised about his disappearance."

A few hundred yards offshore, a white-sailed catamaran skimmed over the Caribbean. Geysers of spray exploded one after another as its twin hulls knifed through the waves.

But Leslie's eyes stared straight ahead. "One thing is clear," she said. "Our friend Jonah never made it to Dunmore Town."

"Maybe he never intended to," I said. "Perhaps that display of righteous indignation when we gave him the cocaine was nothing more than an act. After all, as you mentioned to Dabney, we don't know him well. Jonah may have fled Eleuthera, counting on a certain valuable little sack to buy him a new lifestyle." I nodded at the sea. "He might be on that very sailboat, heading for Miami."

"I think Jonah's already found his island paradise," Leslie said, shaking her head. "I'm certain his reaction on the deck the other day was no performance. He despises the drug trade."

"So, where does that leave us?" I asked. "I'm not sure the local authorities would put much credence in a wild theory advanced by a pair of tourists."

"My hunch is that he got waylaid between his house and Dunmore Town. Somebody learned almost at once that he had that coke in his possession, and then did something about it."

She slowed the Wrangler and left the highway, turning onto a narrow, nondescript road heading east, toward the Atlantic side of Eleuthera.

"Want to tell me where we're going?" I asked.

"One of these little side roads may hold an answer. I want to check 'em out."

"There must be dozens of them."

She glanced at her watch. "We've got five hours of daylight. Plus, I've completed my photo assignment for the magazine. Unless you have a better idea."

Downshifting into first gear, she steered us up the steep, rocky track. It was worse than any of the gut-wrenching backroads I'd ever encountered deep in the Arkansas Ozarks. After five minutes of lurching twists and turns, we topped a rise and, in the distance, saw the Atlantic, its sparkling swells breaking over the distant barrier reef. That was the background. Unfortunately, a dump the size of a city block filled the foreground. Rusting appliances, crumpled car bodies, and heaps of bottles and cans littered the landscape. A column of bluish-gray smoke rose from one edge of the trash pile. It was like discovering an overflowing latrine in the Louvre.

"I don't believe this spot is listed in any of the guidebooks," Leslie said.

A scrawny feral cat slunk from the debris and slipped into the bushes with a limp lizard dangling from its mouth.

Two miles down the highway we took our second side road, a crumbling asphalt lane leading in the direction of the Caribbean. A large gate, half-hidden in undergrowth, had been shoved to the side. Beyond it lay the remains of an abandoned industrial operation, an oil storage facility or power plant from the looks of things. A long row of off-kilter pilings extending into the water indicated a wharf or pier once served the site. It looked as if the place had exploded years ago. The lush, relentless vegetation had overtaken toppled tanks, ruptured pipelines, a roofless warehouse, and most of a parking lot. Misshapen sheets of tin hung from the broken trunks of palms.

"Good grief," Leslie said. "What happened here?"

"My guess, given the devastation, is hurricane damage."

The next two side trips led to houses. The first was a luxurious gated estate, apparently unoccupied, posted with "Keep Out" signs every 50 feet on a heavy-duty fence. The other was a 400-square-foot cinder block hovel with five or six smiling faces gathered around the front porch. We returned their waves and headed back to the Queen's Highway.

"Maybe you're right," Leslie said. "This could take forever." She hesitated when we approached the next side road.

"We've got nothing to lose. Besides, your intuition's been right before."

"Okay," she said. "We'll give it another try."

The rough track meandered for a mile through palmetto thickets before opening onto a pristine and deserted Atlantic beach. A short way offshore a shipwreck, split in two, rose above the waves like a distant skyline puncturing through a bank of fog.

"I can't pass on this shot," Leslie said. "I'll be quick."

While she began her photo ritual, I backtracked 20 yards along the road to examine a papaya tree I'd noticed. The limbs sagged with fruit, most beyond my reach. I'd turned around to hunt for a long stick when an unexpected break in the brush caught my attention. I studied the ground at my feet. A set of recent tire tracks angled off the chalky road and disappeared into the dense growth. Yet the bushes hadn't been beaten down, but stood tall.

That's strange, I thought. I stepped forward and pushed into the scrub, shoving aside the thick, leafy vegetation. It parted easily. Too easily. When I pulled at a pair of the bushy strands, they offered no resistance. None. My eyes followed the stems to their ends. Both pieces had been cut cleanly. And so had several dozen others positioned between me and a large shadowy object.

My heart racing, I trotted to Leslie as she collapsed the last leg of her tripod. "I got some nice shots," she said. "Are you ready to go?" She placed her gear in the back of the Jeep.

I shook my head. "I found something you need to see." I held the branches in front of Leslie.

"What do you mean? What are those?"

"I'm not sure, but it looks as if someone has hidden a bulky object of some sort behind a blind." I tossed the vegetation aside, took her hand, and led her along the road.

"See how those tire tracks vanish into the brush?" I asked. Her eyes followed my gaze to the ground. Shoving our way through the artificial thicket, we almost collided with the tailgate of a dusty Ford pickup. The bed was empty. So was the cab.

"Could it be Jonah's?" Leslie asked.

"I think there's a good chance of that," I said and pointed to a pair of Miami Dolphin stickers on the rear bumper. "We probably shouldn't touch anything."

Both doors stood wide open, their interior panels ripped out. The seat had been removed and slashed from one end to the other. The headliner fabric hung in tatters.

Leslie stared at the cab. "My God! Someone has destroyed his truck."

Yanked halfway off the rim, the spare tire lay on the ground. I walked to the front of the truck and peered under the raised hood. The top to the air cleaner had been removed, its filter smashed almost flat.

"Somebody was searching for something, alright."

Leslie shook her head. "At least there's no sign of blood."

"I wonder if they've searched his house?"

We jumped into the Jeep and bounced back to the highway. Pulling next to our cottage half an hour later, we parked and jogged down the trail to Jonah's home.

"My business card's gone," Leslie said as we neared the deck. But then we spotted it, crumpled at the base of the door.

We didn't bother knocking, but marched straight into the house. It resembled a war zone. The couch had been flipped over and gutted. Bookcases were upended, cabinets emptied, canisters turned upside-down. The bowl of bread dough lay shattered on the kitchen floor. In the bedroom, the mattress and box springs had been sliced open and the closets ransacked. His office hadn't fared any better. Desk drawers had been tossed across the room and files covered the floor. Somebody had cut the telephone cord. And his new modem wouldn't be needed; Jonah's computer looked like a train had hit it.

We trudged through the door and slumped into a pair of sling chairs on the deck. Lost in our own thoughts, we were oblivious to the waves crashing against the nearby shore.

"Where's our pineapple rum?" Leslie said, breaking the silence. "I could use a good shot."

"There may not be enough. We just bought two bottles."

"What do we do? Who do we call?"

The same questions had been racing through my addled mind. Back in Little Rock under similar circumstances, I could phone my friends or neighbors. Or a relative. Or more likely, dial 911. But I wasn't home, and I wasn't even sure what had happened. If we located a policeman, what would we tell him? Was Jonah a missing person, a kidnap victim, or a man on the run? Had his house been burgled or vandalized? And another thought kept nagging me.

"Earlier today you said something that's only now registering," I said. "You suggested that somebody found out about the bag of cocaine…and Jonah has vanished as a result."

"It's the best theory I can offer."

"You're saying that Nigel and the two young men with him would be suspects."

"Along with anybody they might have told."

I puzzled over it for a moment. "Jonah, of course, could have mentioned it to others. Either by phone or e-mail. Dabney, for instance. Or maybe he said something to a neighbor or friend."

"But it's Nigel who gives me the creeps." Leslie stood and stretched. "Let's go sample our rum."

We were halfway across Jonah's lawn aiming for our cottage when a loud "Hello" echoed over our shoulders. Glancing back, we saw a familiar pith helmet bobbing in our direction. Nigel Watlington was 30 yards away and closing.

# ~ NINE ~

"Has our missing land baron yet returned?"

Leslie and I exchanged troubled glances and then turned and met Nigel in front of Jonah's shed.

"No one answered the door," she said. "He's still gone."

"I deduced as much," Nigel said. "That ghastly lorry of his is absent as well."

"Are there other neighbors?" I asked. "They might have an idea of his whereabouts."

Nigel removed his pith helmet, revealing a serious comb-over situation, and ran a pasty hand over his damp scalp. "You could speak with Monsieur Marchant. That is, if he feels like speaking. He and his fascist wife are the French couple living betweenst Jonah and me. Theirs is the tawdry bungalow encased in a chainlink fence and guarded by a loathsome poodle." He actually sniffed when he said it. "But dare not interrupt their daily cocktail hour."

"Thanks for the warning," Leslie said.

Nigel replaced his headgear and turned to the shed. "I'm sure Jonah shan't object if I liberate his wheelbarrow for a day. This bloody yard work will be the death of me yet."

We waved our good-byes and had taken a few steps toward our cottage when an angry shout brought us to a dead stop.

"Bleeding blighters!" Nigel stormed from the shed, waving his thin, pale arms. "Effing vandals!"

"What's the matter?" I asked as Leslie and I trotted back.

"The shop's been ransacked. Everything is turned topsy-turvy."

Leslie and I peeked into the shed and observed a scene reminiscent of what we'd discovered in Jonah's house. The workbench lay on its side, boxes had been upended, and sacks of fertilizer, mulch, and peat moss ripped open. The birdhouses he'd been assembling had been smashed into splinters.

"Shouldn't we call the authorities?" Leslie asked.

"Authorities?" Nigel snorted. "The lazy peelers in Governor's Harbor seldom leave their air-conditioned offices."

A pair of confused expressions gave us away.

"Sorry. Peelers is slang for bobbies. And our bobbies are nice enough chaps, but they're not what you Yanks would call cops. Some sit in the lobby of Barclays Bank and attempt to appear official. Others flit about here and there."

Muttering under his breath, Nigel began sorting the debris, and Leslie and I joined in. Heaving the workbench back into position, we replaced the tools and used duct tape to patch the tears in the sacks. Within half an hour we'd returned the shed to some semblance of normal. I swept up the remnants of the shattered birdhouses and dropped them into a trash bin.

Nigel reached for the wheelbarrow. "Perhaps we shall meet again under more pleasant circumstances." He started to push away from us, but then stopped and looked at Leslie. "Did I understand that you're a professional photographer?"

"That's correct," Leslie asked. "*Southern Living* magazine sent me here to get shots for a feature article scheduled for publication next summer."

"Would you be willing to examine a vintage camera?" he asked. "It was handed down to me from my grandfather. It shan't take but a moment."

Realizing she had no graceful alternative, Leslie smiled, nodded her head, and said, "Sure."

We followed Nigel and the wheelbarrow as he led the way down the narrow track. "Years ago, this used to be the Queen's

Highway, you realize. After a few nasty hurricanes, they relocated the motorway to the Caribbean side of the island."

As we neared a modest house surrounded by a fence, Nigel gave it a quick nod and said, "The Marchant's place." A gleaming silver Peugeot sedan, brand new or close to it, had been parked near a satellite dish. On the porch stood the biggest French poodle I'd ever seen. It was the size of a small pony. Black as coal and groomed to perfection, the beast bounded across the yard in our direction, ears erect and tail wagging. "Don't let the bloody bastard fool you, mates. He'll rip a hole in your arse if he gets the chance."

Stopped by the fence, the poodle growled and showed us a fine set of teeth.

Five minutes later we arrived at Nigel's house. "Estate" might be a better word. Sprawling across most of a handsome knoll, it commanded a 360° view, the Atlantic to the east, the Caribbean opposite. From a distance it looked like a sure choice for *Lifestyles of the Rich & Famous*. Up close, it was even more splendid, obviously designed by an architect who'd been given free rein and enough cash to make the most of a unique setting. Enormous windows stood between towering stone walls, and a terraced deck led to a magnificent infinity pool overlooking the Atlantic. A young man—apparently Nigel's son Gilbert—lounged under the shade of an umbrella. The table next to him held a couple of beer bottles.

"Allow me to store this handy contraption," Nigel said, "and I shall return with that camera."

Leslie and I waited in a garden off to one side of the expansive house. She pulled a business card from one pants pocket and her cell phone from another.

"Who are you calling?"

Glancing at her watch, Leslie said, "I suspect that Dabney's closed her shop by now. Seems to me it might be wise to give her a ring."

Leslie punched in the numbers. "Dabney, this is Leslie Carlisle. We met—" She shot me a worried glance, her ear pressed to the receiver. "Slow down," she said, "and start over. Are you hurt?"

She listened for nearly a minute, nodding now and then. "Randy and I are on the way. Give me directions to your house." As she repeated them to me, Nigel sauntered back into view with a camera in his hand.

"I believe it's German," he said, handing it to her.

Leslie gasped. "You're right. It's one of the pre-World War II Leicas," she said as she examined its body. "This is a very fine camera. A classic with marvelous optics."

"I never caught the photo bug," Nigel said. "And Gilbert's shown absolutely no interest in it. He claims he gets all the photos he wants on his mobile phone."

"I also have a Leica," Leslie said, "although mine's a much newer model."

"Would you like this one?" he asked. "As a gift."

"You've very kind," Leslie said. "But I couldn't possibly accept it. Gilbert might eventually discover his creative side."

"You'll stay for a pint?"

Leslie handed him the camera. "I'm sorry," she said, "but we must be going. I have developed a splitting headache. May we take a raincheck?"

"Most certainly," Nigel said. "A raincheck it is." He seemed disappointed. Maybe he wasn't such a jerk after all. He gave us a hearty wave. "Cheerio."

"What's going on?" I asked once we were out of earshot.

"Dabney's hysterical. When she got home, her front door stood wide open. The house had been turned upside-down."

"She's okay?"

"I think so, but she sounded scared to death. I told her we'd help put things in order."

As we neared the Marchant's house, we spotted Briscoe inside the fence mowing the lawn. When we waved, he returned a shy smile. I must have approached too near the gate; the poodle rushed at us, slamming into the woven-wire fence with a vicious snarl. While I stumbled backwards, Briscoe flashed a big grin, shrugged, and continued with his mowing.

"Maybe I'll let that dog bite me," Leslie said once we were beyond the roar of the mower. "It'd take my mind off this headache."

"There's aspirin in my dopp kit."

Leslie slipped into the Wrangler's passenger side while I trotted to the cottage door. I stepped inside—and stared. Looking back, I should have expected it. A repeat of the scene in Jonah's house and shed. Furnishings turned over, kitchen cabinets rifled, suitcases rummaged through, every room a mess. I started to shout for Leslie and then realized there was nothing she could do. My toilet kit had been emptied, but I found the aspirin under a nightstand.

After tossing Leslie the bottle, I hopped into the driver's seat and started the Jeep. We bounced over the long, rough driveway and got to the Queen's Highway unscathed.

"Remember," she said. "Keep to the left."

Five minutes later, I broke the silence. "I have some bad news. Our cottage resembles Jonah's place. It must have happened during our Gregory Town jaunt."

"I'm worried, Randy. I'm afraid we're in way over our heads." Leslie shut her eyes and massaged her temples. "Thank God we had my bag of camera gear with us."

Minutes passed. To our left, the sun seemed to be considering a colorful departure over the calm Caribbean.

"It's my turn for bad news," Leslie said, nodding over her shoulder. "That white van I saw at Governor's Harbor the other day. I believe it's following us."

## ~ TEN ~

I glanced at the rear-view mirror. Fifty yards back was a dirty white cargo van.

"How do you know it's the same one?" I asked.

"I don't. But the van I spotted in Governor's Harbor had a damaged grill."

So did the one trailing us. "Are you always so observant?"

"I'm a photographer," she said with a shrug. "Noticing things is how I make a living."

I slowed to allow the van to draw closer, but it maintained the same distance. When I accelerated, the driver following us did likewise.

"Any suggestions?" Leslie asked.

"We're not going to outrun it in this Wrangler," I said. "We'd flip anyway. Let's drive into Gregory Town, acting like everything's okay. Instead of going to Dabney's, we'll stop at the restaurant. You can call her from there."

A couple of miles passed. The van kept its position behind us. "Should we have mentioned Jonah's house to Nigel?" I asked.

"I wondered the same thing," Leslie said. "But something about him still unnerves me. Let's wait a bit."

We arrived in Gregory Town a few minutes later, and our pursuers shot past as I pulled in next to Sarah's. The van's tinted windows masked the driver and any passengers. A Chevrolet, it lacked a license plate. I tried not to stare, but noticed it stopped a block down the street and parked in front of a church.

The same lady we'd seen at lunch earlier in the day greeted us with a smile of recognition. "Welcome back," she said.

While I ordered a pair of Kaliks, Leslie stepped into the women's restroom and made her call. I'd knocked off half my bottle by the time she arrived at our usual table.

"Dabney's on the way."

"What about the van?"

"In five minutes, we're to slip out the back door," Leslie said. "Dabney says it's next to the restrooms. She'll be waiting behind the restaurant."

I reached for my beer.

\* \* \*

Ten minutes later, Dabney's Beetle came to a stop in front of an isolated frame house hanging on a hill overlooking the Caribbean. We had sneaked out as planned, with me hunkered down in what passed for Dabney's backseat while Leslie did the same in the front.

My joints aching from the jarring ride, I crawled from the car and stumbled after the ladies toward Dabney's front porch. "I've already dealt with much of the mess," she said as she led us up the steps. "But I appreciate you coming over."

"This is a great home," Leslie said. "The view's incredible."

Dabney nodded. "I thought I'd landed in heaven. Until this happened." She shook her head. "I just don't understand."

On the drive to Gregory Town, we'd decided to take our chances and tell Dabney the whole story.

"Our place got ransacked earlier today," Leslie said. "And Jonah's, too."

Dabney's chin dropped as she placed her arms across her chest. "What's going on?"

"Let's step inside," I said. "We'll tell you what we know."

Back home in Little Rock, realtors would describe Dabney's house as a charming bungalow. Cleverly designed, it made the most of every square foot of space, with built-in bookcases, small closets, pocket doors, and a compact kitchen. The west side, facing the Caribbean, was a sunroom—all glass and screen. She'd converted the spare bedroom into her studio. An industrial-strength sewing machine stood against one wall, opposite a cutting table piled high with bolt after bolt of brilliant cloth. A cluttered sketchpad leaned against an overturned easel. Four headless mannequins lay in a heap to the side with grotesque puncture wounds covering their torsos. Busted arms, legs, and heads lay scattered across the room.

"You're lucky," Leslie said. "They could have wrecked your sewing machine."

Dabney retrieved a fabric remnant from the floor and used it to wipe a tear from her cheek. "You're right, but..." She couldn't finish the sentence.

As we sorted through the remaining disorder, Leslie and I told her everything, beginning with the sacks of cocaine tumbling from the airplane three days earlier.

Dabney leaned hard against the kitchen door. "So, whoever did this is seeking a king's ransom in drugs? Or more?"

"That's our theory."

She bit her lip. "My God, do you think Jonah's okay?"

"I'm sure of it," I said, trying to sound confident. "He knows where the sack is. My guess is that his captors have locked him away somewhere with plans to wait him out. They can't afford to kill him." I didn't mention the obvious; they surely weren't treating him too well, either.

"He's tough," Dabney said. She reached for a tissue. "But these people could be brutal."

"It's time you took us back to the diner," Leslie said after taking a peek at her watch. "We don't want our escorts in the van to get impatient."

"Are you certain you're doing the right thing?" Dabney asked.

"No, we're not," I said. "But we figured we might as well act as if nothing has happened. Maybe we'll get lucky."

Dabney led us onto the porch. To the west, the sun sank into a shimmering sea, but she didn't notice the spectacle. "I'm not sure

57

what I could suggest anyway. Prime ministers come and go, always promising to reduce crime. But law enforcement has never been a priority in the Bahamas," she said with a sigh. "And despite what Jonah claims, corruption is part of the culture."

"Jonah insisted that's history."

"It's what he wants to believe," Dabney said. She shook her head. "But the drug trade is like a cancer that's been in remission the past few years. Under the surface, it's always there, waiting for the right opportunity."

I led us from the house to Dabney's car. I climbed into the backseat as before and slid out of view and Leslie did the same in the front. When Dabney dropped us off behind the restaurant, we promised to stop by her shop the next day.

"It'll be late in the afternoon," I said. "We'll nose around and see if we can uncover anything."

"Thanks for your help," she said. "And be careful."

"You, too," said Leslie.

We returned to our table 35 minutes after we'd left it.

Sarah gave us another smile. "A pleasant evening for a walk, eh?"

"Yes," I said. "We've worked up an appetite."

Leslie stared at the blackboard. "Conch fritters sound pretty good right now."

\* \* \*

As we got in the Jeep to leave Sarah's, I sat behind the wheel. About the time I reached for the ignition, Leslie gave my ribs a gentle nudge with an elbow. "Our chaperone's still on duty."

"That's too bad," I said and pointed over Leslie's shoulder. A huge moon owned the eastern sky. "Tonight's moon has triggered some romantic thoughts."

My ribcage caught another elbow, but this one wasn't so harmless.

The van followed us as we headed south toward Governor's Harbor, its headlights swinging across the pavement some 200 yards behind the Wrangler. Mile after mile passed. When I turned off the Queen's Highway onto the Barracuda Bay road, our uninvited escort briefly slowed before continuing to the south.

I killed our lights and skidded through a gut-wrenching U-turn.

"What are you doing?" Leslie grabbed the roll bar, worried that we'd tip.

"Those bastards are getting on my nerves," I said. "We're going to follow 'em."

"Are you crazy?"

I shoved the Wrangler into second gear as its tires bit into the asphalt of the narrow highway. "Nah," I said. "Just curious."

I shifted into third, pushing us further into our seats. Ahead, the taillights of the van disappeared around a curve.

"What if we meet someone?" Leslie shouted over the roar of the wind.

I gave a slight shrug under the bright light of the moon. "I'll switch on the parking lights."

"And if someone falls in behind us?"

"Nobody's going to catch us."

I kept our vehicle several hundred yards behind the van as it sped south. Eerie shadows crept across the roadway as we shot through the surreal lighting.

Nearing Governor's Harbor, our quarry slowed and we did the same. I saw Leslie gripping the dash and patted her knee. "I promised a memorable honeymoon."

The van drove under the single stoplight on the island and continued through town. Hanging back several blocks, we met an oncoming car. When the driver flipped its headlights at us, I switched our parking lights on but doused them after the car passed.

"Where'd the van go?"

The road ahead was clear.

"It must have turned at the next corner."

I slowed the Wrangler to a crawl as we neared the intersection. Craning our necks to the right, we saw the van parked half a block away near a nondescript tavern. The only other vehicle in sight was a vaguely familiar shiny sedan.

A slight smile crept across Leslie's face. "Things are becoming a bit more interesting, Randy," she said. "I believe that car belongs to Jonah's neighbors. The Marchants."

We stared at the dark vehicles for maybe a minute. The neon sign in the tavern's window flashed "Kalik," first casting a bluish tint on Leslie's face and then red. I heard a faint reggae beat through the open door.

"What are you thinking?" I asked.

Leslie gave me a blue wink. "I'm thinking maybe we should pass on a nightcap."

"You realize this bar is the real thing. Not a tourist trap."

She studied the building for a moment and then turned her gaze to me. "How do you know?"

"The music. It's not a Jimmy Buffett song."

Leslie patted my cheek. I backed up 50 feet, switched on the lights, and pulled another U-turn. Fifteen minutes later we'd returned to our cottage, climbing the steps to the porch.

I'd forgotten that our place looked like a war zone. When I switched on the lights, we both gasped.

"I'm beat," Leslie said, surveying the damage. "Let's get our bed in order and worry about the rest in the morning."

And for the first time since our arrival in the Bahamas, we propped a chair under the knob to the front the door.

# ~ ELEVEN ~

Leslie and I had a long and serious talk over a late breakfast as we dined on fresh mangoes, toast, and coffee. Worrying about yesterday's events, neither she nor I had slept very well.

"Although Nigel hasn't been impressed by local law enforcement, it seems to me that we need to pay a visit to the authorities at Governor's Harbor," she said. "In retrospect, we probably should have done that first thing. I'm sure Jonah's in serious trouble. There's got to be someone we can talk to." She maintained eye contact, waiting for my reaction.

"You're right," I said. "But we must remember that we're American tourists, not Bahamian citizens. We're not high on their priority list." I took a sip of coffee. "And we need to be very careful with what we say."

"Like not mentioning the drug drop?"

"Amen," I said. "In the Bahamas, the drug traffic, tourists, and local cops make for a real bad combination."

After Leslie finished her coffee, she lowered the cup to the table with an understanding nod. "Our report should be about a missing person, no more and no less. One Jonah Jefferson."

A quarter of an hour later, we found ourselves once more on the Queen's Highway, heading south toward Governor's Harbor. It was a brilliant morning, and the Caribbean had never looked better. A pair of fishing boats sped across the distant swells. I tapped Leslie's shoulder and pointed to a magnificent frigate bird soaring high overhead. She grinned and squeezed my knee with one hand while steering with the other. But things were not the same. Our carefree days in the Commonwealth of the Bahamas had ended with Jonah's disappearance.

Leslie parked our Wrangler in the shady lot next to the Administration Building. Holding hands, we walked through the double doors and into a long hallway. A slender young woman stepped from an office marked *Building Permits* and smiled when she saw us. "Are you searching for the Post Office?" she asked.

I returned her grin, enjoying her delightful British accent. "Actually," I said, "we'd like to talk to a police official."

Her eyebrows raised. "Were you in an automobile accident?" she asked.

"Nothing like that," she said, shaking her head. "We have a friend who has vanished."

"An American?" she asked. "A visitor?"

"An American," I said. "But he lives here on Eleuthera."

We'd confused our new acquaintance, but she had a good heart. "Wait here, please," she said. "I will find someone who can help."

As she hurried away, I glanced at the other agencies housed down the hallway. The *Work Permits/Visas* office stood in front of us, with *Public Records* located next door. Behind us was the *Bureau of Transportation*. A *Postal Office* sign hung from the ceiling halfway down the hall.

"I'm afraid this may be more difficult than we thought," Leslie said.

I had the same uneasy feeling.

The young woman returned with an older gentleman dressed in a handsome dark blue suit. Stooped and walking with the aid of a cane, the man stopped in front of us and extended a frail arm. With his thick white hair, sparkling eyes, and rich mahogany skin, he would have been a classic subject for Leslie's camera.

"I am Lyford Robinette," he said as he shook Leslie's hand and then mine. "Perhaps I may be of service."

62

The young woman added, "Mr. Robinette serves in the Bahamas' House of Assembly." With a slight wave, she slipped away and disappeared down the hall. I figured it would be the last time she offered any help to strangers for a while.

After we'd introduced ourselves, Leslie said, "We are sorry to trouble you, sir. But a friend is missing. Jonah Jefferson."

Mr. Robinette studied Leslie with his bright, animated eyes. "I am acquainted with Mr. Jefferson, though not well," he said. "I believe he's a former Miami policeman."

"We were supposed to have had dinner with him two nights ago," I said. "He failed to show, and we haven't seen him since."

He flashed me a bemused smile. "Sometimes we do things on the islands in a different way," he said. "Our schedules, shall we say, are a bit more flexible, a bit more unpredictable, than in the States. Laid back, as the young might claim."

"We should have mentioned that his house has been vandalized," Leslie said. "The same for the cottage we've rented from Mr. Jefferson."

"And we found his truck in a thicket," I said. "It, too, had been stripped."

Robinette's expression changed as he shifted the cane from one hand to the other. "Vandalized, you say? That is cause for some concern." He ran his free hand over his chin, his gaze settled somewhere beyond our shoulders. "My dear friend Sidney Bostwick is our Captain in the Royal Bahamas Police Force. As fine a man as there is."

"Are his offices nearby?" Leslie asked.

"He and his fellow officers are stationed in a beautiful brick building one mile south of town," Mr. Robinette said. "I am responsible for passage of the legislation resulting in our new law enforcement facility."

"Thank you, sir," I said. "We will go see him at once."

"I'm sure there's a logical explanation for Mr. Jefferson's absence," Robinette said. "And I suspect the property damage is the mischief of renegade teenagers. You know how the younger generation is." He paused before giving us his best political smile. "My recommendation is you put these unfortunate incidents behind you and enjoy your visit to Eleuthera."

We thanked Mr. Robinette for his assistance and left the Administration Building, heading south for the local office of the Royal Bahamas Police Force. Lost in our own thoughts, Leslie and I hardly spoke.

\* \* \*

We found the station on our first try. As Mr. Robinette indicated, it was indeed a handsome structure. I parked between two SUVS, both quite new and marked with *Royal Bahamas Police Force* logos. I held the door open and followed Leslie into the lobby. A middle-aged woman smiled as we entered and asked how she could help us.

"We would like to see Captain Sidney Bostwick," I said.

"May I tell him the nature of your business?"

"We want to report a missing person," I said. "A local gentleman by the name of Jonah Jefferson."

Her smile faded as she stood from behind her desk. "Let me see if Captain Bostwick is available." She stepped behind an "Employees Only" door.

"I am so nervous," Leslie said. "I sure hope this goes well."

The receptionist returned less than a minute later, trailing a serious-looking man wearing a khaki uniform. I guessed him to be in his late 30s. He carried a notepad in his left hand.

"Good morning," he said. "I am Inspector Albury. Captain Bostwick is in a meeting, but perhaps I can be of assistance."

"I'm Randy Lassiter and this is my wife Leslie Carlisle," I said, and Albury shook our hands. "A friend has disappeared."

The officer fumbled with his cell phone, placed it in a pocket, and said, "Follow me please."

He led us across the foyer and through a door marked "Conference Room." Leslie and I took seats on one side of a long table and Albury sat opposite us. The wall behind our host held a large framed color photograph taken during the ribbon-cutting ceremony for the facility. A beaming Lyford Robinette stood front and center.

"Matilda says your friend Jonah Jefferson is the missing person," Albury said. "Is she correct?"

"He'd invited us to his home for dinner night before last," I said. "He wasn't there when we arrived and hasn't been back since."

Albury made a few hurried scribbles in his notebook.

"His house and workshop have been ransacked," Leslie said. "And we found his pickup truck and it, too, had been vandalized."

"I take it Mr. Jefferson's truck was discovered elsewhere?"

"It was just off one of those little side roads between here and Gregory Town," I said. "Hidden behind a pile of brush."

Albury set his notebook aside and studied us for several moments. "What is your relationship with Mr. Jefferson? Are either of you connected to him by family? Or by, say, university?"

"We have no ties with Jonah," Leslie said, "other than we've rented his cottage. It's a short distance down the road from his house."

"Were you acquainted with him before you arrived on Eleuthera?"

"No, but—" Leslie said.

"So, you've known him how long?" Albury asked, interrupting Leslie.

"About four or five days," I said. "Less than a week."

Albury bounced the end of his pen against his notebook repeatedly as his eyes shifted from me to Leslie. "I must note that your interest in Mr. Jefferson's welfare seems quite unusual. You've admitted to entering his house during his absence and you also took it upon yourselves to search for his truck." He paused, his gaze settling on me. "Does Mr. Jefferson owe you some money? Are you trying to get back a deposit or a refund?"

Not pleased with the direction of this conversation, I leaned back in my chair and stared at Albury. Seconds passed before I said, "No, nothing like that."

"Are you in the middle of a dispute with Mr. Jefferson?"

65

"We became worried when he failed to honor a dinner invitation," Leslie said, "and later alarmed when we discovered that his home had been vandalized."

"May I see your passports?" Albury asked.

After we gave him the documents, he stepped outside the room and asked Matilda to make copies.

"I will dispatch an officer to Mr. Jefferson's home to investigate the situation," he said. "In the meantime, I assume you can be reached at the nearby cottage?"

"There's a small sign out front," Leslie said. "It's called Barracuda Bay."

As Albury made another note, Matilda opened the door and handed him our passports. He spent a full minute examining one of them before returning it to Leslie. "Arkansas, eh?" he said to me while reviewing the second one. "Bill Clinton was a fine President. He has visited the islands several times in recent years." He smiled, gave me my passport, and then dismissed us.

"That was pretty strange," Leslie said as we stepped to the Wrangler.

"Maybe we should have told him the full story."

\* \* \*

Out of habit more than anything else, we walked to Jonah's house after returning from our stop at the Royal Bahamas Police station in Governor's Harbor. We decided that the mess in our cottage could wait another couple of hours.

As we neared Jonah's deck, a curve-bill ani burst from the brush, startling us with its loud and unexpected flight. When it lit on a colorful birdhouse 30 feet ahead, I slowed to a stop. Something seemed different, I thought. Something had changed. Staring at the birdhouse, I realized Jonah hadn't wasted any time. An involuntary "Huh" escaped from my lips as I shook my head.

"What's the matter?" Leslie asked.

"I know where Jonah hid the cocaine." I paused. "Or at least I think I do."

Her mouth formed a small O. "What do you mean? Don't tell me you've had a vision."

"Sort of," I said and pointed to the ani's perch. "I'm positive that this birdhouse wasn't here on the day we met Jonah. He must have put it up just before he left."

Shielding her eyes with a hand, Leslie stared at the structure. Positioned ten feet off the ground on a slender aluminum pole, the bright pink and turquoise house rested on a thick, rectangular platform. "You're right," she said. "I don't remember it from the first time we visited him."

"It has a much bulkier base than any of the others—and the paint looks fresh," I said. "Ten to one that's where he cached the coke."

I trotted to the pole, noticing the small mound of disturbed soil. Jonah had driven a steel pipe into the ground, and the base of the aluminum post fit snuggly inside the larger shaft.

Leslie followed, glancing around Jonah's yard. After studying the half dozen or so elevated avian apartments, she focused on the new birdhouse. "It's brilliant. Absolutely brilliant."

The ani flew off with a screech as Nigel sauntered into view, pushing a wheelbarrow. He lifted a hand to wave and lost control of his charge, knocking over a birdbath.

"Ruddy contraption!"

We helped him set the concrete basin back in place.

"Thought I'd get my son to have a go at the grounds," he said. "But he's far too busy playing electronic games of one fashion or another with his friend."

"Gilbert's a teenager," Leslie said. "That's the way they are."

Nigel shrugged with the typical frustration of an exasperated parent.

Over breakfast, Leslie and I had debated filling Nigel in on the recent happenings regarding Jonah. I'd argued for it, convinced he was a doubtful player in Jonah's apparent kidnapping. Leslie, though, wasn't so sure, feeling that something about Nigel still tripped her sensors. Nevertheless, we agreed to share some information with the Englishman—while keeping a wary eye in his direction.

I sucked in a deep breath. "Remember what we found in Jonah's shed?"

"Righto," he said. "I hope the rotters are done with their nasty business."

"I'm afraid they weren't," Leslie said. "They ransacked his house, too. They also paid a visit to our cottage."

Nigel's chin dropped. "Tore them apart from wall to wall?"

"Apparently searching for something important."

He furrowed his eyebrows. "Whatever could they be seeking?"

Leslie turned her gaze to me, indicating the ball had landed in my court.

"Think back to a few days ago when you, your son, and his friend first met us."

"'Twas early one morning," he said, scratching his jaw. "We were in Jonah's house."

"In the kitchen to be exact," I said.

Nigel nodded. "The three of you had gathered around the counter. You seemed rather startled at our appearance, as I recall—like we'd caught you with your hands in the cookie jar."

I returned his nod. "You might recall that Jonah was holding something?"

Nigel gave us a nod. "It appeared to be a packet of some sort. I remember Jonah slipping it behind him without comment."

"The packet, to use your word, that you and the boys saw in Jonah's hands was worth a small fortune," I said.

Nigel cracked a small smile and turned to Leslie, expecting her to fill him in on the joke. "Stop playing silly buggers and get on with it."

"We'd found a suspicious bag on the beach, and assumed it was drugs," Leslie said. "We figured Jonah would know what to do with it."

"What with him being an ex-cop," I added. "And he confirmed that what we found was a bag of cocaine."

The smile faded as Nigel's eyes narrowed. "So, this is no jolly story?"

I shook my head. "Jonah's now missing, and we feel it has something to do with the cocaine."

"We're not sure what to do," Leslie said. "We didn't get much help from the authorities in Governor's Harbor."

Nigel massaged his chin for several moments, and then widened his eyes as if struck by an epiphany. "Come with me," he said. "I've a splendid idea." After steering the wheelbarrow into the shed, he turned and headed toward his house at a brisk pace. We fell in place at his heels.

"Do you know someone we can call?" Leslie asked.

"Oh, no," he said. "I have something far more useful. A fresh pitcher of Bloody Mary's."

## ~ TWELVE ~

I'm not much of a Bloody Mary fan, but Nigel served a fine libation. In heavy crystal goblets, no less. I took another spicy sip as I studied our surroundings. The Chart Room he called it, although it looked like a sumptuous private library to me. Framed, antique prints, including a stunning collection of eighteenth-century maps of the West Indies, hung between the six barrister bookcases lining the interior walls. About half the volumes were vintage leather-bound books, the ones interior decorators sell by the linear foot to clients who are often more interested in making a status statement than in furthering their literary pursuits. A predictable mix of contemporary bestsellers made up the rest. It was tacky of me, but when I noticed that several of the newer books had been shelved upside-down, I wondered just how serious Nigel was about his reading.

The exterior wall, facing east, was almost entirely windows. It overlooked the sprawling infinity pool and acre upon acre of perfect lawn sloping toward the Atlantic. Through the tops of towering palms, I saw distant waves crashing over the exposed reefs. Miles away, a tanker provided a small break on the horizon.

Nigel directed us to a handsome sofa. "Let me get this straight, mates," our host said, sitting opposite us in a leather captain's chair. "Jonah has disappeared, and his house and your cottage have been ravaged by ruffians."

"The same for Dabney's place," said Leslie.

His eyes narrowed, Nigel looked hard at my bride and then to me.

"And we found Jonah's truck," I said. "It had been stripped and abandoned on a side road between here and Gregory Town."

"I am stunned by these events," Nigel said. "Stunned." He sighed, drained the last of his drink with a shaky hand, and reached for the pitcher. "Refills, anybody?"

Leslie and I slid our glasses his way. After topping our drinks, he poured the rest of the pitcher into his own before placing fresh stalks of celery in each. This Brit knew his social graces.

"You Americans are always quick with theories," he said. "Also, I might add, you're rather accustomed to crime. What's your reading on this ghastly situation?"

Leslie took the lead. "As far as we know—outside of Jonah and ourselves—you, your son, and his friend were the only ones aware of the sack we found on the beach."

"Does that make me a suspect?" Nigel asked. His eyebrows arched high into his expansive forehead.

I avoided looking at Leslie and shook my head. "We wouldn't be having this conversation if we were worried about you."

"What about my son Gilbert? Or his friend Briscoe?"

Leslie shrugged. "You tell us."

Nigel took a long, slow sip of his Bloody Mary and then pursed his thin lips. "It's true Gilbert hasn't been, shall we say, a Boy Scout. But his problems were petty crimes. Rebellious acts committed by a bored and privileged adolescent—things such as defacing public property, vandalizing restrooms, and the like." He swallowed the last of his drink.

But did that jibe with what Jonah had told us, I asked myself. I'd gotten the impression Gilbert had fallen into more serious troubles in England. Something beyond basic juvenile delinquency. Something requiring a clean slate in another country.

"So, you think Gilbert's innocent?" Leslie asked.

"I don't believe he kidnapped Jonah, if that's the question," Nigel said. "But, and this is nothing but idle speculation, he could have said something to the wrong person. Teenagers do tend to talk."

"What about Briscoe?"

"He seems a solid enough chap," Nigel said. "Not ambitious by any means, but harmless. Besides, neither of them needs the money."

My reaction must have caught Nigel's attention.

"It's true," he said. "Briscoe comes from a well-to-do family, at least by Bahamian standards. And Gilbert receives a generous allowance. Also, he's in line to get a substantial trust fund on his twentieth birthday." He emphasized the word substantial. "Two years hence."

"What kind of crowd do the boys run around with?" Leslie asked.

"The usual suspects," Nigel said with a hollow laugh. "But here they come now. Why don't you ask them?"

Through one of the large windows, we saw Gilbert and Briscoe approaching the rear door, closing in on the kitchen. When we drew even with them, they had just left the refrigerator after grabbing a pair of soft drinks. Looking like the youth of America, they wore their shorts low, exposing the top third of their colorful boxers. Tank tops and designer sandals completed their attire.

"Good morning, boys," Nigel said.

While Gilbert managed a faint nod, Briscoe said, "Good morning, sir" as if he meant it.

Nigel pointed to us. "You may remember Mr. Jefferson's friends. Leslie Carlisle and Randy Lassiter."

The young men, unsure about the direction of this conversation, bobbed their heads, and Briscoe mumbled a greeting. But their eye contact could have been measured in milliseconds.

"They're concerned about Mr. Jefferson." Nigel hesitated, first looking at his son and next to Briscoe. "Our friend Jonah seems to be missing." A long pause followed.

"Perhaps he's returned to Florida," Gilbert said, staring at his feet. "He visits the States every few months."

"Twice a year at least," Briscoe added.

Another long pause.

Leslie cleared her throat. "Do you remember the morning when we first met?"

Gilbert didn't react, but Briscoe nodded his head. "In Mr. Jonah's house several days ago."

"Do you recall anything about the circumstances?" I asked.

Gilbert looked impatient. "Sure," he said. "We went to his house at some god-forsaken hour. Father wished to borrow some lawn equipment." He rolled his eyes.

"Think back," Leslie said. "We were in Jonah's kitchen when you arrived."

The boys lowered their gazes to the floor.

"Did you pay any attention to what was in Mr. Jefferson's hands?" I asked.

While Gilbert rubbed his nose with a fist, Briscoe bit his lower lip. The seconds dragged by.

Finally, Briscoe looked up. Blinking rapidly, he moved his mouth as if attempting to speak. But nothing came out. He coughed and tried again. "I'm not certain what we saw," he said, his voice breaking. "Gilbert and I talked about it later." He glanced at Gilbert who continued to stare at his feet.

"Go on," Leslie said.

"What it looked like…" He paused, searching for the right words. "It reminded me of the days when I was a child." He took a deep breath. "The bad days…when sacks of cocaine fell from the sky."

# ~ THIRTEEN ~

"Do you remember those days well?" Leslie asked.

Briscoe sniffed. "Yes, ma'am." As his head lifted, he looked beyond us, his young, troubled eyes settling on some point in the past. "Two cousins of mine got involved in that business."

I could feel my pulse quickening. "What happened?" I asked.

"What is this?" Gilbert snapped. "A police investigation?" He glared at his father.

Nigel said nothing, but I noticed the muscles in his jaw tightening as he clenched and unclenched his fists.

"It's okay, mon," Briscoe said, patting his friend on the shoulder. "My cousins Wilton and Ezekiel… We never saw them again." He took a deep breath. "But long after they disappeared, we learned that bad things came to them. Very bad things."

"So, when you saw that sack in Jonah's house, you told this story to Gilbert?" I asked.

Gilbert grew red-faced. "What's the fuss? It's all history. Ancient history."

Nigel took half a step forward. "But did you tell anyone what you'd seen?"

"Whatever," Gilbert snorted. He rocked back and forth on the balls of his feet, his arms swinging at his sides. "I didn't realize there was a black-out in effect."

"Who knows about the sack?" Nigel asked. His chin jutted toward his son.

"It's not like we summoned a news conference," Gilbert said, eyes flashing. "It's no big deal."

"We mentioned it to some friends later in the morning," Briscoe said. "Nobody seemed interested."

"And they told their friends, and so on," I said.

Gilbert shrugged. "That's the way the world works."

"Has anyone brought it up again?" Leslie asked.

"No ma'am." Briscoe almost had a smile on his handsome face. "We'd rather talk about girls and cars and music."

"May we be dismissed?" Gilbert stared at his father.

"I have one last question," Leslie said. "Do either of you know anyone who drives a beat-up white Chevrolet van?"

They shook their heads and slunk from the kitchen. Gilbert slammed the door as they left the house.

Nigel wiped his brow with a handkerchief. "I must apologize for my son's brutish behavior."

"Don't worry about it," Leslie said. "It's just a phase he's going through."

"What's this business about a white van?" Nigel asked.

"We're not sure," I said. "It followed us into Gregory Town and back last evening."

"You're quite certain it was trailing you?"

"Like a shadow."

"I'm going into town straightaway," he said. "I shall be on the lookout for that vehicle." He escorted us out the front door and to the gate.

"Thanks for the drinks," Leslie said.

"I am disturbed by these ghastly developments," Nigel said. "Keep me posted, mates." He reached into a back pocket, removed his wallet, and handed me a business card. "Here's my number. I must insist that you call if I can be of any assistance."

\* \* \*

As we neared the Marchant's house on the walk back to our cottage, a door opened, catching my attention.

Leslie noticed it, too. "Let's stop for a chat," she said.

A tall, gaunt woman in a faded blue kimono stepped onto the porch, the enormous poodle prancing at her feet. As she ran a brush through his fur, the dog spotted us and rushed to the fence, covering the 20 or so yards in a heartbeat, snarling with every stride. His attitude about us had not improved.

The lady shouted something in French and stepped to the edge of the porch. The frantic barking ceased and the dog dropped to his haunches.

"Good morning!" Leslie smiled and waved to the woman.

She didn't respond but lit a long cigarette.

Leslie didn't let it bother her. "Could we speak with you for a moment?"

The woman sighed and mumbled to herself before stepping off the porch and trudging in our direction. Bobbie pins held her graying hair in a tight bun. She had dark eyes, a thin upturned nose, and no eyebrows. I placed her age in the late fifties.

"You must be Madame Marchant," Leslie said. "I'm Leslie Carlisle and this is my husband, Randy Lassiter."

The lady wasn't impressed. She exhaled a chestful of smoke through her flared nostrils, then slipped a bony foot from a worn slipper and stroked the dog's back with her gnarled toes.

"Yes," she said, finally. "What is it you want?" Her English carried a heavy French accent.

"We're guests of Jonah Jefferson," I said. "He's—"

"The swine!" Mdm. Marchant's loud interruption startled the dog. She glared at me and slammed her free hand against the fence railing. "A wicked man. Trouble. Nothing but trouble."

The door of the house creaked open and a man wearing a worn yellow bathrobe stepped out. He spoke to his wife in rapid French, and she replied in kind, some urgency to her voice. He grimaced, raised both arms in apparent disgust, and started waddling our way.

Leslie gave me a subtle nod. The Marchants didn't realize my wife had minored in French.

Marchant, who looked to be somewhere in his mid-sixties, eventually reached his wife's side. A foot shorter and about 100 pounds heavier, he needed a shave, not to mention a trim job on tufts of coarse hair protruding from both ears. "What's this trouble you're causing?" His English carried no accent.

"We meant no harm," Leslie said. "We're looking for Jonah—"

"The pig!" shouted Marchant. He spat onto the ground.

At least they're consistent, I thought.

"Nothing but scum," he continued. "Now leave before we turn Jean Claude loose on you." Hearing his name, the dog leaped to his feet and pressed his muzzle against the fence.

Marchant dismissed us with a quick wave of his hand. He and his wife turned without another word and strode away. The dog, though, held his ground, a low growl vibrating through his thick chest.

Leslie grabbed my hand and led me toward our cottage.

"Wow," I said once we were beyond earshot. "What a reception."

She squeezed my fingers. "But something puzzles me, Randy."

Leslie came to a sudden stop, nearly wrenching my arm from its socket, and pointed to the ground. A brown snake, maybe four feet long, slithered across the trail and disappeared into the weeds. Leslie leaned against me, breathing hard.

"No doubt a warning from the gods," I said. "About the Marchants."

Leslie regained her composure. "What's strange is that brief conversation they had in French. She described us to her husband as a pair of nosy Americans, probably searching for their disgusting neighbor." She paused, letting me figure it out.

"And this happened before you mentioned that we're looking for Jonah?"

"Right." Leslie looked back at the French couple's house. "Things don't add up."

## ~ FOURTEEN ~

As we angled across Jonah's property on the way to our cottage, I took Leslie by the arm and steered her toward his darkened house.

"Let's take one more look around."

The quiet, empty rooms made me nervous. I flipped on every light switch I could find.

"What are you looking for?" she asked.

I shrugged. "I'm not sure," I said while rummaging through the mess in the kitchen. "But something, my gut maybe, tells me there's got to be an answer here."

I collected the sticky, pungent mound of bread dough and dropped it into the garbage can. While Leslie made another tour of the bedroom, I stepped over and around the debris and went into his office.

"I don't think Jonah's traveling," she said, catching up with me as I studied the pile of mangled computer components. "His toilet kit's on the floor, along with an empty duffel bag and a pair of matching suitcases."

After peering at the dinged and dented CPU for several moments, I shoved it aside and then spotted an interesting little item halfway hidden under a Miami Dolphins pennant.

Leslie heard me chortle. "What is it?" she asked.

I handed her my find—a bright yellow thumb drive—and gave her an optimistic grin. "We may have uncovered a clue."

That small discovery seemed to energize us. We returned to our cottage and within half an hour restored it to some semblance of order before fixing a lunch of cold cuts and fresh fruit. While I washed the dishes, Leslie dried.

As she shelved the last plate, she glanced at her watch. "We promised to see Dabney this afternoon," she said. "Why don't we go now?"

"We can tell her about our visit with Gilbert and Briscoe."

"And our conversation with the Marchants," she added. "If one could even call it a conversation."

Leslie drove and kept an eye on her rear-view mirror. "Still no sign of the white van," she shouted above the roar of the wind. "Maybe they're no longer interested in us."

I squeezed her knee. "Let's hope so."

Dabney stood outside next to the door to her shop as we stepped from the Wrangler. Her body language wasn't encouraging, despite the short skirt and tube top. Some sort of symbolic tattoo encircled her navel.

"Something the matter?" Leslie asked.

Our friend gazed over our shoulders with worried eyes. "Come on in."

"What is it?" I asked.

Dabney walked to the counter, reached under the cash register, and pulled out an envelope. She handed it to Leslie. "Read this."

The door flew open, its jangling bell startling the three of us. Two middle-aged women, tourists given their tacky animal print outfits and matching sunburns, strolled into the store and removed their designer sunglasses in unison.

Dabney caught her breath and flashed them her best customer service smile. "I'll be right with you."

The ladies nodded and began browsing through the colorful racks of batik blouses and dresses, paying us no attention. They sounded German.

"I found it under the door when I got here this morning," she said, her voice low. "That's all I know. Except that it frightens me."

She sniffed, pulled her arms close to her chest, and approached her customers.

Leslie held the white envelope by the corners, her fingers touching as little as possible. Standard business-sized, it had no address and no stamp. The sole marking was a six-letter word scrawled in black crayon across its front: *DANGER*.

Leslie lifted the flap and pulled out a folded piece of ruled notebook paper, the kind school children use around the world. Her hands trembling, she opened the page. I peeked over her shoulder. The message was brief: *Tell yur new American freinds to go home. This bisness is not there cuncern.* It, too, was written in bold black crayon.

"Great," she said, trying to smile. "Bad guys who can't spell." She handed the items to me.

I flipped the piece of paper. Blank. I smelled it. Nothing. Just the two sentences, their meaning unmistakably clear.

Meanwhile, Dabney shuttled clothing to and from her dressing rooms at a furious rate. Within a matter of minutes, she'd sold $1,500 worth of merchandise to the pair of European visitors. She wrapped their purchases, escorted them to the door, and wished them a safe trip home.

A safe trip home... That's what we need, I thought.

Dabney shut the door and walked toward us, her steps dragging. "What a strange day." She shook her head and leaned against the counter. "First, I get that disturbing note. And now the biggest sale in weeks."

I handed her the envelope. "Any ideas about this?"

"I know it wasn't here when I left yesterday. Now and then I get a political flyer or an announcement about a church supper slipped under the door." She paused and rubbed her eyes. "But never anything of this sort."

"Let's change subjects," Leslie said. "What can you tell us about the Marchants?"

After staring at Leslie for a few seconds, Dabney nodded. "Oh, you must mean Jonah's difficult neighbors. The woman came in here once, soon after they moved to Eleuthera a couple of years ago. When I asked that she not smoke in the shop, she stormed out and hasn't been back. I know Jonah's not fond of the Marchants."

"What's his problem with them?" I asked.

"A property dispute," she said. "When they announced plans to build a tavern on their land, Jonah fought it. He felt it'd ruin the neighborhood."

"What happened?" Leslie asked.

"Jonah's attorney discovered that every deed in his area carries a restrictive covenant prohibiting commercial development." She paused for a moment. "And that put an end to their project."

"We made an unsuccessful attempt at visiting with the Marchants earlier this morning," I said. "Plus, we talked with Nigel's son Gilbert and his friend Briscoe."

Dabney raised her eyebrows. For the first time, I noticed a small silver ring in each.

"The boys admitted to telling some of their friends about the sack of cocaine," Leslie said.

"Wonderful," Dabney muttered. "Now the entire island knows." She tossed the envelope to the counter. "What do we do about this?"

"My photography assignment's finished," Leslie said. "I'd hate to leave with things in limbo, but it may be time for us to go."

## ~ FIFTEEN ~

We climbed into the Jeep, waved good-bye to a tearful Dabney, and pulled away from the dress shop. Leslie slowed to let a small flock of scrawny chickens scurry across the narrow road.

"Are you serious about leaving?" I asked.

Leslie shifted into second. "What if we left—temporarily?"

"I'm not sure I follow."

"Let's return to the cottage, pack our things, and catch the next plane to Nassau," she said. "We're scheduled to depart tomorrow, but should be able to book an earlier flight."

This didn't sound like the same person I'd married only a few weeks ago. The spunky, independent woman who rooted for every underdog, who never gave up. "And just wash our hands of this entire affair as if Jonah didn't exist?" I asked as a warm flush spread over my face.

"That's the way it'll look to those guys." She jerked her head backwards.

I glanced over my shoulder and saw the white Chevrolet van 200 yards behind us. It closed the gap, riding our bumper like a Manhattan cabbie, but I couldn't see any faces through the glare of the windshield.

Leslie acted as if we had the road to ourselves. "When we get to Nassau, we'll stash most of our gear—including my photo equipment—in an airport locker. We can then return to Eleuthera via the daily hydrofoil ferry serving Dunmore Town."

She was referring to the exclusive resort community at the island's extreme north end.

"So, we'll continue our search, but from a different location?" I asked.

"Not only that," she said, patting her pocket, "we'll get the local computer expert to open that thumb drive you discovered in Jonah's office."

When Leslie turned onto the Barracuda Bay road, the van roared past, spewing a trail of blue smoke in its wake. They're getting bold, I thought, making sure we get the message.

An hour and a half later, after furiously packing, we pulled in at Governor's Harbor Airport. While I turned in the Wrangler's keys to the rental car manager, Leslie went to the BahamasAir counter and handled the ticket situation. Within an hour we stepped through the gate and filed across the blinding tarmac with a dozen or so other passengers to our plane. I felt Leslie's elbow against my ribs.

"Don't stare, Randy," she said. "But there's a familiar vehicle parked near the fence to your right."

I swung my head toward and then past the bustling terminal. The white van sat at the edge of the lot, backlit by the afternoon sun. I thought I saw two silhouettes through the dark glass, but maybe my imagination was working overtime.

The plane took off to the south. Within moments I spotted our cottage, Jonah's house, the Marchants' place, and Nigel's estate. Leslie leaned over to peer out the window. "There's where it all started," she said, pointing to the long and empty beach. The small grove of palms looked quiet and peaceful.

* * *

An uninspired calypso band greeted us in the terminal at Nassau's International Airport. I'd opened my mouth to make a sarcastic remark when Leslie's eyes met mine and she shook her head. "Just how many times a day could you play 'Day-O' to rude and arrogant tourists before losing your enthusiasm?" Given her uncanny ability to read my mind, I knew better than to look at the young women in their short and sexy sundresses.

We stored most of our bags in an airport locker before catching a cab to an inexpensive inn recommended by Leslie's guidebook. Following a restless night, we hired another cab and arrived at Nassau's harbor by 7:30 the next morning, ready to board the ferry to Dunmore Town.

A modern, sleek-looking craft, the hydrofoil appeared about half-full, with most passengers decked out in tourist attire. The steep fares apparently discouraged inter-island commuters. After a blast from the horn, the captain surprised us and pulled away from the pier at eight, right on schedule. Once he throttled up, the ferry seemed to fly over the waves, eliminating the rolling motion I'd dreaded. Two hours and 75 miles later, we had returned to Eleuthera. I never even reached for my seasickness bag.

Dunmore Town was far more developed than the other communities on Eleuthera. More restaurants, more shops, more resorts. The sidewalks teemed with people while the streets were busy with golf carts—the favored mode of transportation—and motor scooters. Leslie pointed to a Tourist Information Center across the street from the docks, next to a bustling straw market. "There's a good place to start."

The helpful clerk gave us the names and telephone numbers of half a dozen rental car possibilities. Not an Avis, Hertz, or Alamo on the list, but instead a Mr. Cooper, a Mr. Robertson, and so on.

"One more thing," I said as we started to leave. "Can you recommend a handy computer expert?"

The lady behind the counter flipped through a ragged Rolodex. "We have two," she said. "There's a Radio Shack two blocks from the harbor."

"And the other?" Leslie asked.

"An individual," she said. "Mr. Malcolm McDaniel."

That name sounded familiar, and Leslie must have had the same reaction. "Could we have his address and telephone number, please?" she asked.

As we left the center, Leslie grabbed a brochure featuring Dunmore Town walking tours. A handy street map filled the middle panel.

"It looks like McDaniel's place is no more than five minutes away," she said after studying the map for a short while. "Let's make him our first stop."

His shop occupied a small building situated between a laundromat and a liquor store. Built of cement blocks, it looked classically Bahamian with a pale green exterior and turquoise trim. A bell chimed as we walked in. Dell, IBM, and Apple boxes lined the walls to our left and right while a collection of cables snaked across the concrete floor and through racks of metal shelving full of computer components. The rear of the store housed a long workbench covered with parts and tools.

"Morning!" The owner of the pleasant voice had yet to appear. "I'll be right with you."

A few moments later, a tall skinny guy with a buzz cut emerged from a back room carrying a monitor. He placed it on the workbench and then turned his attention to us. A wrinkled Michigan State T-shirt topped his khaki cargo shorts. A pair of vintage Birkenstocks completed his outfit.

"What can I do for you?" His bright eyes bounced from me to Leslie.

She reached into her pocket and removed the flash drive. "We'd like to read what's on this," she said.

McDaniel took the device and gave it a quick once-over. "That should be no problem," he said. "I assume it's in a standard format?"

"We think so," I said, hesitating a moment. "It's not actually ours."

Leslie gave me a look indicating that I'd perhaps shared too much information.

"You're not trying to get me in trouble, are you?" McDaniel asked. A grin stretched across his face.

"We're friends with one of your customers," Leslie said. "Jonah Jefferson."

McDaniel's smile broadened. "Jonah's a great guy," he said. "I've got a modem waiting on him right now." He nodded toward a shelf loaded with boxes.

"We're also waiting on him," I said. "We'd rented his cottage, but Jonah has…well, he's…we just can't seem to locate him."

"We've been working with him on a project," Leslie said, again giving me a look. "He left this thumb drive with us, but… uh…my laptop got stolen." I'd forgotten how quickly she could concoct stories.

McDaniel pursed his lips. I could sense his enthusiasm for our project waning.

"Dabney Attleman recommended that we visit with you," I said. "She claimed you're the best on the island." I hoped I hadn't been too effusive with my praise.

McDaniel's smile returned. "Best in the Bahamas, she meant. Come on back." He grabbed two folding chairs along the way and led us to a desk. After shoving aside a pile of parts, he slipped the small drive into a computer. His fingers danced over a keyboard and the monitor sprang to life. "It's a basic text file," he said. "No security features." He sounded disappointed as he stood and left the machine to us. "Give me a shout if you need any help."

## ~ SIXTEEN ~

Jonah's flash drive contained a dozen or so files. Leslie scrolled down the cryptic titles as I stood behind her.

"What do you think?" she asked, staring at the screen.

Peering over her shoulder, I read down the list, and shrugged. None of them looked very promising. "It'll take a while, but we might as well be thorough. Let's start at the top and work our way down, checking each one."

I slid into the chair and scooted next to Leslie.

The first held a summary of Jonah's mutual fund investments, updated every month. He had a diversified portfolio that provided a comfortable but unspectacular income. It was a far better nest egg than Leslie and I had assembled, but nothing to raise eyebrows. Leslie closed it and opened the second file.

It appeared to be a rough draft of an incomplete but comprehensive history of Eleuthera. Jonah hadn't mentioned this project, but it explained his familiarity with the island and the helpful photo leads he had given Leslie. Double-spaced, the manuscript totaled almost 50 pages. Taking the Michener approach, he had just wrapped up Christopher Columbus' 1492 visit to the Out Islands of the Bahamas. He had another 500 or so years to summarize.

The next file, much more personal than either of the others, featured a collection of poetry. Using traditional verse, Jonah had attempted to capture the beauty of a morning rainbow, the power of an electrical storm, and the grace of a dolphin. Other poems were in various stages of completion. After reading these innermost thoughts, I found it hard to believe Jonah Jefferson had been a cop.

"Randy, I feel like such a creep," Leslie said as a tear slid down her cheek. "Are you sure we should continue?"

"Right now, it's the only thing we've got."

We spent over an hour pouring through the rest of Jonah's electronic records, with the hard metal chairs growing more uncomfortable by the minute. We found a list of items he'd purchased over eBay, most of them additions to his collection of Miami Dolphins memorabilia. We located a chatty form letter he sent to his cottage visitors once they returned home, and the correspondence he'd exchanged with his attorney regarding the legal controversy with the Marchants. There was even a mailing list of contacts to receive Christmas cards. We discovered maintenance schedules for his house and the cottage, plus an inventory—complete with photos—of his birdhouses along with dates of construction and what species had taken residence. The newest birdhouse, I noticed, hadn't been added to the list. Another file contained a detailed record of every repair and expense regarding his Ford pickup. He'd computed the miles per gallon following each fill-up since he'd bought the truck. Our friend Jonah seemed a tad on the anal-retentive side.

"I'm having doubts about this," Leslie said. She stretched her arms and rotated her neck. "And my body is complaining."

"Two more files and we're done."

The next one surprised us. It represented an attempt at building a family tree, but the Jefferson bloodline had come to an end. A quick review revealed Jonah had no immediate kin. He was an only child, had no offspring of his own, and his parents had died over a decade ago. His sole surviving relative was a second cousin in South Carolina well into her seventies. A dashed line led to a godson who had a Washington, D.C. address.

Leslie sniffed and wiped away a tear. "There's nobody out there to even miss him," she said and closed the file.

The last file—labeled "Beach News"—sounded like another dead end. I assumed it was something on the order of a neighborhood e-newsletter. Leslie centered the arrow over the icon on the screen and clicked the mouse. Text filled the monitor.

Leslie leaned forward. "What have we here?" Her low voice carried a hint of discovery.

I leaned across her shoulder and read some disturbing words.

The first few paragraphs—under a *Situation* heading—comprised what Jonah might have called "an incident report" back in his days as a policeman. They described how an unusual sack of Robin Hood "flour" came into his possession earlier that morning. Omitting our names, he recounted our story, noting that two young men had apparently retrieved the other eight bags of cocaine and delivered them to persons unknown.

As my eyes skipped down the screen, my pulse raced when another heading—*Potential Suspects*—came into view. Several groups or individuals were bullet-pointed, with what appeared to be a short description or explanation following each. The list continued to the bottom margin and evidently onto a second page.

"Oh, my God," Leslie said. She pointed to the first name on the list: *Marchant*.

McDaniel surprised us, appearing at our backs. "How's it going?" he asked. "Any luck?"

Leslie's shoulders jerked, and she dropped a fist to my knee.

"We may have found something," I said, trying to sound calm and wondering if he could see the flush spreading across the back of my neck. "Any chance we could use a printer?"

He peeked behind the computer, grabbed a cable, and followed it to his workbench.

"Looks like we're hooked up," he said. "Go ahead and give it a try."

Leslie reached for the mouse, her hand trembling. She moved the cursor to the print icon and double-clicked.

McDaniel cocked his head toward the printer. "It's on the way."

I hopped to my feet and maneuvered through the stacks to the back of the shop. Bent over his bench, McDaniel worked on another project as two sheets emerged from the printer. I snatched them from the tray and slipped the pages into a pocket as Leslie came to my side.

"How much do we owe you?" I asked.

McDaniel gave us a toothy grin. "Nothing," he said. "I enjoyed your company."

"Did you say you have a modem waiting for Jonah?" Leslie asked.

McDaniel nodded. "A speedy little devil," he said. "Jonah will love it."

Leslie held the flash drive in front of McDaniel. "Could you put this with it?" she asked. "That way it'll get back to him."

She's way ahead of me, I thought. The drive should be safe in this shop.

He took it from her. "No problem."

We said "Thanks" at the same time and then stepped into the brilliant afternoon sunshine of Dunmore Town.

\* \* \*

"How 'bout a quiet lunch somewhere?" I asked.

Leslie scanned through her brochures. "Sally's sounds just right," she said. "And it's not more than a few blocks away."

The narrow, winding street led us past two whitewashed churches with fading pastel green shutters. Arriving at Sally's, we ducked under a fragrant arbor of bougainvillea and entered a quaint dining room with eight empty tables. Leslie guided us to one in a corner where we ordered dauphin burgers and hand-squeezed limeades from a shy, barefooted waitress sporting dreadlocks bedecked with bright ribbons.

I removed the two sheets of paper from my shirt pocket, unfolding them across the bright red tablecloth.

"God," Leslie said. "I'm so nervous."

Our heads almost touching, we studied the top page.

I reread the first portion of Jonah's notes. He'd remembered every detail we had told him, from the time of day to the mysterious twin-engine aircraft to the two young men, armed with shotguns, who had awaited the drop. He noted why we were on the beach at that hour of the day, and that we had stashed the unclaimed sack at the base of an agave near the grove of palms before retrieving it the next morning and leaving it with him. The last sentences of his summary made my skin crawl:

> *The nine sacks in this drug drop have a street value of approximately $5 million. The individual or group behind this operation should be considered a major threat to the Commonwealth of the Bahamas—and a real danger to any civilians who get in the way.*

Leslie gasped, her hand at her mouth. "Randy, this is awful," she said. "Jonah may have written his own obituary."

My thoughts, exactly.

# ~ SEVENTEEN ~

Our young waitress appeared without a sound and startled us both. "Your limeades," she said with a smile before retreating to the kitchen. Whispering when she spoke, she'd yet to make eye contact. I took a sip and then swung my gaze back to the paper, dropping down the sheet to Jonah's list of *Potential Suspects*.

At *Marchant*, he had written these thoughts: *French couple rumored to have ties with underworld in Nice; secretive; occasional late-night guests; paranoid about household security. But all this may be coincidental…*

Leslie and I looked up at the same time.

"This sounds unusual, Randy," she said. "How would he have heard rumors of their activities in France?"

I didn't have an answer.

"And what does his last sentence mean?"

"I wish I knew. Maybe he's trying to give them benefit of the doubt."

We went to the next item on the list, and it surprised me. Another neighbor's name appeared: *Nigel Watlington*.

"Hmmm," Leslie said. "We may have been right to suspect our English friend."

Jonah's comments were brief: *Aggressive UK businessman with extensive experience in imports; claims to have many international contacts; drawn to opportunities to make a fast buck; seems restless, and is looking for challenges; believes he's blessed with superior intelligence.*

I whistled through my teeth. "Jonah didn't mince any words with his assessment."

Leslie thought about it a moment. "His law enforcement background is showing," she said. "But I feel much of Nigel's persona is just a veneer. My gut tells me he's a big softie underneath a corporate raider image." After a pause, she gave me a slight shrug. "Of course, Jonah knows him better than we do."

"Nigel is an enigma," I said. "Although I get the impression that he's still working on the transition to island time."

"Meaning," Leslie said, "he may lack the patience this cocaine job required?"

"Not only that, he's trying to keep Gilbert on the right track. Maybe I'm wrong, but I don't think he'd risk losing his son."

"Besides, I doubt if he needs the money."

"On the other hand," I said, "many wealthy folks never seem satisfied with their position in life, always seeking more."

Leslie slid the papers aside as our meals were delivered with an embarrassed grin. After asking our waitress to refill my limeade, I reached for the steaming dauphin burger. A few bites convinced me that I'd never enjoyed a tastier sandwich.

As we scraped the last crumbs from our plates, I pulled the pages between us. "Ready for the second sheet?" I asked.

Leslie wiped her chin with a napkin and nodded. I flipped the top sheet over, expecting to see another full page of text. But a surprise awaited us. Down the left margin of the second page were numbers three through five. The one word on the piece of paper was *Baines*, mysteriously placed after number three.

"My gosh," Leslie said. "I expected more. Lots more."

"My guess is that Jonah left for Dunmore Town before he had time to finish," I said after thinking about it for a moment. "He must have stashed the coke in his customized birdhouse first thing, did a little stream-of-consciousness typing at the computer—"

"And then headed this way, planning to pick up the modem from Malcolm McDaniel and talk with his law enforcement contact," Leslie said. "Only to be kidnapped along the way." She stared at the wall, her eyes transfixed by a bright print of a school of tropical fish. Moments later she turned my way. "But who is this Baines character?"

"Maybe Dabney knows."

"That reminds me," Leslie said. "I should give her a call, let her know where we are and what's going on."

"While you're calling Dabney, I'll find us a rental car," I said, leaving a small wad of cash on the table.

We agreed to meet half an hour later outside the tourist bureau.

\* \* \*

"Any luck?" Leslie asked as we convened on the sidewalk.

I waved a key ring in front of her. "We'll be driving one of the biggest cars in the Caribbean," I said. "A ten-year-old Ford Crown Victoria parked on the other side of the bay. The owner said there's a minor crack in the windshield and that the body has a little rust, but he gave me a ten-dollar discount. After all, we're no longer on your expense account."

Leslie shook her head. "At least we won't be mistaken for rich tourists."

"What about Dabney?" I asked.

"She was both surprised and glad to hear we're still around," Leslie said. "She asked if she could meet us for supper at seven here in Dunmore Town and even recommended a place. Irene's Deli."

A shadow passed through my mind. "But what if she's followed?"

Leslie's chin dropped. "That never occurred to me." She turned on her phone and tried calling both the shop and Dabney's house. Her frown told the story; no luck.

Once we'd rented a room in a small hotel several blocks from the waterfront, we spent the rest of the afternoon roaming through Dunmore Town by foot. Each time we turned a corner, we discovered a splendid garden, an architectural curiosity, or a unique window display in one of the boutiques. Half a dozen times Leslie complained about leaving her professional camera gear in Nassau although she took a few snapshots with her compact Leica. After exploring most of the quaint narrow streets and visiting a handful of shops, we found ourselves at the harbor. Against a setting sun, the fleet of water taxis raced back and forth across the bay like noisy waterstriders on a giant pond.

Leslie looked at her watch. "Dabney should be arriving by one of those boats in about an hour. Why don't we get a drink?"

We found a quiet little bar overlooking the docks and ordered a pair of Kaliks. I was thirsty, but the taste hadn't improved. Leslie found her local map and spent a few minutes studying it. "Here's where we are," she said, pointing to a spot at the harbor's edge. "And Irene's is six blocks away. On the other side of town."

"When it gets closer to seven, why don't you head for the restaurant," I said. "I'll wait here for Dabney."

"So, Randy, you'd rather escort her than me?" My beautiful bride arched her eyebrows and gave me an inquiring smile.

"Only if she's wearing one of those cute short skirts," I said moments before the sharp toe of Leslie's sandal connected with my shin. "Actually, I'd planned to lurk here in the bar to make sure she hasn't acquired a tail," I said with a grimace.

"Good idea," she said. She leaned over and kissed my cheek. "I'll be a block or two beyond Irene's. We can enter together."

"If no one's trailing Ms. Attleman."

\* \* \*

Hidden in the shadows of the bar, I watched Dabney arrive ten minutes after Leslie left for Irene's Deli. Except for an older couple in matching polyester outfits of an unnatural color and stretched to unreasonable dimensions, Dabney was the sole person to get off the boat. Dressed rather conservatively, at least by her standards, she wore a long, wraparound skirt and a light sweater over a white blouse. She paid her water taxi captain and gave him a hesitant wave before turning and heading toward the street, walking at a determined pace. She glanced back halfway down the block, then again as she reached the streetlight at the corner. She looks nervous, I thought. Nobody fell in place at her heels.

I remained at the bar, feeling like a spy, as I nursed my tepid Kalik. Two more boats docked soon after Dabney's landing, but the passengers appeared harmless. The first group was a touring family, to include a sulking teenaged boy. The second boat discharged two couples who'd already had a little too much to drink. The men and women spent a few moments arguing about the direction of their next destination before the men wandered off heading one way and the women going another.

After paying for the beers, I set out for Irene's. The streets and sidewalks teemed with pedestrians enjoying the cool night air and sociable surroundings. I saw Leslie window-shopping a block past the restaurant. I stopped and watched. She was the prettiest woman on the island, I thought. Tall and slender, she moved with the grace of a dancer. As I walked closer, she turned and beamed a big smile in my direction. I got a nice kiss on the lips before we entered Irene's Deli.

It was a strange place, sort of a combination restaurant, bar, and souvenir stand. An eight-track tape player sat between the cash register and a stack of tapes. Through a pair of tinny speakers, I heard the theme song from *Saturday Night Fever* playing at about 75 percent of the recommended speed. At least we'd been spared another Jimmy Buffett tune.

Dabney waved to us from a corner table. Her smile seemed forced.

"Am I glad to see you," she said as we sat. "I thought you might've forgotten."

Leslie patted her arm. "Sorry we're late."

"It's my fault," I said. "We wanted to make sure no one was tagging along behind you."

Dabney's head bobbed up and down. "That's just it. Somebody followed me home when I left my shop in Gregory Town."

## ~ EIGHTEEN ~

Leslie brought a hand to her mouth. "What happened?"

Before Dabney could answer, a smiling young man with a handsome gold front tooth appeared at our table, menus in hand. "May I get you something to drink?"

I decided to swear off Kaliks and followed the ladies' lead and ordered bottled water.

"I closed the shop at the usual time," Dabney said as soon as our waiter departed. "About halfway home, I realized someone was following me."

"The white van?" I asked.

"A black car," Dabney said, shaking her head. "Something low and sporty. Maybe a Firebird or Camaro."

"You're sure it was trailing you?" Leslie asked.

"Certain," she said. "It kept back a good distance, but continued past my house when I pulled in. Nobody ever goes up there. The road dead ends a few blocks beyond my driveway."

"But it didn't follow you here?"

Dabney's eyes showed a bit of life. "I gave 'em the slip."

I must have looked more than a little skeptical.

"I left some lights on at my place, then snuck out the back door and trotted down a path to a friend's house a block away and borrowed her car. I pulled off the road several times on the way here, killed my headlights, and waited a couple of minutes," she said. "Nobody passed."

"I watched as you got off the boat," I said. "You seemed to be in the clear."

"What?" Dabney asked. She gave me a quizzical look.

"I was in the bar next to the harbor."

"Back to the black car," Leslie said. "Any idea who was in it?"

"I don't pay much attention to cars," Dabney said. "But I don't recall seeing it before."

After delivering drinks, the waiter took our orders. Following his hearty recommendation, we opted for broiled lobster with rice and chick peas.

"Thanks again for coming back," Dabney said. "Jonah needs our help."

I handed her the sheets of paper. "Here's something you should read."

"We retrieved it from a flash drive that we found near his computer," Leslie said.

Dabney scanned the first page, nodding as she read. A frown appeared as she went to the second. "It looks like he intended to expand this," she said, "but never got around to it."

Leslie explained our theory about the abbreviated list. Dabney nodded while re-reading the papers.

"Does the name Baines ring a bell?" I asked.

She thought about it for a moment. "I know of two men named Baines. A father and son. I'd guess the father's in his late fifties, the son in his early to mid-twenties."

"What can you tell us about them?" Leslie asked.

"They live in Governor's Harbor," Dabney said. "The father is widowed and stays with his sister and her family. He's a retired customs agent for the government. A nice guy, well liked for the most part."

"And the son?" I asked.

Dabney puckered her lips. "I know him by sight, nothing more. Sort of a rough looking dude. I'm not sure what he does."

"Is Jonah acquainted with them?" Leslie asked.

"Jonah knows everybody," she said with a chuckle. "Unlike most others who have relocated to Eleuthera, he's an active member of the community. In fact, Jonah'd much rather mingle with the locals than hang around with the smug and snobby expatriates."

The arrival of huge steaming plates of lobster interrupted the conversation. An involuntary groan followed my first bite.

"What's the matter?" Leslie asked. "Is something wrong with the food?"

I shook my head. "The lobster's great. But that music…"

In the background, Jimmy Buffett's *Cheeseburger in Paradise* struggled through the tape player, sounding like a tropical dirge.

"Please show some respect," Dabney said with a grin. "You're disparaging our unofficial national anthem."

As we scraped our plates, Dabney glanced at her watch. "I should head home soon. It's an hour's drive back to Gregory Town, not counting the water taxi ride to the car."

Our signal to ask for the check came when Irene's eight-track stereo belched out Tom Jones singing a garbled version of *Delilah*. While our waiter left with my credit card, the hostess led two men wearing identical navy-blue windbreakers to the rear of the crowded restaurant.

As they passed our table, Leslie gasped. "Tell me I'm imagining things," she said.

I glanced over my shoulder. The backs of both jackets had DEA stenciled in large white letters. The men disappeared into the adjoining dining room.

Dabney, too, had noticed the newest customers. "Those initials stand for Drug Enforcement Administration, right?" she asked.

I nodded, thinking perhaps our luck was about to change.

Leslie and Dabney headed for the restroom, promising to meet me outside on the street. I added a respectable tip, signed the credit slip, and then followed an impulse and walked toward the DEA duo.

The hostess had given them the last open table, a four-seater next to the swinging door leading to the busy kitchen. The men broke their conversation as I approached, looking at me with alert, wary eyes.

I reached for an empty chair. "May I visit with you for a moment?" I asked.

The heavier of the two deferred to his partner who hesitated a moment before responding with a disinterested shrug. "Have a seat."

"I'm Randy Lassiter," I said, extending my hand. I got two firm grips in return but no names. I scooted my chair closer and leaned across the table. "My wife and I witnessed…uh…an unusual incident on the island a few days ago," I said, keeping my voice low. "We'd like to talk with you about it."

They gazed at me for what seemed like a minute. Maybe they were sniffing the air for liquor, watching my face for a nervous tic, or waiting for me to say something even more bizarre. But I stared back, my eyes never wavering.

"What happened?" asked the same one who had spoken earlier. While he fiddled with his cell phone, his companion pulled a pamphlet from a pocket and opened it. The brochure was a guide to the historic sites of Dunmore Town.

"A drug drop," I said. "From an airplane."

Both men looked up, their eyes widening.

"A drug drop?" The man holding the brochure lowered it to the table. "You're sure about this?"

"Positive," I said. "No doubt whatsoever."

"This is not a good place to talk," he said. "We've just ordered our lobster dinners. But—"

"We're escorting a friend to the harbor in a few minutes," I interrupted. "Could you meet us at our hotel later this evening?"

Again, the long penetrating look. He reached inside his jacket and pulled out a pen. He handed it to me and slid a cocktail napkin my way. "Why don't you write down your name and the place where you're staying?" he asked. "We'll stop by once we finish our meals."

Instead of using the napkin, I removed a business card from my wallet, jotted down the information he requested on its back, and handed it to him. "Thanks," I said, rising from the chair. My heart seemed to be in overdrive as I left the deli.

Leslie and Dabney stood across the street, window-shopping at a women's clothing store.

"Ready to go?" I asked.

We ambled through the dark streets, more or less in the direction of the docks.

"We're staying here in Dunmore Town tonight," Leslie said to Dabney. "We'll rent a place closer to Governor's Harbor tomorrow. Something convenient, but still out of sight."

"Why don't you let me help?" Dabney asked. "I can get phone numbers for a couple of decent but out-of-the-way cottages."

"That's a good idea," Leslie said. "We'll give you a call when we get a chance."

We stepped aside to let a pair of sociable drunks meander up the sidewalk.

"And I'll gather what I can about Mr. Baines and his son," Dabney said.

A water taxi waited under a bright light at the end of the pier, bobbing on the waves beneath a cone of flying insects and circling nighthawks. Dabney gave each of us a hug before stepping into the boat.

"And watch out for that black car," I said.

Dabney's boat hadn't gone more than 50 yards when I took Leslie's hand. "We need to return to the hotel," I said. "Guests will be arriving soon."

"Guests?" she asked. "We have friends here?"

"Let's hope so. I invited the two guys in DEA jackets to stop by and see us."

We hustled to our small inn and walked into the lobby. I halfway expected the DEA agents to be waiting on us, but the front desk clerk had the place to himself. He kept his eyes glued to his computer screen as we passed.

"Let's make a quick run to our room," Leslie said. "I'd like to freshen up."

We climbed the dark narrow stairs to the second floor. Our room was at the end of the hall. I slipped the key into the lock and

101

shoved the door open. The overhead light had been turned on, and sitting on the couch against the opposite wall were the two men we'd seen in the restaurant.

"Come on in, Mr. Lassiter and Ms. Carlisle," one said. He gave us a faint smile.

"And lock the door behind you," said the other. "Please."

# ~ NINETEEN ~

I closed the door and twisted the deadbolt into place.

"Do you mind if we sit?" Leslie asked, her voice icy. Apparently, she didn't approve of the liberties taken by our guests. I had similar thoughts.

One of the men gestured to the two chairs they had moved to face the couch. "Have you enjoyed your honeymoon?" he asked.

"With one exception," I answered, taking a seat next to Leslie. "And I'm feeling a bit uncomfortable now."

A hand stretched out. "I'm Jack Stroble," said its owner as we shook. "And this is my associate, Donnie Bruno." The second man followed Stroble's lead.

As the agents exchanged handshakes with Leslie, I looked them over. Stroble was slender and taller than Bruno and wore his blond hair in a classic military cut. Bruno appeared to be in his early thirties, maybe a dozen years younger than his partner, and 20 or so pounds heavier; all muscle. His thick, black curls grazed his ears and collar. I don't believe he had a neck.

"I guess we could assume you're with the DEA," I said. "But I'd prefer to see some identification." The jackets we'd spotted at the restaurant were not in sight. Stroble nodded and pulled a handsome gold badge from his wallet. Bruno did the same. With an eagle perched above an ornate circle containing the words *US Drug Enforcement Administration: Special Agent*, they appeared authentic to me.

"Why the windbreakers earlier?" Leslie asked. "Don't you guys usually work undercover?"

Stroble slid his wallet back into a pocket. "We do some of both," he said. "Right now, we're operating out of Eleuthera at the invitation of the Commonwealth of the Bahamas." He paused a moment. "Our objective at the restaurant this evening was to send a message."

"A message?" Leslie asked. "To whom?"

"We've been told that word spreads fast here," Bruno said. "From one end of this island to the other, folks tonight are learning that the DEA is nosing around."

"And this news will discourage certain…businessmen?" I asked.

"That's the theory," Stroble said. "But we're here tonight to collect details about your alleged incident."

I didn't appreciate his use of the word "alleged." Leslie's harsh glare indicated she didn't much care for it either.

Bruno reached into a small pack at his feet, removed a compact tape recorder, and placed it on the coffee table between them and us. "Why don't you start with your arrival on Eleuthera," he said, switching on the machine. "Unless you noticed something out of the ordinary on Cat Island."

"Or Andros," added Stroble.

Leslie stared at them, slowly nodding. "Just how much do you know about us?" she asked.

Stroble shrugged. "You're a successful free-lance photographer. Your husband of less than a month owns an advertising agency in Little Rock. Name of Lassiter & Associates. You've been in the Bahamas for a couple of weeks shooting for *Southern Living*. You have no criminal record." He stopped and gave her a shrug. "Outside of the occasional speeding ticket."

Leslie blushed. She'd gotten her latest citation the morning of our wedding while hurrying to pick up a floral arrangement.

Stroble lifted an iPad for us to see and smiled. Sort of. "We have access to some apps not generally available over the internet."

Bruno cleared his throat and I took that as a signal to proceed.

"We flew into the Governor's Harbor Airport on November third," I said. "After checking into our cottage, we spent the afternoon in town."

"I used the rest of that day to scout locations for potential shots," Leslie said. "The dock, the cemetery, and a few other sites in Governor's Harbor."

"Did you see anything unusual or suspicious?" Stroble asked.

I shook my head. "No, but the next morning all hell broke loose."

"What happened?" Bruno asked.

"I needed the obligatory sunrise shot," Leslie said. "We rose before dawn and got to the beach about 6:15 or so."

"Where's this cottage?" Stroble asked.

"It's on the Atlantic side of the island, about halfway between the airport and Governor's Harbor," I said. "We walked north up the beach, maybe a mile or so."

Bruno reached down and retrieved a thick file from his pack. He removed a bulky paper item and began to unfold it. "Here's an aerial photo of Eleuthera," he said. "Can you get us oriented?"

"I'd noticed a promising grove of palm trees the previous afternoon," Leslie said. After studying the photo for several moments, she pointed to a spot. "Here it is."

"As you walked along the shore, did you see anyone?" Stroble asked.

"We had the beach to ourselves," I said. "Leslie had just finished getting her camera gear in place when a plane flew overhead, real low and heading south."

"Can you describe it?" Stroble asked.

"Twin engine," I said. "Probably a King Air. No lights. We didn't catch any markings."

"What happened next?" Bruno asked.

"Something crashed through the palm trees and landed in the sand near my camera bag," Leslie said.

"We later found out that it was a sack of cocaine," I said. "Eight others—all similar—fell to the beach just south of us."

105

"A total of nine bags of cocaine, huh?" Stroble asked. He crossed his arms and leaned back into the couch. He looked skeptical. "I guess some people appeared out of nowhere and hauled these unexpected goodies away?"

"All the sacks but one," Leslie said. "They didn't find the bag landing in the grove near us."

"So, these 'businessmen,' as you call them, ignored both of you and strolled away, leaving a very valuable sack of cocaine on the beach?" Bruno asked. He shot an impatient look at his partner.

Their attitude annoyed me. "They didn't see us," I said, "because we were scared out of our wits and grabbed our gear and hid. And they didn't find that last bag because a palm frond had fallen on top of it."

"What can you tell us about your drug runners?" Stroble asked.

"Two young black men," Leslie said. "I'd think they were locals, given their accents. We overheard them talking a bit on the beach."

"And they were armed," I said. "Shotguns."

"Back to that ninth bag," Bruno said. "Where is it?"

"We're not sure," I said. "We think—"

"Not sure," Stroble grumbled, shaking his head. He sighed and rolled his eyes. "I cannot believe we cut our dinner short to listen to this crap." He stood and nodded toward his partner.

Leslie jumped to her feet and took a few steps back. "Not so fast," she said, blocking the door. "A friend is missing as a result of all this. You have to hear the rest."

Stroble glared at her and shifted his withering gaze to me before glancing at this watch. He slumped onto the couch. "Make it quick," he said. "We have work to do. *Important* work."

"We remained hidden for about an hour after the men left the beach. After Leslie found the sack, I buried it in the dune," I said. "When we returned the next morning for another try at the sunrise shot, it was still there."

"And then what?" Stroble asked, not bothering to disguise his irritation.

"The guy who owns our rental cottage is a retired Miami policeman," I said. "We figured the best thing to do was to tell him what we'd seen."

"And give him the bag," Leslie said. "He's the one who determined it contained cocaine."

Suddenly, we had Bruno's full attention. He stared at us as his drawn face paled. "This man," he said. "Is he the one who's missing?"

"That's right," I said. "His name is Jonah—"

"Jefferson," Bruno said, shaking his head. "One of the nicest people you'll ever meet."

"You know him?" Leslie asked, her eyes wide.

"You could say that," Bruno said. "He's my godfather."

# ~ TWENTY ~

I stared at Bruno, my mouth gaping open. "Your godfather?" I asked. "You've got to be kidding."

"Jonah Jefferson is the very reason I went into law enforcement," Bruno said. "I've worshipped that man since I was a kid. After my dad died, he was a surrogate father."

"He's the former neighbor that you've told me about, right?" asked Stroble. "From your childhood days in South Carolina."

Bruno nodded. "He coached my Little League team, helped me bury my first dog, and read me the riot act when my grades started to slip in high school." He held his right hand in front of his chest, showing us a thick, heavy ring. "I never would have gone to Clemson, much less graduated, without Jonah's help."

"When did you last see him?" Leslie asked.

"It's been a couple of years," he said. "When I received this assignment, I gave Jonah a call. We'd planned to get together soon, but just hadn't got around to it yet." He slammed a meaty fist against the arm of the couch.

I shut my eyes and tried to recall the skimpy family tree Leslie and I had discovered on Jonah's flash drive earlier in the day. I hadn't thought much about it at the time, but I seemed to remember that it had included a godson.

"So, he knew you'd been assigned to Eleuthera?" Leslie asked.

"I e-mailed him a little over a week ago," Bruno said. "Told him in vague terms about our new posting and where we'd be based."

"I suspect he was on the way to see you," I said, "when he disappeared."

Stroble ran a hand through his hair. "Let's hear the rest of your story," he said. "What happened after you left the cocaine with Jonah?"

"We drove to the opposite end of the island so Leslie could photograph an abandoned lighthouse," I said.

"Jonah already had business to tend to here in Dunmore Town, and also told us he planned to talk to a contact—perhaps you—about the drug drop," Leslie said.

"He invited us to stop by for dinner later that night and said he'd fill us in on what happened," I said.

"And then what?" Bruno asked.

"We waited for an hour on his deck that evening and he never arrived," Leslie said. "We haven't seen him since."

For the next 30 minutes, we described how we'd spent the past six days, beginning with our delivery of the sack of cocaine to Jonah early on the morning after the drug drop. We told Stroble and Bruno about the unexpected appearance of Nigel, Gilbert, and Briscoe in Jonah's kitchen with the bag of coke in full view.

"Did they realize what they were looking at?" Stroble asked.

"We didn't say anything, of course, and Jonah slipped it behind him," I said. "But I'm afraid that we looked guilty as all get out."

"At the best," Leslie said, nodding, "it was a very awkward situation."

"And at the worst?" Bruno asked.

"Who knows?" I answered with a shrug. It was a question that had been worrying me for days.

We then mentioned our brief conversation with the Marchants, described the Chevrolet van we'd seen following us, and recounted our experiences with Dabney Attleman, including the threatening note she'd received. After Leslie advised them of Jonah's dismantled truck, I pinpointed its location on the aerial photo the agents spread across the coffee table. And we noted the ransacking of Jonah's house and shed, our cottage, and Dabney's home.

109

"His kidnappers are still looking for the coke," Stroble said. "I'd say that's a good sign."

Bruno leaned forward and twisted his head from side to side. I heard bones in his neck popping. "No doubt Jonah concealed the cocaine—and must have done a damn good job," he said. "Do you have any idea where it is?"

When Leslie looked at me, Stroble and Bruno followed her gaze. I cleared my throat. "I have a theory," I said. "Jonah builds birdhouses. He—"

"Jonah has always loved birds," Bruno interrupted. A sad grin crept across his face. "He taught me to build feeders and bluebird houses when I was in Cub Scouts."

"We think Jonah stashed the sack in the base of a new birdhouse," I said. "He apparently put it in place later that same morning after we gave him the coke."

"This particular house has a much thicker platform than any of the others," Leslie said. She used her hands to show its approximate dimensions.

"That sounds like Jonah," Bruno said. "Anything else?"

"We had dinner tonight with Dabney," I said. "She told us that a car followed her home after work. A black, sporty model of some sort."

"And I almost forget about this," Leslie said. She reached into her purse, pulled out the two sheets of paper, and handed them to Stroble. "Jonah's computer was destroyed, but we managed to find a thumb drive. This was on it."

Stroble studied the top page, his eyes taking in Jonah's summary and analysis. As he handed it to Bruno, he glanced at the second sheet. He looked to us with a frown. "Is this all?"

"Our reaction, too," I said. "We suspect he stopped writing at that point and headed this way." I paused a beat. "Perhaps to see you."

"Only," Bruno said, gesturing to the aerial photo, "to be abducted before he got halfway here."

"Do you still have the flash drive?" Stroble asked.

I shook my head. "We felt it'd be safer out of our possession so we left it with Malcolm McDaniel," I said. "He's a computer expert with a shop just a few blocks from here. Jonah's original reason to visit Dunmore Town was to pick up a new modem from McDaniel."

After Bruno made a note, he turned and looked to his partner. Stroble clinched his jaw several times and then massaged his temples. "The hard drive on Jonah's computer might be worth looking at," he said. "We have technicians in Atlanta who can extract every last keystroke from those units." He sighed before glancing at his watch. "It's getting late," he said. "Let's call it quits for now." He and Bruno stood. "Will you be staying here much longer?"

We hadn't told them we'd flown to Nassau yesterday, planning to continue a surreptitious search for our friend. As far as they knew, Leslie's photo assignment required this jaunt to Dunmore Town. "We'll head south tomorrow," I said.

"Somewhere around Hatchet Bay or Gregory Town," Leslie added with a nod.

Stroble stared at us while reaching for his wallet. He handed me a business card and gave another to Leslie. "This has my cell phone number. I want you to call me every day and check in," he said. "Every single day. If I'm not available, leave a message. And don't do anything foolish."

Bruno folded the aerial photograph and replaced it and the tape recorder in his pack. After a quick round of handshakes, the agents left our room.

Leslie locked the door behind them and slid the safety chain in place. I looked at my watch. It was almost one o'clock. We soon doused the lights and went to bed. I must have gone to sleep at some point, but it was a restless night.

*　*　*

The following morning, after a late breakfast, Leslie and I had a gut-wrenching water taxi ride as we crossed the choppy bay. Every wave we hit exploded in a drenching spray. The boat felt like a roller coaster in a driving rainstorm, and I'm no fan of amusement parks.

111

Another minute or so and I would have had a second—and decidedly unpleasant—experience with a big stack of pancakes. We didn't remove our life jackets until we'd clambered onto the dock.

Each of us carrying a small duffel, we located our rental car behind a radiator shop. I double-checked the scrap of cardboard I.D. hooked to the key ring, hoping I'd made a mistake. But the license plate matched the number on the ring. It had two months to go before expiring.

Other than the metallic blue left front fender, our Crown Victoria was of an indeterminate color. The lower panels of all four doors displayed various stages of terminal rusting, and the front bumper didn't exist. A meandering crack bisected the windshield and the back seat had been removed, replaced by a trio of mismatched milk crates lashed together with a frayed rope to form a makeshift bench. A piece of baling wire held the trunk closed while a modified coat hanger served as a makeshift radio antenna. It made the little red Wrangler seem like a luxury vehicle.

After Leslie took a slow walk around the car, she gave me a wink. "Looks like the honeymoon is over." She tossed her bag next to mine on the milk crates and climbed into the passenger seat.

I stuck the key into the ignition, expecting the worst. But the engine fired at once, growling under the wide, mottled hood like an awakening beast. Maybe it had been a police cruiser in a former life, I thought. I shifted into drive, tapped the accelerator, and we shot forward like a dragster. Leslie grabbed for a missing seat belt.

"Keep to the left!" she screamed.

I swerved to the proper side of the road, waved at a wide-eyed driver skidding to a dusty stop on the opposite shoulder, and reached for the radio. I needed my Jimmy Buffet fix. But someone had removed the knobs. Leslie loosened her death grip on the dash and found our map of the island. "South," she said, breathing hard. "Stay on this highway and head south."

As if we had any options. There was but one single narrow road running the length of Eleuthera with the occasional drive or track angling off into the brush.

We drove south toward Gregory Town.

# ~ TWENTY-ONE ~

We'd been on the road about 20 minutes when we passed through a small, unidentified community. Three churches, a tiny grocery store, and a beauty parlor were scattered among a dozen or so modest cinder-block houses. A basketball backboard and goal hung from a power pole over the asphalt pavement and I eased off the accelerator to let a group of adolescent boys fight for a rebound.

Watching the game in the rearview mirror, I felt a hand on my elbow. "Turn around, Randy," Leslie said.

"Let me guess. You want to shoot some hoops."

"I just had an inspired idea."

I gulped. "Want to tell me about it?"

"I think we need to work on altering our appearances."

As we backtracked, interrupting the basketball action again, I noticed Leslie studying the buildings ahead of us, paying particular attention to the beauty shop. The front door stood open and a pair of window fans blew into the small shop. A young boy dashed out, followed by a girl a couple of years older wielding a fly swatter. She took a wild swing and missed as the boy whooped and sped around the corner.

"Park here."

I pulled off the road, stopped the car in the dust next to the *Vernita's Beauty Boutique* sign, and turned to my bride. "I'm afraid to ask what you're thinking."

She grinned and tickled my neck with her fingers. "Here's your chance to fulfill one of my fantasies," she said with an impish wink. "I've always wanted a blond boyfriend."

"Will this be a quid pro quo arrangement?"

"Meaning?" Leslie asked.

"Meaning that you'll be willing to work with me on one of my fantasies?"

"Maybe," she said, giving me a mischievous smile. "It depends upon the type and degree of perversion. We can negotiate later."

Leslie stepped from our Detroit road hog and strolled to the entrance. Trudging along behind her and growing more nervous with every step, I reluctantly walked through the doorway. Strange smells attacked my nostrils, reminding me of several unsuccessful experiments in my high school chemistry class. While my nasal passages reminisced, I prayed that the appointment ledger was booked solid for days. Two women looked up as we walked in. One sat in the ceremonial chair reserved for customers while the other stood behind her with a comb and pair of scissors. They smiled. My hopes sank.

The hairdresser nodded to Leslie. I'd never seen a larger woman. Not obese, just big. Standing at least six three and weighing maybe 250 pounds, she had beautiful mahogany skin, brilliant eyes, and sparkling teeth. "Would you like braids, miss?" she asked. "I can make you a real Bahamian beauty."

Leslie chuckled and shook her head, her hair brushing her shoulders. "Do you style men's hair?" she asked and pointed to me. I felt like a common commodity.

"Of course," she said. "Let me finish with Myrtle."

Less than five minutes passed before I climbed into the warm chair. The outgoing proprietor, who introduced herself as Vernita, draped a clean sheet around my neck and patted my shoulder. "What can I do for you?" she asked.

Leslie had found an empty seat under the nearest window and pretended to be absorbed in a magazine.

I ran a hand through my generic brown hair. It grazed my ears and had started to curl a bit above the collar. "Go ahead and cut it short," I said after a moment's pause. "Moderately short. After that, I'd like it dyed blond."

Vernita gave me a big smile. "A new start, eh?" she asked. "You will be even more handsome!" She gave me a colorful brochure. "While I trim," she said, "I want you to pick out the shade you'd like. We have many blonds to choose from."

My mind wandered as large clumps of hair tumbled to the floor. At some point during the ordeal, I noticed a small hand-lettered sign across the room: *Ears Pierced*. What the heck, I thought. If Leslie was so insistent on changing our looks, I might as well go for the full effect. And given our location, I felt compelled to opt for the *Golden Tropic* tint.

I remained pretty stoic throughout the hair styling process, but found the outpatient surgery on my ear rather uncomfortable. In fact, it hurt like hell. As Vernita put the bloody needle aside, I thought about other piercing options and shivered.

When she held a mirror in front of me an hour and a half later, I didn't know what to think. I recognized the worried eyes, the gaping mouth, the nose, and the top three-fourths of my right ear, but the rest belonged to an imposter. Before I could hyperventilate, Leslie squeezed my arm. "You look great," she said. And then she pushed me aside and slid into the chair.

"I'd like a short, layered cut," Leslie said. "Something like this." She showed a photograph from the magazine to Vernita. "And I want you to color it black. As dark as you can get it."

Vernita slid her fingers through Leslie's thick reddish-brown hair. "It is so beautiful," she said. "You are certain you want to do this?"

"Yes, ma'am. I, too, am ready for a new start."

I tried to read an out-of-date tabloid, but instead found myself watching Leslie's wonderful locks cascade to the worn linoleum. She wouldn't resemble the beautiful woman in our wedding photographs, I thought. Not even close. When I shook my head, she flashed her dimples and shrugged. "I'm okay," she mouthed.

We left about three hours after we'd arrived, giving Vernita a generous tip for her services. I kept wondering about the nervous stranger staring back at me in the rearview mirror as we drove out of town. And I continued to glance at the vaguely familiar passenger who sat in the adjacent seat. Leslie caught me looking and patted my knee. "Don't worry," she said. "These changes are temporary. They're for a good cause." Her eyes shifted to my throbbing ear. "And I like your gold stud." I yelped as she touched the tender lobe.

We'd gone a few miles when she reached into her purse. "I almost forgot," she said. "I bought several props in Dunmore Town." She handed me a pair of wrap-around, mirrored sunglasses. "You can be a rock star!"

I slipped them on and peered into the mirror. Not bad, I thought. Maybe this blond will have more fun.

Leslie pulled another pair of glasses from her purse. With clear lenses and thick, black frames, they appeared to be reading glasses. She put them on and turned to me, her eyes wide. "What do you think?"

"I'm seeing a female Buddy Holly," I said. "Cute, but sort of serious." I braked to let a herd of goats amble across the road. "The question is: will anyone recognize us?"

Leslie opened our map and held it in her lap. "We'll know in about 20 minutes," she said. "Let's hope that Dabney's in her store."

\*\*\*

We entered Gregory Town, and for once the mysterious white van wasn't in sight. I parked our Crown Victoria next to Dabney's Volkswagen and followed Leslie into the dress shop. The bell on the door chimed as we entered. In the throes of assisting an apparent mother-daughter duo, Dabney glanced at us. "Good afternoon," she said, forcing a smile. "I'll be with you in a moment." She hurried into her stockroom.

While we waited, Leslie sorted through rack after rack of clothing, picking out a pair of pretty sundresses to try on. She stepped into a dressing room as Dabney rang up an impressive sale to her other customers. When they left the store, Dabney walked over and stood near me. "Enjoying your trip to Eleuthera?" she asked. She never made eye contact but began rearranging a stack of blouses.

"We're having a grand time," I said, wondering how a rock star would answer. I tried lowering my voice. "An absolutely fabulous vacation. The beaches are superb. Almost as good as those in… uh…Fiji. And along the Riviera." I tilted my new earring toward Dabney, hoping that she might comment on it. But she had me out-pierced about ten to one and paid it no attention.

Leslie returned from the changing room, slipped one dress back into the rack, and handed Dabney the other. "I'll take this one, please," she said.

Dabney stared at her for several seconds before turning and making her way to the cash register. As she keyed in the sale, her gaze returned to Leslie. "Have you shopped here before?" she asked.

A faint smile appeared between Leslie's cheeks as she removed her glasses and her dimples surfaced. Dabney gasped and almost dropped the dress to the floor. "It's you!" she shouted. "I cannot believe it." She gave Leslie a big hug before stepping back and taking in my bride's new look, shaking her head in disbelief.

Dabney then turned her gaze to me and studied my face and head, her mouth wide open. I hoped that I might also receive a nice, lingering embrace but it never materialized. She leaned forward and tousled my hair instead.

"What a transformation," Dabney said. "You two are unrecognizable. It's amazing, completely amazing."

# ~ TWENTY-TWO ~

After Leslie paid for her new sundress, Dabney folded it and placed the garment in a sack. Following the obligatory chitchat about hairstyles, Dabney turned serious. "I've found you a place to stay," she said. "It's a compact house, but clean, convenient, and fully equipped. The owner is a fussy German businessman who won't be back 'til Christmas."

"Where is it?" Leslie asked.

"And how expensive?" I added.

"About five miles south of here, right on the Queen's Highway. The house has a great view of the Caribbean," Dabney said. "It's $750 a week—or some 30 percent off his usual rate."

That kind of money would get you a furnished mansion in Little Rock. World-class snorkeling, palm trees, ocean breezes, and fresh grouper don't come cheap, I realized.

"Could we take a look at it?" I asked.

Dabney drew a map on the back of a blank receipt and handed it to me. "If you come to a cement block plant," she said, "you've gone too far. The key's hidden under a conch shell next to the back porch."

"We'll return soon," Leslie said as we angled to the door. "Thanks for your help."

As I backed our rusting land yacht into the street, Leslie gave my knee a pat. "Let's stop at the local grocery as we leave town," she said. "This girl missed her lunch."

I glanced at my watch. A quarter before two. My saliva glands kicked in. After purchasing enough food for a small feast, we headed south out of Gregory Town. Dabney's directions delivered us to the rental property ten minutes later. Before stepping inside and inspecting the house, we yielded to a more urgent need and detoured to a weathered picnic table on the deck and fixed ourselves gourmet ham and cheese sandwiches.

"I could enjoy this setting for hours," Leslie said, nodding toward the emerald waters of the Caribbean. She stared at the horizon, lost in her own world. I wondered what she was thinking. Had we made a mistake choosing the Bahamas for our honeymoon? Were we foolish to continue our search for Jonah Jefferson?

I built another sandwich and scanned the property. The house stood on a knoll 20 or 30 feet above sea level. An impenetrable thicket surrounded the two sides and back of the lawn. The front yard, boasting several key lime trees laden with fruit, sloped down to the ragged highway paralleling the shoreline.

As we finished our meal, a gentle breeze jostled a set of wind chimes hanging from the eave of the roof. A curious lizard climbed atop the other end of our table and gazed at us through dark, beady eyes for a moment before scurrying out of sight.

Leslie began packing away our leftovers. "Although we've haven't yet toured the house, I'm beginning to like this place."

The interior sparkled, about what I'd expected from a German landlord. As Dabney had noted, the house contained all the modern conveniences: a spacious master suite with a nice bathroom, roomy shower, dishwasher, disposal, washer and dryer, television, satellite dish, CD player, wet bar, and even a small library, although most of the works were in German. Large picture windows overlooked the sea.

"Let's take it," Leslie said. She locked the door and slipped the key into her purse. "We can afford this house for a week."

"And there's another feature," I said, pointing over her shoulder. A covered hot tub sat on the corner of the stone patio. I fiddled with the controls for a moment and managed to turn the heater on. "If we're going to stay here," I said, "we might as well take full advantage of the amenities."

Leslie arched her eyebrows. "How long before it heats up?"

"Four or five hours," I said. "Maybe sooner."

\* \* \*

As we drove back toward Gregory Town, Leslie pulled out her phone. "I owe the DEA guys a call." She had to leave a message, giving them directions to our rental house.

When we returned to the dress shop, Leslie handed Dabney a check. "I'll deposit this in the owner's account," Dabney said, placing it in her register. "Any news on Jonah?"

I nodded. "Remember those two DEA agents we saw at the restaurant last night? We visited with them after you left."

Dabney's eyes grew wide. "What's their take on things?"

"We're not sure," Leslie said. "Other than they warned us to be careful. The younger of the two has known Jonah since he was a kid. We told them we'd keep in touch every day."

"What's next?" Dabney asked.

"We've talked about driving into Governor's Harbor tonight," I said. "There's a local dive we'd like to check out."

Leslie ran her fingers through her short ebony locks. "I don't think anyone will remember us."

Dabney grinned and shook her head. "You'll be just another anonymous tourist couple," she said. "In the meantime, I'll do more research on those two Baines characters who were included on Jonah's list."

\* \* \*

We made a more serious pass through the local market before returning to our new cottage. After stocking the refrigerator and pantry with groceries, we unpacked our meager belongings. While I grabbed a paperback thriller, Leslie took a shower. Twenty minutes later—wearing her bright new sundress—she joined me on the deck.

"Wow!" I dropped the book into my lap. "How 'bout a date?"

After Leslie kissed my forehead, she stood behind me and massaged my neck and shoulders. "Surely you weren't planning to ply me with liquor?"

"Followed by wild suggestive dancing," I said. "Let's go."

The sun had set by the time we arrived at Governor's Harbor. We cruised through the quiet town before stopping at the tavern. For the first time we noticed its name: *The Jellyfish Lounge*. As before, the neon "Kalik" sign in the single window flashed first red and then blue. None of the nearby vehicles looked familiar.

Remembering that we were on a date, I trotted around the car and opened Leslie's door. She slipped on her glasses and took my hand. "Shall we?"

We entered the smoky dive, pausing to let our eyes adjust to the dim lighting. A well-stocked bar stood to the left and a small stage filled the opposite end of the building. A dozen cocktail tables, a third or so occupied, surrounded a worn dance floor. I didn't recognize any of the faces. I led Leslie to the nearest empty table, arranging our chairs so we faced the door.

"This way we can see who comes in," I whispered.

A tall, attractive waitress appeared as we sat. "Good evening," she said. "What may I bring you tonight?" I could have listened to her lilting accent for hours.

Leslie asked for a gin and tonic. I settled for bottled water with a twist of lime. And we ordered a platter of conch fritters for supper.

The Marchants arrived half an hour later, about the time the band began setting up. They shuffled past us, landing at a table for two next to a cigarette vending machine. While Mme. Marchant dropped a handful of coins into the slot and selected a pack, the waitress delivered two tall beverages topped with plastic umbrellas to their table.

"They must be regulars," Leslie said, nursing her drink. "They didn't even have to place an order."

The Marchants visited with the waitress several minutes before she excused herself to tend to other customers. More couples had wandered in, several of them guests of the nearby Club Med complex if their shirts were reliable. The band members tuned their instruments and started with a Bob Marley medley bringing everyone but the Marchants to the dance floor. Ten minutes later Leslie and I collapsed into our chairs and ordered a second round.

As the waitress brought our drinks, two young black men strolled in, teasing the waitress as they passed, and settled at an adjacent table. Something about them seemed familiar.

Leslie's knee knocked against mine. "Don't stare," she whispered. "But those are the guys we saw on the beach."

I felt the hair on my neck begin to rise as my head slowly turned their way. "The ones at the drug drop?"

"Yep," she said. "The same. But they had shotguns then."

# ~ TWENTY-THREE ~

I glanced at the men. Young and black with intense eyes and perfect smiles, they didn't appear much different from about half the crowd in the bar. "How can you be sure?"

Leslie leaned closer to me. "I wouldn't swear on it," she whispered. "But look at the one to the right and check out that fine piece of jewelry hanging around his neck. One of our beach commandos wore a heavy gold necklace with that exact same pattern."

I tried to keep my squinting discreet. "A dragon?"

"I'd forgotten all about it until moments ago," she whispered, giving me a slight nod. "But when I saw the necklace, it clicked."

I stood and scooted my chair against the table.

"Where are you going?"

"Outside," I answered, my voice low. "It might be worth examining the vehicles in the lot."

Nearly blocking the door, a shiny Peugeot with a fleur-de-lis decal in a corner of the rear windshield occupied the prime spot. That one must belong to the Marchants, I told myself. Six or eight other cars, including our unique Ford Crown Victoria, filled the remaining parking spaces. But I didn't see a decrepit white Chevrolet van. Following an impulse, I walked on out to the dark street and looked both directions. Half a block away in the distance, I spotted a familiar cargo van parked under a streetlight and trotted toward it. After glancing back to confirm no one was watching, I tried all doors and discovered, not surprisingly, that they were locked.

"You found it, didn't you?" Leslie asked when I returned to our table.

"The very same, complete with defective grill. Locked tight, but no license plate." I tilted my head toward the next table. "Anything going on here?"

Leslie put an arm around my neck and whispered into my ear. "They've been flirting with a pair of young women, but haven't said a word to our French friends." She leaned back, eyed my new hairdo, and ran her fingers across my scalp. "You make a pretty cute blond."

The musicians reappeared on the stage and launched into another reggae tune. Leslie smiled and jerked me to my feet. When we slid into our seats minutes later, the Marchants had departed. A serious Japanese threesome now occupied the same table. Meanwhile, the young Bahamian men and their two female friends had a spirited party underway as another round of Kaliks arrived at their table.

We'd just ordered more beverages ourselves when the band began playing a slow calypso song. I led Leslie onto the dance floor and wrapped my arms around her. Somebody had the good sense to dim the lights another notch as eight or ten couples swayed to the music. My hands slid down Leslie's back, coming to rest at her waist. Strange, I thought; I hadn't felt the bump of a bra strap. My fingers eased a bit lower and made another discovery. A most interesting and intriguing discovery.

"You aren't wearing anything under this dress, are you?"

"Do my sandals count?"

I pulled her close.

Leslie nuzzled my neck for a moment. "We seem to have gotten out of the honeymoon frame of mind," she said. "But I'm not ready to give it up." She pressed her firm, warm body against me.

The song came to an end, much to my dismay, and we returned to our table. The young men and their acquaintances had disappeared.

"These glasses are giving me a headache," Leslie said. "Maybe it's time for us to call it a night, too."

I signaled to our waitress.

On the drive back we discussed what, if anything, we'd learned at The Jellyfish Lounge. Leslie argued against a connection between the Marchants and the two men with the white van. "They never made eye contact, much less engaged in a conversation," she said. "I got the impression they're not even acquainted."

"But that doesn't remove the Marchants from our list of suspects."

"You're right. They all could be playing it cool, not openly recognizing each other."

After parking the car next to the house, I led Leslie to the dark patio. The Milky Way stretched over the heavens like a glistening band, and thousands of more distant stars twinkled across vast, incomprehensible galaxies. When we came to a stop at the hot tub, Leslie dropped my hand and lifted the sundress above her head.

"Did I ever mention my fantasy about a blond boyfriend?" she asked, tossing the dress over a bench. She stepped out of her sandals.

In seconds, I stripped and then shoved the cover of the hot tub aside. With jets of warm water pulsing against our bodies, we made love under the deep night sky of the Bahamas.

\* \* \*

A downpour awoke us the next morning. We'd just finished breakfast when a car turned off the highway and crept up the drive to our cottage.

"Who could that be?" Leslie asked.

Two men sprinted from the sedan, ducking their heads as they tried to block the driving rain with their forearms. I recognized the blue windbreakers as Stroble and Bruno leaped to the deck. With Leslie standing at my side, I slipped on my mirrored sunglasses, flung open the door, and motioned for them to enter.

"Thanks," Stroble said, wiping the water from his face. He looked at me before turning his gaze to Leslie. He took a step back and bumped into Bruno. "I'm sorry. We must have made a mistake."

Leslie, wearing her new eyeglasses, reeled off something in French. Hands on her hips, she looked and sounded upset. Choking back a laugh, I played with my earring.

125

Bruno peered around his partner. "We're looking for an American couple," he said. He spoke slowly, almost shouting, as if that would help bridge the language barrier. "They've rented a place in this area."

My clever bride replied with more rapid French phrasing and gave them a classic European shrug.

Stroble gave us a feeble wave, forced a small smile, and said, "Please excuse us." He turned and reached for the door.

I waited until they'd stepped onto the deck. "How 'bout some coffee?" I asked and took off my shades. "We're always hospitable—to our DEA friends."

The men froze, staring at me for seconds, as water from the roof dripped onto their stunned faces. Leslie giggled and removed her glasses with a grin.

"I'll be damned." Stroble studied us as if we'd just climbed from a spaceship. He shook his wet head. "I'll be damned…"

As the agents came back inside, Leslie handed them a pair of towels. "While you dry off, I'll get the coffee."

"I suppose I should thank you for yesterday's call," Stroble said. "But I don't remember any mention of this disguise routine."

"We're going to be here a while longer," I said. "We didn't want any more hassles."

Bruno tossed me his towel. "You're not planning on doing something stupid, are you?"

Leslie snorted. "Do we look like heroes?"

Stroble's eyes searched our faces while he sipped his coffee. "You can be heroes by helping us recover the cocaine and Jonah's computer. Are you available for a trip to Jonah's house?"

"What if someone shows up?" Leslie asked. "Like Nigel?"

A cryptic smile appeared on Bruno's face. "Don't worry," he said. "We'll have the place to ourselves."

Within five minutes Leslie and I had piled into the backseat of the agents' car. We held hands the entire way as we passed one familiar landmark after another. A few miles north of Governor's Harbor, Leslie pointed ahead to the sign for Barracuda Bay. "There's the road," she said. "It's got some serious potholes."

Bruno turned off the highway and bottomed-out within seconds. "No worries," he grunted. "This is a rental car."

We drove past the quiet, empty cottage before stopping in front of Jonah's home. A deserted beach stretched beyond the house. Wave after wave spilled across the sands and, further out, breakers surged over the barrier reefs. As Stroble stepped from the car, he whistled. "Man, what a spread," he said.

Bruno took his time surveying the surroundings. "For years Jonah worked hard, dreaming of a place like this." He clinched his jaw. "I owe him a lot."

Stroble began walking toward the deck, eyeing the birdhouses as he went. "Let's get the computer first."

While Leslie and I disconnected the severed cords to the computer and brushed the dust off, Stroble and Bruno toured the rooms. Bruno had been assigned to photograph the house; occasional flashes reflected down the hall. A few minutes later they joined us in what remained of Jonah's office. "Those sons of bitches sure did a number on this place," Stroble said. "I hope to participate in the payback."

After he took half a dozen quick shots of the room from various angles, Bruno grabbed the hard drive with one arm and headed to the car, the rest of us following in his wake. While he stored it in the trunk, I looked to Stroble. "How could you guarantee Nigel wouldn't barge in on us?"

"We have a skilled associate," he said, glancing at his watch. "An attractive young woman. She dropped in on him a bit earlier, unannounced and desperate for help with directions. I understand he has a fondness for talking with females."

"Maybe he just likes good conversation," Leslie said.

Stroble opened his mouth, and then wisely opted not to challenge her. Instead, he inspected Jonah's collection of birdhouses, stopping beneath the newest addition. "This must be it."

"That's our theory," I said.

After taking a series of photos, Bruno gave the digital camera to Stroble and wrapped his thick arms around the post and pulled.

He lifted the house a couple of feet and startled an ani, causing it to leap from one of the holes and fly away with a squawk. The rest of us helped lower the house to the ground.

"Let's take this into his shop," I said and pointed to the outbuilding. Leslie trotted ahead and opened the door. We placed the birdhouse on its side atop Jonah's workbench. While Bruno again went through his photographic ritual, Stroble found a pipe wrench and removed the pole. Using Jonah's electric drill, we took turns extracting eight long screws from the base. When the bottom piece of plywood fell away, a burlap bag tumbled onto the bench.

# ~ TWENTY-FOUR ~

I reached for the burlap sack.

Stroble caught my elbow. "Not so fast," he said. "Sometimes these things are packed with very nasty tricks. Rude surprises that go boom."

"I don't think Jonah would have booby-trapped this little item," Bruno said, "but it's better to play it safe."

The DEA agents spent a few minutes studying the bag, eyeing it from every angle. While Stroble gently poked and prodded it with a screwdriver from Jonah's toolbox, Bruno took a series of close-up photographs before setting his camera aside. After a nod from Stroble, Bruno lifted the bag from the workbench and unfolded the thick layers of burlap. When the rough fabric fell away, the remaining object in Bruno's hands appeared to be wrapped in a black plastic garbage bag. He removed the plastic and a familiar portrait of Robin Hood stared back at us.

"What have we here?" Stroble's eyes widened as he smiled at his partner. "I don't believe our civilian friends mentioned this unique packaging." He arched his eyebrows and shifted his gaze to us.

"What do you mean?" Leslie asked. "Is the Robin Hood image significant?"

Bruno nodded, aiming his camera at the bag. "Let's just say it's the calling card of a certain malevolent entrepreneur from South America. A very ambitious and elusive—and successful—master criminal by the name of Alarico Villarreal. You might've seen his name in the media over the years. We didn't realize he operated in the Bahamas." A flash from the camera temporarily blinded us.

"Up to now, he's funneled his merchandise through Jamaica or the Caymans," Stroble said, rubbing his chin. "Or via Mexico, from time to time. This is an unexpected but interesting development. Extremely interesting." A few moments passed and he reached into his jacket and pulled out a small plastic box. "Let's take an independent sample," he said and handed the item to his colleague.

Bruno opened the compact container and extracted a metallic instrument about the size of a penlight. He pressed a button and a needle emerged from the base. Bruno then slipped the sharp point into the cloth and held it steady for a few moments.

"I thought you could just touch a sample to your tongue," Leslie said. "That's what Jonah did."

Stroble snorted. "Back in the old days we could. But the bad guys soon started sabotaging the occasional bag with strychnine. That little high-tech item," he said, pointing to the tool in his colleague's hand, "is a godsend."

Bruno studied a series of small dials on the device for a moment and then looked to Stroble with a telling nod. "Pure, uncut, unadulterated coke," he said, almost repeating Jonah's exact words from days earlier. "It doesn't come any better." After cleaning and storing the gadget, he returned it to Stroble and rewrapped the plastic and burlap around the bag.

"I'm going to lock this in the trunk," he said.

"You can't be serious," I said. "It would make Jonah's situation even worse."

"What do you mean?" Stroble asked. "Do you expect us to leave this cocaine in the birdhouse?" He didn't bother to hide a heavy measure of sarcasm.

I didn't much care for his attitude. "That's exactly what I expect *us* to do. Jonah may find himself in a position where he has no choice but to tell his captors about the bag's location."

"Randy's right," Leslie said. "If Jonah is somehow forced to bring them here to retrieve the cocaine, they'll kill him if it's not where he said it'd be."

"They might do that any…" Bruno said and paused, unwilling to finish his sentence.

"But we've got to take the chance," I said. I stepped forward to the workbench and started to replace the sack in the base of the birdhouse.

"Let's put a little insurance policy in place first," Stroble said. "I believe my young but talented colleague can make a minor modification, one that will somewhat put our minds at ease."

Bruno pulled a small case from a pocket and extracted an item not much bigger than a toothpick. "Something like this, I assume?"

"What's that?" I asked.

"His little device," Stroble said, "is an electronic transponder. Agent Bruno will conceal it within the bag and we'll be able to track it from a long distance."

Once Bruno completed his handiwork, Leslie and I returned the sack of cocaine to its secret compartment within the customized birdhouse and screwed it in place. With the agents' help, we carried the birdhouse from the workshop and installed it in the original position in Jonah's yard.

Stroble stepped back and gazed at Jonah's latest example of avian architecture. "I suspect we're looking at the most valuable birdhouse in the history of the world."

"I have another idea," Bruno said. "Something to give everyone some additional comfort. It's also from our bag of electronic goodies."

"I'm all ears," Stroble said.

"Let's take our infrared camera unit, mount it on the shed, and aim it right here," Bruno said. "It's motion-activated and solar powered—and will transmit a video feed straight to your laptop in real time."

With Stroble's quick assent, Bruno jogged to their car and removed a duffle from the trunk. He spent a few moments sorting

131

through the bag before trotting to the shed where he installed a small housing, appearing to be an electrical outlet, on the exterior wall. Bruno next slipped a miniature camera lens into place. He then attached an inconspicuous solar panel to the roof on the opposite side of the building, providing power to the camera via a thin cable.

Fifteen minutes after first suggesting the idea, Bruno finished his work. "I believe we now have an acceptable solution."

While Bruno placed his camera and duffle bag in the trunk of their car next to Jonah's hard drive, Stroble opened his laptop and tested the infrared camera system. "Donnie Bruno," he said. "You are a miracle worker." He held the screen for Leslie and me to see. While the image was a bit grainy, there was no doubt what we were viewing.

Stroble pulled a cell phone from his pocket and punched in a number. "Good morning, Allie," he said. "We have completed our expedition. You may now bid Mr. Nigel Watlington a heartfelt goodbye." He closed the phone and slid into the passenger seat as Bruno got behind the wheel. "Let's hit the road." Leslie and I climbed into the back.

"I suspect you have a photography assignment to complete, Ms. Carlisle," Stroble said as we bounced across the rough road to the highway. Leslie didn't say anything but squeezed my hand. "While you're getting your shots, with your husband's capable assistance, of course, Agent Bruno and I will see what we can discover on this unexpected Villarreal connection to Jonah's disappearance." He swung around and faced us. "I again must request that you stay in daily contact with us."

They dropped us off at our cottage with perfunctory good-byes and headed north, returning to Dunmore Town. Or at least that's what they told us they'd be doing. I noticed Stroble had the cell phone pressed to his ear as Bruno backed down the driveway.

\* \* \*

We fixed a light lunch of soup and salad and took our plates to the picnic table. A breeze swept up from the Caribbean and awakened the wind chimes. Five hundred yards offshore, a pair of fishing boats bobbed in the swells. Miles beyond them a line of towering thunderheads loomed on the horizon like a distant mountain range. A flash of lightning zigzagged between the clouds, too far away to be heard.

Leslie stared into space, sipping her Coke. Her food hadn't been touched.

"Lost in thought?" I asked.

She blinked and turned to me with a questioning look. "I wish we could search the Marchant's property," she said. "If for no other reason than to eliminate them as suspects."

"Maybe we can," I said. "Our young friend Briscoe handles their yard work. Perhaps he'd be willing to help us out."

"Hmmm…I hadn't thought of Briscoe." She nodded and nibbled on a cracker. "Something else is troubling me," she said between bites.

I waited, figuring she'd tell me. It didn't take long.

"Perhaps I'm worrying when I shouldn't be, but something about Dabney doesn't seem…quite right."

"I thought you liked her."

"I do," she said. "She's smart, creative, and no doubt's a lot of fun. Yet she doesn't seem very upset with Jonah's disappearance, given the history of their relationship." She shrugged. "Maybe my intuition's running amuck, but I'm getting warning signals. Subtle, but they're still present."

"Meaning you think she could be…involved…in it?" I asked. "What about her ransacked house and the threatening letter slipped under the door to her shop? And that car following her home the other evening?"

"She could've upended her furniture herself and written that note for all we know. And fabricated the story about the mysterious car." Leslie took a long sip of her drink and then looked me in the eye. "I find it rather curious that her dress shop hasn't been touched."

That also struck me as peculiar.

133

"There's something else I noticed when we helped get her house back in order the other day," I said. "Something that didn't quite jibe. I should've mentioned it earlier, but I forgot all about it 'til now."

"Go on," Leslie said.

"There was a rolled-up sleeping bag tucked away in one corner of her sunroom."

"So? Dabney doesn't seem the outdoorsy type, but maybe she enjoys spending a night on the beach."

"That's just it," I said. "Camping is illegal in the Bahamas."

"Are you sure?"

"The national government outlawed it many years ago to preserve a higher-class tourist experience," I said.

"In other words," Leslie said, "to discourage the riffraff."

"That's what our guidebook claims," I said. "And one other thing puzzled me. When I went into her bathroom to wash my hands, I saw a razor, a can of shaving cream, and a stick of deodorant—the masculine varieties. I didn't think about them much at the time, but I doubt if Jonah left them there."

"Do you think she has a male houseguest?"

"I think it's a distinct possibility. Too bad we didn't have a chance to take a peek into her closet."

Leslie took another drink of her coke. "Also, her insistence on meeting us night before last for supper in Dunmore Town seems odd," she said.

"I've wondered about that myself," I said. "There appeared to be no reason to see us, other than to commiserate. The alleged incident with the mysterious car didn't occur until after we'd agreed to meet."

"My point precisely," Leslie said. "Could our dinner date have been an opportunity for her to determine if we'd learned anything new? And to figure out what we'd be doing next? Remember how she volunteered to find us a house?" Leslie swung an arm across the deck. "And here we are."

"So, you feel there's a likelihood that Dabney's hoping we can lead her to the missing cocaine?"

"It's a wild theory," Leslie said, gazing at the sea. "A long shot. But if she's behind all this, I'd sure like to turn the tables."

"In other words, let Dabney lead us to Jonah."

Leslie rewarded me with a clever little smile. "Let's play dumb a bit longer."

That, I felt certain, would not be a problem.

# ~ TWENTY-FIVE ~

After lunch Leslie and I walked down the sloping yard and across the narrow, desolate highway to the rugged shoreline. Hand in hand, we stepped over and around the sharp and jagged rocks, spotting crabs as they scooted sideways and searched for cover in the shallow tidal pools. Waves surged against the eroded ledge, throwing a fine mist into the air with every small watery explosion. The steady breeze pressed our clothing against our bodies.

We stopped and gazed out to sea. Miles away a tanker inched across the horizon. Closer by, a pair of gulls sailed overhead, their heads pivoting as they scouted for food.

I squeezed Leslie's fingers. "Do you think we can trust Nigel?"

Leslie continued to stare at the distant swells and rubbed her chin with her free hand. She turned to me with a slight smile. "I've given a lot of thought to good old Nigel," she said. "I don't care much for him; he's arrogant and a hopeless chauvinist." She hesitated for a moment and looked back to the sea. "But I think we can trust him. Why do you ask?"

"You said something earlier about inspecting the Marchants' house. With Nigel's help, we might be able to recruit Briscoe's assistance."

"It's an idea worth checking out," she said. "Do you still have that business card Nigel gave you?"

"It's in my wallet on the dresser. Let's give him a call."

As we turned to go back to the cottage, Leslie made a sudden stop and studied the shoreline. Stooping at the water's edge, she picked up a long chunk of driftwood with an unusual twist at one end.

"You've found a beautiful souvenir," I said.

She flipped the weathered piece over in her hands and held it high for me to see. "Let's hope it's a good omen concerning Jonah," she said. The stick of driftwood formed a perfect J.

When we stepped through the front door, I made a beeline for the dresser. I found Nigel's card and handed it to Leslie. "He'd probably much prefer talking to you," I said as she keyed in his number.

Explaining that we wanted to hire a local guide, she asked Nigel if he could arrange for us to meet Briscoe later in the afternoon. After a few seconds had passed, Leslie placed her hand over the mouthpiece. "Things may be falling into place," she said. "Briscoe's there right now, and Nigel is checking with him." Nigel apparently returned to the phone and she asked a few more questions before ending the conversation.

"Any luck?" I asked.

"The deal's arranged," she said. "In one hour, we are to meet Briscoe in front of the Administration Building in Governor's Harbor."

\* \* \*

The drive toward Governor's Harbor was uneventful. I glanced at the rear-view mirror; no one was following us.

"What spiel are we going to give Briscoe?" I asked.

Leslie reached across the seat and placed a warm hand on my thigh. "My female intuition tells me that we need to level with him. I believe Briscoe admires Jonah and will be pleased to help us try to find him."

We passed the airport and then the road leading to Barracuda Bay before entering Governor's Harbor proper. I drove us a block past the Administration Building to the deserted dock where we parked. The appointed time was ten minutes away.

Leslie reached for the pack she'd tossed in the back before we had left. "I'm afraid he wouldn't appreciate my new look," she said, placing a baseball cap on her head. It hid most of her hair. What was left of it, that is.

"There's our man," I said. Briscoe appeared on the opposite end of the building, walking on the sidewalk next to the bay.

Leslie leaned over and planted a kiss on my cheek. "Wish me luck!" She stepped from the car and began striding in the direction of our young Bahamian friend.

Even from a block away, it was clear Briscoe didn't recognize Leslie when their paths first intersected. He stopped several feet short of her and cocked his head a time or two before drawing closer and extending his hand. They talked for four or five minutes, Leslie's gestures meeting with a series of nods from Briscoe. A couple of kids wheeled by on bicycles and a pair of cars drove past as they conversed, but no one other than me seemed to be paying them any attention. Moments later, after they exchanged waves, Leslie turned and began walking back to the car and Briscoe headed in the other direction.

Giving me a "thumbs up" as she closed to within 50 feet, she slipped in the passenger door with a sigh. "I explained what we wanted to do and he's agreed to help," she said. "We're to meet him here at six o'clock."

I glanced at my watch. "That's about an hour and a half hour from now."

"Briscoe says the Marchants will arrive at six sharp for their regular cocktails at The Jellyfish Lounge—the honky-tonk where we saw them earlier."

"He'll take care of the poodle while we check out their house?"

"Right. But he doesn't want any part of going inside."

"How is he going to keep the dog under control?"

Leslie shrugged. "He said not to worry."

We killed the extra time wandering through the nearby cemetery. As I studied the old, worn tombstones, I realized we should have picked another diversion. Looking at one gravesite after another when a friend is missing can be a discomforting experience.

\*\*\*

Briscoe arrived right on schedule. Leslie had mentioned to him earlier about my altered appearance, but Briscoe still stared at me for several moments before extending his hand.

"I would not have recognized you, sir," he said. "You look… uh…younger."

The kid was no fool, I thought, giving him a smile. "Thank you for agreeing to help us."

"Mr. Jonah is a decent man," Briscoe said. "We need to find him."

Leslie pointed to our car. "Let's get started."

She sat in the middle as the three of us piled into the front seat.

At Briscoe's suggestion, we first drove past The Jellyfish Lounge. The Marchants' silver Peugeot sat near the tavern's entrance.

"You should have an hour," Briscoe said. "Perhaps more."

We left Governor's Harbor, heading north on the Queen's Highway. As we neared the side road leading to the Marchants' house Leslie turned to our guest. "How will you deal with their dog?" she asked.

Briscoe grinned and reached for the sack he'd placed between his feet. "Jean Claude may appear vicious, but he is still a puppy in the heart." He lifted a Frisbee from the bag, its edge rough with teeth marks. "He and I will play toss while you do your…investigation."

I pulled in near the Marchants' gate. Jean Claude raced to the fence and leaped against the chain-link, snarling wildly, before the car came to a stop.

Leslie gave Briscoe a worried look. "You're sure that we'll be okay?"

He stepped from the car and whistled, bringing the poodle's aggressive antics to an instant halt. When Briscoe walked to the fence, the dog almost moaned in excitement, his tail wagging back and forth. "Jean Claude," he said. "You are the best of the best." Briscoe turned to us and gestured with an index finger. "Give us a moment, please."

Leslie and I waited in the car as Briscoe opened the gate and scratched the poodle's back and shoulders. After commanding the dog to sit, he flung the Frisbee across the lawn. Like a rocket, Jean Claude shot after the soaring disk. He leaped high into the air, snagged it with his mouth, and brought it back, strutting like a star NFL cornerback following an interception. Briscoe held the dog by the collar and nodded to us. "I've got him."

Leslie and I slipped out of the car and, giving Briscoe and the dog a wide berth, stepped through the gate. Halfway up the sidewalk to the Marchant's house, I stopped and looked back to Briscoe. "Do you have a key?" I asked.

"They do not lock their home," he said. "Jean Claude is their... how you say...security."

Briscoe was right; the front door was unlocked. We marched in like we owned the place, Leslie heading to the right while I angled left. A minute later we converged in the dining room overlooking the Atlantic. I'd passed through a living room and bedroom and observed nothing out of the ordinary. Except that every room smelled like an overflowing ashtray.

"Just a spare bedroom, a bath, and the kitchen on my side," Leslie said.

As I gazed through a picture window at the ocean, I realized that the room stood ten or twelve feet above ground level. "Look how high we are," I said. "There's got to be a basement under this place."

We almost missed it. On my second tour of the house, I glanced into the kitchen's big walk-in pantry. A narrow wooden door occupied most of the back wall. A vintage padlock hung from a hasp above the knob.

I tugged on the unyielding lock. "Damn!"

Leslie studied the shelves. "The key's got to be right here," she said. "I just know it." She searched under a few cans, lifted several boxes of crackers and cereal, and then reached under a stack of folded dishrags. A worn brass key was her reward.

# ~ TWENTY-SIX ~

Leslie handed me the key and I slipped it into the lock. After a gentle twist, the heavy mechanism fell open in my trembling hands. Leslie replaced the key under the dishrags while I removed the lock from the hasp. I then set it aside and shoved the door open. A steep staircase led down into a dark and quiet room.

"Jonah!" After a second's pause, I shouted his name again. Nothing.

I glanced at my watch. "The Marchants have been at the lounge half an hour," I said. "Let's make this quick."

When I flipped a light switch near the top of the stairs, a bare bulb hanging above the landing ten feet below us glowed brightly. I crept down the rough wooden stairway, gripping a worn handrail with Leslie at my heels. As I reached the bottom step, I pushed another switch lighting the entire room.

I stopped—and stared. Leslie did the same.

"My God," she said. "What is this?"

The floor of the windowless room was a thick pile carpet, sort of a pale blue. A pair of black leather ottomans provided the sole furnishings. A floor-to-ceiling mirror covered the entire wall on the left side of the room. In front of us, a large flat-screen television filled much of the space, with speakers suspended from either side. In one corner—between a pair of portable lighting units—stood a compact movie camera mounted on a tripod. Behind the tripod, I saw a small bookcase housing a dozen or so videocassette tapes.

My eyes next swung to the strange wall to our right. Covered by the same carpet that stretched across the floor, it offered additional amenities a bit beyond the ordinary: a pair of leg and arm shackles.

"Do you think the Marchants could have held Jonah captive down here?" Leslie asked.

I walked across the room and opened the first of two narrow doors near the bookcase. Not much bigger than a pantry, the room contained a tiny washbasin, a toilet, and a towel rack, nothing more.

"Given this set-up, it's certainly possible," I said.

Behind the second door we found a walk-in closet. It held a videocassette player and stereo, plus a cabinet filled with lotions and oils and an impressive inventory of whips, paddles, feathers, and blindfolds. And several devices I didn't recognize, although a phallic theme was obvious. Nearby was a small basket with an assortment of batteries. A portable clothes rack displayed an extensive wardrobe of gauzy lingerie.

"I think this little dungeon is for the Marchants' private enjoyment," I said.

"An S & M kind of thing?" she asked. "Maybe some bondage?"

I turned and looked at my bride. "What?"

She grinned and offered a shrug. "You'd be surprised what a girl can learn from the articles in *Cosmo*."

I continued to stare at her, my mouth still gaping wide.

"No personal experiences," she said as her face turned a bright pink. "Not yet, at least."

I selected a VHS-tape from the top shelf of the bookcase and inserted it into the player. A moment later I found a remote for the big-screen TV and switched it on. "This may not suit your tastes," I said, pushing the *Mute* button. "Or perhaps you'll be intrigued."

We returned to the main room where Leslie perched on one ottoman and I sat near her on the other. An image flashed onto the screen. Facing the camera, Madame Marchant leaned against the wall to our right, her thin arms and legs bound by the restraints. Blindfolded and covered for the most part by a flimsy gown, she shook her head, apparently in response to a question we couldn't hear. Her husband soon edged into view, wearing a loincloth and leather gloves. He held a paddle.

"Okay," Leslie said, "I think I've seen enough."

I turned the television off, returned to the closet, and rewound the tape. After replacing everything in their original positions, I examined labels on other videotapes. As expected, they were all in French. "Leslie," I said. "Got a second?"

She left the ottoman and met me at the bookshelf. I pointed to the tapes. "Can you make any sense of these?"

She studied the collection, shaking her head. "Let's see," she said. "We have *A Very Special Birthday*, *A Midsummer Night's Dream*, and others in a similar vein." She picked up one, slowly shaking her head. "And here's one, with apologies to Queen. It's titled *A Bahamian Rhapsody*."

As we turned to leave, something halfway hidden under the staircase caught my eye. It was a ball cap. I picked it up—and found myself holding a hat featuring a familiar *Miami Dolphins* logo.

"Wow! Is that Jonah's hat?" Leslie extended her hand. "May I see it?"

"There's no guarantee this is Jonah's, but it sure resembles the one we've seen him wearing."

Leslie examined the hat, and then handed it back to me. "I cannot understand why the Marchants would have anything like this down here—unless they'd held Jonah prisoner. I seriously doubt if it's a prop for any of their home movies."

With more than a bit of reluctance, I replaced the hat where I'd found it. We switched off the lights, climbed the stairs, and fastened the padlock. Convinced we'd left no visible signs of our visit, we stepped to the front door. Briscoe saw us and collared the oversized poodle. He motioned for us to come ahead.

Leslie and I trotted to the car, followed soon after by our guide. As we backed away from the fence, Briscoe waved to the dog. "Good-bye, Jean Claude. I shall see you again soon."

143

Within minutes we were on the Queen's Highway, returning to Governor's Harbor.

"Did you have any success?" Briscoe asked.

"We did not find our friend," Leslie said, telling the truth if not the whole story. "But we are not giving up."

"What do you think of the French couple?" I asked. "The Marchants."

Briscoe mulled the question over in his mind for seconds before answering. "They are a strange pair, those two. I should not speak ill against them, for they pay me well to trim their grass." He swung his head toward the sea and gazed at another fabulous sunset.

"But the Marchants don't like Jonah, do they?" Leslie asked.

Briscoe smiled and arched his eyebrows. "This is true. They despise Mr. Jonah very much." He shrugged. "But they despise everyone. Everyone but the young waitress at the lounge. And perhaps myself."

We drove in silence for another mile. As we neared Governor's Harbor, Briscoe once more turned to face Leslie and me. "I am glad you checked their house," he said. "But I cannot believe the Marchants are involved in Mr. Jonah's disappearance."

"Why is that?" Leslie asked.

"They are old and feeble," he said. "And although they are mean and often rude, I believe it is mostly…how you say…an act. For show."

I wondered how he'd react if he knew about the cap.

We were almost to the Administration Building when Briscoe suddenly ducked to the floorboard. Half a block ahead, I saw the Marchants approaching in their Peugeot. Busy talking and gesturing, neither of them paid us any attention as the vehicles converged and then passed.

"It's clear," Leslie said.

We dropped Briscoe off moments later, thanking him for his assistance. Leslie tried to give him some cash, but he refused.

"It was nothing," he said with a smile. "I will be pleased to help again if you need me."

\* \* \*

I drove to the deserted dock so we could enjoy the final display of the setting sun. Leaning against the fender, we let the salty breeze tickle our skin. We'd been there several minutes when Leslie looked over her shoulder and pointed to the harbor.

"Was that yacht here earlier?"

# ~ TWENTY-SEVEN ~

Four hundred yards to the right, anchored in the middle of the harbor, was an enormous yacht. Mesmerized by the spectacular sunset, I hadn't noticed the big ship. Over the years, I'd had occasion to sail on a few large private boats, but this multi-level thing dwarfed them all. At least 150 feet long, and more likely 200, the sleek vessel looked like the prized possession of a dot.com billionaire. Although the light was fading, I could see what appeared to be two or three people milling around on the open deck. A dinghy bobbing in the water next to the bigger boat seemed like a bathtub toy in comparison.

Leslie stared at the impressive craft, her eyes in a tight squint. "My guess is a group is getting ready to come ashore," she said.

We soon heard the whine of an outboard motor. The dinghy pulled away from the mega-yacht and headed our way. As we watched the small boat approach, a vehicle sped past the Administration Building and turned to the harbor toward us, its headlights sweeping across the dock. The car stopped well short of our location.

Leslie gasped, then threw her arms around me, her lips pressed against mine. I'd always enjoyed her spontaneity although she caught me by surprise this time. But I managed to hold my own. Half a minute later she pulled away and stared over my shoulder.

The sound of the motorboat had been replaced by the murmur of voices. I started to glance behind me, but Leslie nixed that notion with another unexpected but passionate embrace. When we broke apart, I heard the outboard again.

"The car that just now drove up," Leslie said. "It's Dabney's."

I spun around and saw a pink Volkswagen parked under the only streetlight on the dock.

"She climbed into the dinghy and left with two guys."

"Do you think she saw us?" I asked.

"This ugly car is all but invisible," Leslie said and shook her head. "Dabney never looked this way and even if she had all she could see was a couple making out. Our dressmaker friend was so eager to meet those fellows she all but ran to the edge of the dock."

By now the dinghy had motored halfway to the yacht. Several lights shone from the larger boat and someone on board waved a lantern back and forth near the bow.

Bright lights suddenly illuminated a raised flat expanse at the yacht's stern. A man shouted and soon half a dozen bodies scurried about. They seemed to be removing tables and chairs from the deck.

I took a step back and cocked my head toward the bay. A distant thump-thump-thump had caught my attention. "I think things are about to get even more interesting," I said.

Leslie also heard the helicopter; she scanned the heavens and gave me a knowing nod. Seconds later I saw its flashing lights suspended against the dusky sky a mile or two to the west over the Caribbean. Meanwhile, the dinghy reached the yacht and its passengers climbed aboard and disappeared into the cabin. Lights poured from every window.

The small chopper made a noisy swing around the harbor and rousted a flock of seagulls from an abandoned pier. It flew overhead, the roar of its engine assaulting our ears, and hovered above the yacht before gently settling onto the landing pad. I tried to read the registration number on the tail but couldn't make it out in the darkness. Two people stepped from the aircraft, bent low to avoid the wash from the still-spinning main rotor, and hurried into the bowels of the immense boat.

"Do you think this could tie in with Jonah?" Leslie asked.

I stared at the yacht. "It's difficult to say. I'm puzzled by Dabney's possible involvement. Something tells me these folks aren't here to discuss investments in her line of sportswear."

"Rather than risking an awkward encounter with Dabney, let's head on back to our place," Leslie said. "I'm not sure how much more we can learn this evening."

"Are you sure the person you saw was Dabney?" I asked as we climbed into the car. "I never got a good look at her."

Leslie's brow furrowed and she pointed to the Volkswagen convertible as we drove past. "Well, that's her Beetle, right?"

"Yes, but remember we saw some evidence at Dabney's place that she might be hosting a guest."

"Now that you mention it, I guess it could've been someone else who borrowed her car. What I saw was a slender figure making a mad dash from the Beetle to the dinghy—and I assumed it was Dabney Attleman."

We soon passed a Jeep Wrangler parked further down next to the seawall. Leslie's head pivoted as we passed the Jeep, her eyes locked onto the compact vehicle. She reached across the seat and touched my arm.

"Randy, I'd swear the person in that car is spying on the yacht."

"Spying? What do you mean?"

"The woman—or at I least I'm pretty sure it was a woman—had a pair of binoculars at her face and they're aimed at the boat."

I pulled over when we reached the parking lot of the Administration Building. I found the Jeep in my rearview mirror but couldn't see into its windows. "Do you want me to turn around? We could make a loop across the dock."

Leslie shook her head. "I'm afraid we'd be obvious. But I'd sure like to know what's going on."

I took another look in the mirror. "The Wrangler appears to be new," I said. "Ten to one it's a rental vehicle like the one we drove."

"An indication that its driver probably isn't local," Leslie said. "This situation is growing more complicated by the hour."

\* \* \*

Leslie and I left Governor's Harbor for the cottage, following the dark and empty highway as it meandered through the elongated countryside of Eleuthera. We discussed our latest observations, feeling more confident with every mile that the yacht's sudden arrival was somehow related to Jonah Jefferson's disappearance. But the apparent binocular-wielding spy left us both baffled.

"I'll have to admit you threw me for a loop with your lusty attack on the pier," I said as we turned off the road and entered our driveway.

Leslie patted my arm. "My primary objective was to keep us out of Dabney's sight. Or whoever it was. But I noticed you didn't seem to mind."

When I stopped the car, Leslie leaned over the seat and pulled my face next to hers. "If you'd like, we could continue where we left off."

"And what, my dear, might be your objective this time?"

"A mutually satisfying experience." She wriggled out of her tank top and dropped it to the floorboard with a mischievous grin.

Half an hour later we emerged from our Ford Crown Victoria, giggling like a pair of teenagers. We'd made the most of its spacious front seat. Leaving our clothes strewn throughout the car, we walked barefooted across the dark lawn, holding hands and wearing nothing but contented smiles. We stood on the deck for minutes, staring across the highway at the Caribbean, lit by ten billion stars.

"I love you, Leslie Lassiter," I said and pulled her warm body next to mine. "And we're going to find Jonah."

\* \* \*

As we finished breakfast the next morning, we heard a vehicle approaching on the driveway. Leslie walked to a window.

"It appears we have a guest," she said. A car door slammed. "Ms. Dabney Attleman has arrived to pay us a visit."

Leslie met Dabney at the porch while I rinsed the last of our breakfast dishes.

"Good morning," Dabney said. She stepped inside and handed Leslie a little sack. "I thought you two might enjoy some fresh papayas."

For five minutes we went through the small talk routine before Dabney's expression turned serious. "I guess you've heard the latest weather report?" she asked.

Leslie and I shook our heads.

"There's a large tropical storm about 850 miles southeast of here," Dabney said. "Somewhere off the coast of the British Virgin Islands. Hurricane Nikita is not a threat right now. But it could pose major problems, especially if it follows the predicted path."

"What should we do?" I asked.

Dabney shrugged. "Nothing right now, unless you're good with prayers. We'll know more in the next few days." She glanced at her watch and grimaced. "Gotta run. I have a big pile of blouses and skirts to price and stock before I open the shop this morning."

She'd walked halfway to the door when she stopped and turned back to us. "Any word from those federal agents?"

"Nothing at all," Leslie said.

Looking thoughtful, Dabney bit her lower lip. "Let's hope they discover some answers."

"Have you had a chance to follow up about the Baines men?" I asked. "The father/son duo Jonah seemed to reference in his notes?"

For a second Dabney's face registered a blank reaction, but she soon recovered. "As I mentioned earlier, the elder Baines is a respected member of the community. He retired early due to some sort of work-related injury. Local gossip has it that he got a sizeable cash settlement, not to mention receiving a nice government retirement check every month."

"What about his son?" Leslie asked.

"Like many of the young men here, he's often unemployed. I can't recall any outright problems, although he's known to mouth off on occasion. I've seen him on a loud motorcycle."

"Was Jonah right to have suspicions about him?" I asked.

"I just don't know," Dabney said. "I'm told he's belligerent at times and has a quick temper, but I really can't say."

Leslie and I followed her onto the porch. After giving Leslie a hug, she extended a hand in my direction. As we shook, I asked, "Did you happen to notice last night's sunset? It was incredible."

Dabney hesitated a moment before running a hand through her hair. "I wish. A terrible headache plagued me most of the afternoon. After closing the shop, I went straight home and climbed into bed."

"I hope you're feeling better now," Leslie said.

"It must have been some sort of allergy," Dabney said. "I'm doing great this morning." With a final wave, she stepped to her car and pulled onto the otherwise deserted highway.

We watched the pink Beetle head in the direction of Gregory Town. As it vanished from view, Leslie took my hand in hers and leaned against me. "Maybe you were right," she said. "Maybe it wasn't Dabney in her car last night, but someone else. But who?"

"And there's another matter bothering me," I said. "I don't believe she'd given a moment's thought to those Baines characters until we her asked about them minutes ago. And while we'll enjoy the papayas, I'm beginning to think that the sole purpose of her unannounced stop this morning was to learn if we'd heard anything from our DEA buddies."

Leslie responded with a slight nod. "But what may be even more disturbing is her news about the weather. A hurricane could be trouble." She tightened her grip on my hand. "Real trouble."

# ~ TWENTY-EIGHT ~

Shortly after Dabney left, Leslie and I departed for Governor's Harbor. Although we realized it would be a futile effort, we wanted to check Jonah's house one more time. Also, we needed to fill the tank of our gas-guzzling behemoth. Other than making the obligatory call to the DEA duo, we weren't sure what we'd do with the rest of the day. The lack of direction bothered us both.

We turned down the narrow lane at the Barracuda Bay sign and drove past our former cottage. The place was just as we left it: quiet and empty. The same for Jonah's home. Half a dozen or so birds perched on the birdhouses and twice as many flitted back and forth across the yard. There was no other sign of life.

I climbed from the car, faced Jonah's shed, and waved.

"What are you doing?" Leslie asked.

"Putting DEA's hidden camera to a test."

I stepped back into the car and Leslie and I drove into Governor's Harbor, stopping at the BP station. A white Jeep Wrangler was parked on the other side of the pump, and a young woman stood next to the vehicle. Once her tank was topped off, she replaced the gas cap and collected her receipt. When she removed her purse from the Jeep and walked into the shop, Leslie trotted to the rear of our car where I continued to watch as gallon after expensive gallon flowed into what seemed more and more like a bottomless tank.

"She's the one I spotted at the harbor last night," Leslie said, her voice low. "The woman checking out the big yacht with binoculars."

"Are you sure?" I asked. "It was pretty dark out there."

"I distinctly remember the silhouette of her head. She wore a baseball cap with a ponytail."

When I continued to fill our tank, Leslie made a surreptitious pass by the Wrangler and glanced into the vehicle. I noticed the slightest hint of a smile before she slid into her seat in our ancient Ford.

The Jeep's driver emerged from the shop with a six-pack of bottled water. She returned to her vehicle, giving us a sociable nod as she passed, and slipped behind the wheel. An orange Texas Longhorns baseball cap covered her head and her hair dangled out the back in a bouncy ponytail.

When I rejoined Leslie in the car, she flashed me a smug grin.

"Inconclusive," I said. "Half the female tourists on this island sport such a look at one time or another."

"But, my dear skeptical husband, how many of them have a pair of binoculars in the front seat of their car?"

I stared at her. "Are you making this up as you go?"

"Nope. Plain as day, right in the middle of her passenger seat."

"In that case, we need to figure out who she is," I said. "And why she's here."

"I have given those very matters some thought—and just had a scintillatingly brilliant idea, if I must say so myself."

"Let's hear it."

"We need to manufacture a situation where we can encounter this mysterious woman again," Leslie said. "At that time, I'll mention she and I undoubtedly have some acquaintances and experiences in common."

"How can you be so sure?"

"Remember her burnt orange cap? I am a proud alumna of the University of Texas."

Somehow, I'd managed to forget that troubling aspect of Leslie's background. Or maybe as a University of Arkansas graduate, I'd exorcized the fact from my memory banks.

"No doubt you're familiar with the six degrees of separation theory?" she asked.

I nodded. Thank goodness she didn't ask me to elaborate on it.

"With University of Texas graduates, it's more like two degrees of separation. Or maybe three. Everybody is connected to everybody else."

I started to opine the mere wearing of a UT hat didn't confirm that our woman in question had graduated from the school. Nor did it indicate she'd ever even visited Austin, or the state of Texas, for that matter. But I took a safer approach. "Tell me how we're going to arrange what will appear to be a chance meeting with this Longhorn-loving woman?"

Leslie shook her head. "Those are details still to be worked out."

But her suggestion got my mind racing. "I suspect she'll be hanging around the harbor," I said. "Why don't we mosey toward the waterfront and see if we can spot her?"

"That's a good start. We can then play it by ear."

\* \* \*

When we approached the harbor, the first thing we saw was the mother of all yachts, anchored as before. The second thing we spotted was the white Jeep Wrangler, parked near the Administration Building. Its driver sat nearby on a bench in the shade and seemed to be engrossed in a book, the binoculars at her side.

"Okay," Leslie said. "Here's our plan. Drive on down the pier as we did yesterday and park. While you remain with the car, I'll walk back to our unsub and—"

"Unsub?" I asked, interrupting her. "What are you talking about?"

"Unknown subject."

"Are you serious?"

"It's a term used in all the crime shows on TV," she said. "The FBI profilers in particular."

Once again, my bride had surprised me. First it was S & M. Now this. I nodded and said, "So, when you encounter this 'unsub,' what will you do?"

"I'll initiate a conversation with her and will then ferret out as much information as I can." She shrugged. "Piece of cake."

If anybody could befriend a total stranger, it'd be Leslie. I had long suspected her ability to establish rapport with almost everyone she met contributed to her success as a professional photographer. That, plus she was damn good with her compositions and exposures. Whether or not she could charm an unsub remained to be seen.

Following Leslie's recommendation, I drove to the dock and parked to ensure that I had a good view of her likely route. She pulled a compact Leica—what she called her fun and games camera—from her purse. "I might break the ice by asking her to take a picture of me with that obscene yacht in the background." She leaned across the seat, gave me a peck on the lips, and stepped from the car.

"Good luck. I'll wait here for further instructions."

Rather than making a beeline for her unsuspecting unsub, Leslie wandered about the pier, taking an occasional photograph, and slowly approached the Administration Building. She looked like a curious tourist with some time to kill.

I turned my gaze to the monstrous boat. Like a tiny duckling snuggling up to its mother, the dinghy bobbed in the gentle swells next to the yacht's massive hull. But the helicopter, I noticed, had left. A handful of people scurried across the various decks working on unknown tasks. I wished for a pair of binoculars.

When I glanced back toward town, I saw Leslie pause and take a photograph of the picturesque government building. As she neared the bench, the woman raised her head, set her book aside, and gave Leslie a wave. Leslie stopped ten or twelve feet away and they apparently began a conversation. A minute or so later they crossed the street where Leslie posed next to the seawall and her new friend took the requisite photograph. They changed places and Leslie snapped a similar shot of the unsub in front of the harbor with the colossal boat behind her.

But Leslie didn't head back to our car as I thought she might. Instead, she and the other woman returned to the bench and began what proved to be a half-hour conversation. The longer it lasted, the more animated they became. Several vehicles drove to the pier and soon departed as did an elderly man on a rusty bicycle. A trio of small fishing boats left the harbor and motored into the Caribbean. On the yacht, the crew arranged tables and chairs on one of the decks.

The car door opened and Leslie slid onto the seat next to me. "Well," she said. "That was interesting." She placed the camera in her purse and removed a tube of lip balm. After adjusting the rearview mirror to her satisfaction, Leslie applied the salve to her mouth. She then turned to face me with an impish grin on her beautiful face. She outwaited me.

"Let me guess. We're going to have to play 20 Questions if I'm to learn anything."

"Now there's an idea!" Leslie reached over and playfully pinched my check. "First things first," she said. "Our unsub, and my new best friend, is Channing Creekmore. She's a Denver native and is a couple of years younger than I am."

Meaning Ms. Creekmore was in her mid to late twenties, depending upon Leslie's definition of "couple."

"She is indeed a UT grad"—Leslie patted me on the shoulder at this point—"and took several journalism classes from professors I'd had. She went on to grad school and got her master's from the University of Missouri at Columbia."

"It sure looked like you hit it off nicely," I said. "But did you learn anything of value?"

"For one thing, she's an investigative reporter and is here trying to follow a lead on a European drug ring."

"Good lord. Do you think we can convince her to work with us?"

"Maybe so," Leslie said. "We're supposed to meet her for lunch in 20 minutes."

# ~ TWENTY-NINE ~

I turned on the ignition and was about to shift the transmission into "Drive" when Leslie touched my arm.

"Let's leave our gas hog here," she said. "We're to meet Channing at Baby Sue's, and it's only three blocks away. We can walk."

I killed the motor and Leslie and I began the short stroll to our luncheon date.

"How are we going to handle this?" I asked.

"Let's take things slowly at first," she said. "I want you to get acquainted with her before we divulge too much. If you're comfortable with Channing, we can share more. But if your intuition says otherwise, we'll make it a quick meal and be gone."

"May I assume she's already passed your test?"

Leslie looked at me and nodded. "I could tell she was also trying to get a take on me. But she seemed truthful and never averted her eyes or hemmed and hawed when I asked questions. Besides, she's a UT grad. I'm positive we can trust her."

"I hope you're right. We're running out of time. Hurricane Nikita is getting closer by the hour."

Leslie reached over and took my hand in hers. We walked another block along the quiet street. "According to Channing, the restaurant is just around the corner."

We turned at the next intersection and spotted Baby Sue's, but restaurant was too fancy a term for the place. Back home we'd call it a joint, which is not necessarily a bad thing. Given its peeling paint, patched roof, and mismatched and crooked shutters, Baby Sue's was an establishment that had been around for a while, one with genuine character. We opened the screen door and stepped inside.

The interior was primitive yet clean: a worn wooden floor, light fixtures with bare bulbs, and plywood walls painted a sky blue. A selection of native art—mostly seascapes—hung between the windows. Three tables occupied most of the available space.

A young woman at one of the tables glanced up and waved. Her orange Texas cap led me to believe she was Ms. Creekmore. That plus the fact that the other two were vacant.

"Channing," Leslie said, "this is my husband, Randy."

She was quite a bit taller than I expected, just a shade less than six feet, and shared a firm, confident grip. Her tank top and shorts revealed the hard, chiseled constitution of an athlete. I wondered if her body fat even registered. Leslie's slender but attractive figure looked voluptuous in comparison. Given her narrow hips and small bust, Channing had the appearance of a veteran marathoner.

"My pleasure," I said and she responded with something similar. She had bright brown eyes and a pleasant smile.

Seconds after the three of us had taken our seats, a waitress appeared with water and menus. Probably twelve, maybe as old as fourteen, she recorded our requests for drinks and darted through a door into the kitchen.

"Leslie mentioned that you own an advertising agency back in Little Rock," Channing said, "but you're not at all what I expected."

"Are you surprised by my trim physique or intelligent gaze? Or perhaps both?"

Channing laughed and shook her head. "Let's just say your spiked hair and ear stud look more Off Broadway than Madison Avenue."

"The industry continues to evolve," I replied with a wink. "Management must remain ever vigilant."

"Leslie also told me your combined honeymoon and photo excursion has evolved into something altogether different."

So much for taking things slow. I studied Channing for a moment, trying to gauge her motives. She took a sip of water but maintained eye contact all the while.

"We've experienced an unexpected development," I said. "A man we met just a few days ago has vanished under mysterious circumstances."

"I told Channing that we assume Jonah Jefferson's disappearance was related to our inadvertent discovery of some valuable contraband," Leslie said, her voice low. "Some very valuable contraband."

Their conversation had progressed further than I realized. "Does Channing know the details of what we found and what's happened since?" I asked.

"Not yet," Leslie answered. "But I think it's time we filled her in."

Over the next few minutes, we told Channing how we happened to be on the beach that fateful morning and what we observed. We explained how we'd hidden the remaining bag in the sand and recounted Jonah's reaction when we brought the sack of cocaine to his house the following morning. We'd just finished describing the awkward incident with Nigel and the two young men when our waitress delivered a tray of drinks to the table. With a nervous giggle she placed the beverages in front of us and took our orders for sandwiches and chips before skipping away.

"So, 90 pounds of pure cocaine landed on the beach, and the bad guys recovered all but one bag," Channing said. "You'd think they'd be okay with getting eight out of nine, but these guys are never satisfied."

"It's greed," Leslie said. "Nothing but human greed."

"My math may not be dead on," Channing said, "converting pounds to kilos and all and taking into account the usual product cuts by middlemen. But with a street value of $650,000 or so, even one bag is worth some extra effort."

"You now know the beginning of our story," I said. "We can bring you up-to-speed later, but first we need to know more about yours."

Channing gave me a faint but knowing smile. "I'm sure Leslie told you I'm an investigative reporter."

I nodded. "Working for whom?"

"I can't disclose my client's name now," she said. "A few weeks ago, I was on the job in western Europe, spending much of the time between Saint-Tropez and Antibes along the French Riviera, with an occasional trip to Monaco."

"Tough duty," I said.

She shook her head. "Except for my assignment to expose a hush-hush drug ring catering to the rich and famous."

"Your approach sounds rather unusual for a reporter," Leslie said. "I'd think you'd write about an operation like that *after* the authorities had busted it. From the safety of an office, police headquarters, or a hotel room."

"You're right," Channing said. "This situation is atypical. But my publisher, a wealthy and powerful man in his own right, has a daughter about our age—his only child. She got entangled in the drug underworld of the privileged class in France last year while modeling. Her addiction was touch and go for a while, but the doctors report she's going to be okay."

"And your publisher," I guessed, "is hell-bent on doing something about it."

"You've got it," Channing said. "Especially when the Police Nationale showed no interest in his allegations. The last straw occurred when the Director-General refused to take his calls."

"I'm curious," I said. "Why did you leave the Mediterranean and travel all the way across the Atlantic to the Bahamas?"

"I'm following that ostentatious yacht now anchored in this harbor. Two weeks ago, it was sailing from port to port along the Riviera with the proprietor and his entourage of beautiful people."

"What happened?" Leslie asked.

"The owner, a rich playboy industrialist from Germany, left the ship—something he does on a regular basis. He rents it out for an extravagant sum and goes back to one of his many fine homes where he'll tend to various business interests for a few months."

"Your theory," I said, "is that in this instance he's rented it to drug traffickers, right? Who is on it now?"

Channing rubbed her chin. "You've asked the million-dollar question. Perhaps literally."

"Let's make sure I'm straight on this," Leslie said. "You're under the impression the yacht has dropped anchor in this harbor to take delivery of certain illicit drugs and to transport them to Europe?"

"In a nutshell, that's it," she said.

"How sure are you about all this?" I asked.

"I have two very good contacts in France who have described the big picture to me," Channing said. "Unimpeachable sources with firsthand knowledge, but because of their positions they're unable to act or come forward. My task has been to weave all the disparate parts together."

"What else have they told you?"

"My sources believe the 'big man'"—and at this point Channing made quote marks in the air with her fingers—"is aboard the yacht. He evidently opted to cross the Atlantic on this luxurious boat and enjoy a few days here in the Caribbean. Like you two, he's combining business with pleasure."

"Do you have any idea who he is?" Leslie asked.

"Yes, but I'd rather not say. Not for now, at least. But I'm told this is a very rare occurrence for him to be personally involved, what with the risk and all. The crappy weather along the Riviera for the past month may have influenced his decision to make this trip." Channing paused, took a deep breath, and exhaled. "I'm also told his outfit has indirect links to Al Qaeda and its mayhem."

Leslie and I looked at each other. Channing's last statement surprised us both. That a drug drop on an isolated beach on a remote Caribbean island could be tied in with global terrorism was almost beyond my imagination.

"To summarize, I've spent months and months on this," Channing said. "I've studied international boat registries, worked undercover as a waitress and bartender, attended ultra-exclusive private parties in Cannes, shadowed suspected couriers, and crewed for a short time on another yacht. I've interviewed several dozen key individuals. And I managed to acquire a set of schematic plans for the mega-yacht anchored about a quarter of a mile from here."

"You have the blueprints for that boat?" I asked.

"On a flash drive," she said and gestured to a small handbag on the table. "My brother-in-law, who's a marine architect in Florida, somehow pulled a few strings and got them for me."

"What's next?" Leslie asked.

"Good question," Channing said. "Using his political connections, my publisher went through the diplomatic channels and asked for Interpol's help—to no avail. I'm stymied."

"What about DEA?" I asked. "The U.S. Drug Enforcement Administration."

"I don't believe they have any jurisdiction beyond the United States," Channing said. "Seems to me, they're charged with keeping illegal drugs out of the US and aren't interested in Europe's problems."

"We're unfamiliar with their authority," Leslie said, "but there are at least two DEA agents working out of Eleuthera right now."

"You're sure about this?" Channing asked. Her eyes widened. "Absolutely certain?"

"We met with them yesterday," Leslie said. "And we're supposed to make contact with them again by phone later this afternoon."

Our waitress reappeared with three baskets of sandwiches and chips. She arranged the meals in front of us and asked if we needed anything else.

"This is perfect," Leslie told her. "Thank you very much." She got another shy smile from the girl as a reward.

For several minutes we ate in quiet, each absorbed in our own thoughts. I enjoyed my snapper sandwich and the homemade chips. Before we could resume our conversation, a loud group of eight walked into Baby Sue's and surrounded the remaining two tables. Given the mix of individuals and the wide range of the logos displayed on their shirts—Disney World, Temple University, Green

Bay Packers, and Cancun, among others—I assumed a vacationing family had commandeered the place. The apparent matriarch barked out seating assignments and the tables soon filled. I covered our check, left a generous trip for the helpful waitress, and Leslie, Channing, and I exited into the afternoon sunshine.

Leslie pulled out her cell phone and attempted to call the DEA agents. Not only did she fail to make contact, she was unable to leave a message. We agreed that she'd try again later.

As we walked from Baby Sue's, Leslie and I filled Channing in on the rest of our discoveries. She seemed quite interested in Dabney Attleman and, like us, wondered about her connection to Jonah and the missing cocaine.

The harbor soon came into view. The dinghy had left the yacht and was motoring toward the pier. Channing motioned for us to stop and we watched the small watercraft cutting through the gentle swells. I counted what appeared to be four heads on the boat.

"I'm told it's an all-male crew working on the yacht," she said. "If that's the case, we might encounter some guys eager for—shall we say—female companionship." She looked at Leslie. "Are you game for a sexist yet harmless social experiment? We can put our feminine wiles to the test."

Leslie turned and looked to me. "Are you okay with this?"

"If you're willing," I said, "go for it. We need to make some progress and this may be a unique opportunity."

Channing grabbed Leslie by the elbow and they trotted to her Jeep. Leslie looked back and suggested that I "blend into the scenery." I ambled over to the bench near the Administration Building and took a seat.

Two or three minutes later, the two women emerged from the Wrangler and walked to me. "Here's something to keep you occupied," Channing said and tossed me a thick paperback book. A slightly altered appearance underneath her thin tank top let me know she'd ditched her bra. Same for her cap. And the ponytail was gone.

Leslie bent over and gave me a quick kiss—and I couldn't help but notice she'd undone another couple of buttons on her blouse

163

and had also removed a traditional undergarment. I then caught a waft of fresh perfume. "Here," she said, handing me her engagement ring and wedding band. "Take these—and guard them with your life." When Leslie walked away to join Channing, I saw that she'd rolled up the hem of her shorts to reveal a considerable expanse of upper thigh. Her mother would not have approved.

They refreshed their lipstick, turned and gave me a pair of subtle waves, and began a meandering saunter in the general direction of the waterfront. They could have been a pair of college girls on spring break. In the distance beyond them, I saw three men climb from the dinghy and step onto the dock.

As the two groups converged, I wondered what my bride had gotten herself into. Then, more accurately, what the three of us had gotten ourselves into.

# ~ THIRTY ~

I took a gander at the paperback book that Channing had chucked into my lap. It was a heavy thing and also carried an onerous title: *Drugs and Security in the Caribbean: Sovereignty Under Siege.* I flipped the book open to a random page and here's what I read:

> "In the case of the Bahamas, its geography makes it an excellent candidate for drug transshipment…Although most of the Bahamian islands could be used for drug smuggling, the trade has been concentrated over the years in a few strategic places:… Cat Island…Eleuthera… For a typical cocaine-trafficking mission, aircraft depart from the north coast of Colombia and four to five hours later arrive in the Bahamas, where their cargo is dropped. The cargo is then either transferred immediately to waiting vessels for the final run to a U.S. port of entry or is collected and held for later shipment."

Enough of that. I placed the thick volume beside me on the bench and gazed toward the harbor. Things appeared to be going as planned. Leslie and Channing had encountered the all-male trio from the yacht and apparently put their feminine charms to immediate use. After one of the men turned and gestured to the big boat behind them, I heard a chorus of laughter. All five soon began walking in my general direction, engaged in a sociable and spirited exchange.

I returned to the paperback and studied the back cover. The author, a professor named Ivelaw L. Griffith, had impressive credentials. He'd written a number of books and twice as many articles on Caribbean-related topics over the course of his distinguished career, most of them addressing the illicit drug trade in one fashion or another. He'd penned all those tomes, I noticed, from the safety of his quiet academic environment at Miami's Florida International University. I wondered what he'd think of our predicament.

When I raised my head, Leslie and Channing and their newfound friends—some 75 feet away and closing—had several conversations going. The loquacious young men were tanned, handsome, and casually dressed—and grinning as if they'd won the lottery. I didn't much care for their bright-eyed enthusiasm. Or what were no doubt some overly optimistic expectations for the evening.

Opening my book, I flipped through the pages, all the time keeping my head down. Moments later, they passed by with nary a glance in my direction. I had indeed blended into the landscape. Given the gestures, laughter, and eager dialogue, the group appeared to be having a great time. English dominated the talk, although the men now and then offered something in French. Leslie spoke the language quite well, but Channing's linguistic abilities remained unknown to me.

Once again, I regretted my embarrassing lack of language skills. Other than English, the peculiar vernacular of the advertising community remained my only other lingo, and it wasn't much to hang one's hat on. It hadn't done me any good on Eleuthera.

Following a self-pitying sigh, I glanced at my watch. It was almost 3:00. If the men from the yacht had expressed interests typical of sailors on shore leave, I suspected Leslie would lead her charges to The Jellyfish Lounge. The smoky joint was within easy walking distance—not to mention the only real bar we'd discovered in Governor's Harbor. I figured that I had two hours, maybe two and a half, to become an expert on drug trafficking in the islands before the women returned and reported on their successes—if any—with the visiting yachtsmen.

I opened the 295-page book and began at the preface, which was probably a mistake. While Griffith was an unequalled authority on his topic, he suffered from the usual problems of an ivory-tower expert: stiff prose, repetitive arguments, and a pretentious vocabulary. Or perhaps I was suffering from the predictable frustrations of a man stuck in a nerve-racking quandary in a foreign country whose beautiful bride had only minutes earlier had trotted off with a likely band of horny drug smugglers—and lacked focus. In any event, it was a tedious read.

\* \* \*

A little over three hours later, laughter in the distance inspired me to set the magnum opus aside. After several false starts, I'd succeeded in working my way through the first third of it and was now somewhat better informed than I'd been earlier in the afternoon. Griffith made many good observations, of course, yet I felt fortunate to have acquired the book following Channing's reading. She'd highlighted a number of salient points with a yellow marker, and I appreciated a series of caustic notes she'd penned in the margins, some complete with double exclamation marks.

In addition to diligently tending to my studies over the past few hours, I'd enjoyed a pleasant conversation with a gracious tourist couple from Nebraska who'd mistaken me for a local and asked for help finding the airport. After I got them more or less pointed in the right direction, I'd talked to one of the community's fishermen just before he and his buddy went out for lobsters. The previous day he'd attempted to sell a fine selection of fresh grouper to the cook on the yacht, but had been shooed away from the boat by a pair of overbearing and insulting deckhands. He would have sworn, he told me, the unpleasant fellows had pistols tucked under their shirts, adding that handguns are illegal in the Bahamas. Plus, I spent some quality time with a sociable hound, giving her large head a serious petting.

The source of the laughter grew closer, and the same animated gang that had strolled past hours earlier approached. More boisterous than before, they could have been a college group back in the States celebrating a gridiron victory. Walking erratically, they drew closer to the harbor with almost every step—for the most part avoiding bushes and lampposts. It was good they were afoot rather than behind the wheel of a car. One man had an arm draped across Leslie's shoulders while Channing seemed comfortably sandwiched between the other two.

I got a hearty if somewhat inebriated "Salut" from one of the guys as they passed by and I responded with a wave and smile that weren't half as sincere as they appeared. In the distance, the annoying din of the dinghy's outboard motor carried over the harbor. A few minutes later the young men had climbed aboard the small boat and headed back to their yacht with a flurry of waves and shouts to Leslie and Channing. The women turned and, silhouetted by another extraordinary sunset, began the long walk back to my quiet station on the bench.

* * *

"Be careful around her," Channing said when they got within earshot. "Your bride is enjoying a nice buzz." Given the slight slurring of her words, Channing had little room to talk.

Leslie gave me a lop-sided grin. "Don't believe a word from that shameless hussy!" She and Channing looked at each other and then burst out laughing.

When they got closer, I could tell neither of them felt any pain. I gave Leslie a hug and noticed the stench of cigarette smoke permeating her hair and clothing.

She must have read my thoughts. Again. "I know," she said. "I'll take a shower as soon as we're back. Back to our place. Wherever it is," she said with a giggle.

"But first," Channing said, "we need to give you a complete account of our exciting afternoon at The Jellyfish Lounge." She snickered again and Leslie did the same.

"All in all," Leslie said, "they were pretty good guys."

"Except for Phillipe," Channing said. "He kept patting me on the butt."

"Dang!" Leslie tried to pout, but seemed to have trouble getting her lower lip to cooperate. "I thought Phillipe liked me."

"No, sweetie," Channing said. "I'm sure it was Marcel who liked you."

"Why don't you ladies sit down," I said, steering them to the bench, "and you can fill me in."

Leslie managed to hit the bench square on, but Channing misjudged the angle and toppled over sideways into the grass. Leslie laughed so hard that she snorted—and then did it again. Her companion struggled to her feet, sniggering the entire time.

"I think we each had one beer too many," Channing said when she got situated. She wiped the tears from her face.

I nodded and chose not to quarrel with her estimate on their alcoholic over-consumption.

"Are you sure it was Marcel?" Leslie asked. "What about Anton?"

I cleared my throat. "Okay, ladies, let's start from the beginning. When we—the three of us—last talked, you were headed to the harbor to meet the visiting sailors. Let's take it from there."

"I need to pee," Channing said. "Can we hold this brediefing a little later?" She laughed again and shook her. "I'm feeling a little light-headed. I meant debriefing."

"My rings," Leslie said. She gave me a stern stare and tried—without success—to snap her fingers. "I want my rings back."

I retrieved the items from my pocket and returned them to my bride. Her hand-eye coordination wasn't yet back to normal and she fumbled with the jewelry for a full minute before indicating she needed help. I slipped the rings onto the proper finger, repeating a ritual I'd done a few weeks earlier with a minister supervising the action.

Realizing the hopelessness of my situation, I located Channing's keys, guided the women into the Wrangler, and got us to the BP station. Retrieving their bras from the backseat, they stumbled into the restroom, giggling as they went. I bought bottled water and an assortment of snacks and then drove us to the nearby cemetery, figuring it might help them get sober. We sat on the seawall under a streetlight facing the gravesites with our backs to the Caribbean. I shared the food and water.

"So, what happened?" I asked. "What did you discover?"

"Several things," Leslie said. "Their yacht is a French vessel and it sailed straight to Governor's Harbor from the Mediterranean. It's named *Vulpecula*, a word meaning 'the fox.'"

How she was able to say "*Vulpecula*" in her condition was beyond me.

"I think it's a reference to the owner," Channing said. "His last name is Fochs." She spelled it for me—one slow letter at a time: F-O-C-H-S.

Leslie raised her hand, as if asking for permission to speak. I guessed she might have had three beers too many. Maybe four. "And we also learned their captain runs a very tight ship," she said.

"She's right," Channing said. "Tonight was the first time any of these men had been allowed to go ashore, and they had strict instructions to meet the dinghy at 6:30 on the dot." She waved her index finger at me to make the point.

"They kept checking their watches so they'd be back to the pier on time," Leslie said. "They were not going to risk the wrath of the captain."

"Oh, but here's the best part," Channing said. "I'd told Leslie earlier I spoke a little French—so before we met the sailors, she suggested that we stick with English, not letting them know we were bilingual." Somehow, she managed to stretch "bilingual" into four syllables.

"It worked, too," Leslie said. "The first words we heard were 'Parlez-vous français?'"

"We each gave them blank looks," Channing said. "As luck would have it, their English was pretty good."

"But," Leslie said, "over the course of the evening they said several things to each other they wouldn't have shared with us in

English." She took a drink of bottled water and dribbled a few drops down her chin.

"Like what?" I asked.

"Well," Channing said, "they all agreed that Leslie's ass is better than mine." She slapped her thigh and giggled again. "But that reminds me. I heard the word 'mamelon' bandied about now and then, but I'm unfamiliar with it."

Leslie smiled and patted Channing on the knee. "I believe those precious boys were discussing our chests," she said. " Mamelon' means 'nipple.'"

Channing glared at me and shook her head. "You men are so weird."

"But did they say anything of substance?"

"We learned they'll depart soon," Leslie said. "The day after tomorrow as it stands now."

"The crew will spend much of tomorrow getting the boat ready and taking on provisions," Channing added. "A load of groceries and other supplies is scheduled for delivery mid-morning."

"We also hinted we'd like to visit the yacht," Leslie said. "Several times, in fact."

"We were aggressive," Channing said. "We more or less begged to be allowed onboard—with no luck."

"One of the guys, I think it was Anton—or maybe it was Marcel—pulled me aside at the dock and apologized for not letting us join them on the boat," Leslie said. "He stated, more or less, that the *Vulpecula* would normally welcome, in his words, 'such beautiful women,' but certain parts of the yacht were now 'off-limits.'"

That was an interesting revelation. "Anything else?" I asked.

Leslie shook her head, but Channing looked at me with a slight nod. "There was a strange comment I heard in the background moments before the men stepped into the dinghy and returned to their ship. We'd made one last plea to board the yacht, and Phillipe again told us it just wasn't possible. One of other guys—and I don't know which one—muttered something in French, and I'm almost certain his words were 'that damn prisoner.'"

## ~ THIRTY-ONE ~

Channing was in no shape to drive and neither was Leslie. Luckily, Ms. Creekmore had booked a room in a bed and breakfast about half a mile from the harbor. After coaxing the ladies into the Wrangler once more, I managed to extract vague directions to the inn from Channing. Still woozy, she also had acquired a cacophonous case of hiccups, much to her dismay—and Leslie's amusement. We drove to the quaint B & B where I parked and locked the Jeep. Leslie made sure Channing got safely inside her second-story room, and then she and I began the long walk back to the pier where we'd left our car many hours earlier. Behind us, we could hear Channing's loud and intermittent spasms through her open window, each one eliciting another giggle from my wife.

"As long as we don't move too fast, this stroll should do me good," she said once we were a block beyond Channing's inn. "But tomorrow morning will be rough. I hope I remembered to pack some aspirin."

She stumbled and would have fallen had I not caught her. I wrapped my arm around her waist and we walked along the darkened roadway toward our car.

"There's at least one thing we still have to do this evening," I said. "Besides the aspirin."

"What's that?"

"Stroble and Bruno are expecting a call from us." I glanced at my watch. "It's not quite eight o'clock."

We scooted off the pavement to let a car pass.

Leslie pulled her phone from a back pocket and—after several attempts—managed to dial Agent Stroble's number. No answer. She tried to leave a message but the connection failed.

"Channing's recollection about 'that damn prisoner' comment... Did you overhear any of that?" I asked.

Leslie shook her head. "No, but there was a lot of talking going on—in both French and English." She paused a moment, evidently collecting her thoughts. "Channing might have caught the phrase while one of the other men spoke with me."

"Do you believe her?"

"The French term for prisoner is 'prisonnier,'" she said. "It's pretty distinctive. She has a good ear for the language and I can't imagine her confusing the word with something else. Even if she was a little tipsy."

We walked in silence for a minute or so.

"Besides," Leslie said, "we did everything we could to get invited onto the yacht. I'm sure the guys wanted our company, but they told us more than once the boat was off-limits."

"Which would be consistent with having a prisoner aboard," I said. "Do you think Jonah could be held captive on the yacht?"

"Assuming Channing's right on her reference to a prisoner, I think it's a strong possibility."

Ten minutes later we arrived at our car. Leslie buckled herself into the passenger seat and fell asleep about the time we left Governor's Harbor. After we pulled in at our cottage, I guided her to the bed, removed her sandals, and tucked the sheets around her limp body. While she slept, I sat on the porch and listened to the gentle waves lapping against the shore. Far up in the heavens, I saw the flickering lights of an airliner heading east, a redeye flight bound for somewhere in Africa. For a moment I wondered about the passengers and their final destinations.

But my mind soon wandered back to Professor Griffith's book. I recalled his grim statistics on crime, and remembered how the murder rate within the Commonwealth of the Bahamas had skyrocketed following expansion of the country's drug culture. Was Jonah Jefferson the latest addition to an already horrific collection?

* * *

The next morning was, without question, the worst since our marriage. In fact, the only one, so far, registering on the negative side. Leslie woke with a relentless pounding headache. I made the mistake of dropping the metal lid to a pan while searching through a kitchen cabinet, and my normally cheerful bride nearly went ballistic as it careened across the tile floor.

"Perhaps you should wait outside on the porch," I said in my perkiest tone. "Get comfortable in the rocking chair and I'll bring you a copy of coffee."

"I do not want to sit in your damn rocking chair and I don't want any coffee either. Do we have any ginger ale?" She spoke in a whisper, but it was not of the romantic variety. When she stepped to the porch, Leslie let the screen door slam behind her. She muttered a response that, like yesterday's rolled-up shorts, would not have resonated well with her mother.

The gods must have sensed my anxiety. I discovered a bottle of the requested beverage in a back corner of the pantry. I walked outside, careful to catch the door before a repeat offense, and found Leslie sitting on the porch decking, sunglasses on, with her feet planted on the steps leading down to the driveway. She grabbed the iced-down ginger ale with unsteady hands and took a hearty swig.

"How about some scrambled eggs" I asked. "And bacon."

Leslie's face blanched. "Why don't you go back inside, very soon and very quietly, and fix your own nutritious breakfast and leave me alone?" After a pause, she added, "But first, bring me some more aspirin. Please."

So, being a perceptive and cooperative husband, I did as she requested.

Half an hour later, Leslie took a long, hot shower and, in her words, "rallied" herself out of the hangover. She gave me a hug and apologized for her behavior. "I haven't overindulged so badly in years. Remind me to never do it again."

"But it was for a good cause," I offered.

\* \* \*

Leslie was nibbling on saltines in the kitchen when a familiar car pulled onto our driveway.

"We've got guests," I announced. "The federal posse has arrived."

"What?"

"Stroble and Bruno have reappeared."

We met the DEA agents on the porch.

"It's about time," I said. "We've been unable to reach you for a couple of days."

"Let's go inside," Bruno said. He held the screen door open for the rest of us. "Things have changed since we last saw you."

Similar to our initial meeting with the men in Dunmore Town, Leslie and I occupied two side chairs while Stroble and Bruno filled the couch. Sitting on the edge of their cushions and leaning forward, our guests seemed eager to see us this time.

"Agent Bruno is correct," Stroble said. "When we shared news of the Robin Hood motif on the bag you salvaged, our superiors in DC became quite interested." He paused. "Intrigued enough to summon us both back to headquarters for what we'll call an extended strategy session."

"There's more," Bruno said. "A reliable agency source in South America indicates Alarico Villarreal has taken an unprecedented personal interest in this European connection. Our analysis indicates the shipment you saw fall from the plane was bound for France—and this particular buyer is among his newest and most-valued customers."

"What do you mean by 'personal interest'?" I asked.

Bruno looked at Stroble who responded with a faint shake of his head. "We aren't at liberty to share any details," Bruno said. "But the situation is very fluid and could get even more complicated."

"How's this for a scenario?" Leslie said. "Villarreal is so eager to cultivate a strong relationship with this nefarious business partner that he's coming to Eleuthera for a face-to-face get-acquainted session."

Stroble stared at Leslie for several seconds. "That's nothing but wild speculation on your part," he said, but his faint smile indicated Leslie's hypothesis wasn't far off the mark. It was nice to see that her cerebral functions had returned.

"Let's assume, theoretically of course, that Leslie's suggestion is more or less on target," I said. "Where might such a rendezvous take place?"

Bruno shook his head. "Unfortunately, DEA doesn't have much intelligence on the ground. Our budget's been slashed and our team is spread thin. But should such an encounter take place, there are dozens, even hundreds, of potential locations."

"We may be able to help," I said. "We've made some progress on our own."

"But first," Leslie said, "we should mention that it appears Jonah was held captive for a short time by the Marchants, the French couple we told you about several days ago."

"Interesting," Stroble said. "How do you know this?"

"We took a quick tour of their house," I said, "and discovered a Miami Dolphins cap that we're almost positive belonged to Jonah. It was in a secure basement room."

"And how did you manage to search their home?" Bruno asked, arching his eyebrows.

"That's not important," Leslie said, waving a hand through the air. "What's important is that we've also encountered an investigative reporter who's spent months trying to identify the players in a major European drug ring."

"She's on the island now tracking the movements of a yacht that arrived from the French Rivera in recent days," I added.

Both agents took notes as we spoke.

"Who's this reporter?" Stroble asked. "And where's the yacht?"

"Channing Creekmore," Leslie said. "The boat's anchored in Governor's Harbor."

"What else have you learned?"

"Time is running out," I said. "The yacht will take on provisions today. Given the approaching storm, I'm sure it'll set sail sometime in the next 48 hours."

Bruno made another notation on his pad and then looked up. "Have you shared news of Ms. Creekmore's arrival with Dabney Attleman?"

Leslie shook her head. "We've begun to have our doubts about Dabney."

"No red flags for her so far," Stroble said. "But we've learned Ms. Attleman has a family member who may be involved in whatever's going on."

He got to his feet and signaled for Bruno to do the same. "Where is this Channing Creekmore?" he asked. "We need to see her at once."

# ~ THIRTY-TWO ~

Leslie and I slipped into the backseat of the agents' car as Stroble and Bruno took their usual positions in front.

"Where to?" Bruno asked.

"Channing's rented a room at a bed-and-breakfast in Governor's Harbor, and I'd recommend that we check there first," I said. "But I suspect she's driven near the pier and parked close by so she can keep an eye on that big yacht and any related activities."

Bruno pulled onto the Queen's Highway and pointed the car south.

Stroble spent less than a minute with his iPad before turning in his seat to face us. "While I'm doing an internet search on this Creekmore woman, what else can you share with us about her?" he asked.

"Channing's told us she's spent a lot of time trying to piece the story together," Leslie said. "Her publisher has a daughter who got involved in the high-society drug scene in Europe. The girl seems to be okay now, but the dad is determined to expose the ringleader."

"Before she arrived on Eleuthera, Channing was following leads along the French Riviera," I said. "Sometimes working at bars or crewing on yachts."

After studying his electronic tablet for a moment, Stroble cleared his throat. "Here's what your federal government knows about Ms. Channing Creekmore. She's 28, is single, a University of Texas graduate, and now lives in Atlanta. She's a legitimate journalist—with a master's degree, in fact, from the University of Missouri—and her articles have appeared in major regional and national publications. Along the way Ms. Creekmore has earned a handful of awards for her investigative work and, based on her tax filings, makes a decent living. Right now, she's listed as a free-lancer."

Stroble's quick summary made me feel better about our decision to confide in Channing. Leslie squeezed my knee and gave me a slight smile.

"She's convinced the guy running the European ring has deviated from his usual routine and has sailed to Eleuthera to accept a shipment," I said. "Channing's guess is that he's ensconced on that large boat anchored in Governor's Harbor."

"By the way," Leslie said, "the yacht is owned by Bernard Fochs, a prominent German businessman, and it's named the *Vulpecula*. He leases it on occasion."

Stroble again played with his tablet. "Fochs," he said. "Bernard Fochs is indeed an entrepreneur of the first order. A very rich dude. He owns four or five companies outright and serves on the boards of half a dozen other multi-national corporations."

"Anything in there about the yacht?" Bruno asked. "And its weird name?"

Stroble scrolled down and then nodded. "Damn, it's a huge boat." He held the screen so Leslie and I could view a photograph. "Is this it?"

"The very one," I answered.

"Here are some details, including an answer to your question, Agent Bruno," Stroble said. "'*Vulpecula*' is a Latin word meaning 'fox.' The ship is 230 feet long and is powered by twin Caterpillar diesels. Its dining room seats 12, there's a library, theater, conference room, wine cellar, and health spa, and the master suite includes a Jacuzzi and walk-in closet. There's even a landing platform for a helicopter."

"Speaking of which," I said, "we saw a small chopper set down on the yacht night before last."

That comment drew Bruno's attention. "Did either of you happen to notice a registration number on the tail?"

Leslie shook her head. "It was too dark, although we watched two people get off the helicopter."

"What about other living arrangements on the yacht?" I asked.

Stroble again studied the small screen in his lap. "Six guest cabins and eight double-crew cabins. And a gourmet kitchen."

Bruno softly whistled. "It's a floating palace."

"We suspect one of those cabins has been converted into a holding cell," I said. "Leslie and Channing got acquainted with three members of the crew last night and learned that part of the yacht is off-limits."

"A secured area doesn't necessarily mean there are captives aboard," Stroble said.

"But we're pretty sure one of the crew mentioned something about 'a damn prisoner'," Leslie said.

"We do have one bit of good news about the yacht," I said. "Channing managed to acquire the architectural details of the boat. She has them with her."

The agents looked at each other, their surprise obvious.

"That might be a game-changer for us," Stroble said.

"Back to Dabney… You said something earlier about a family connection that sounded troubling," Leslie said.

"We decided to do a little background research on Ms. Attleman," Stroble said, again studying his iPad. "Everything appears to check out. She has a degree in fashion design and merchandising along with retail experience in Florida working at an upscale clothing boutique for women."

"Finances?" I asked.

"We examined those frontwards and backwards," Bruno said. "She's current on her taxes and there's no unusual activity in any of her accounts."

"So, who caught your attention?" Leslie asked.

"Her younger brother," Stroble said. "Brock Attleman has chalked up a series of minor brushes with the law in recent years—to include two arrests for cocaine possession. He was busted the first time when police in Tallahassee found five grams in his car. He claimed to not know anything about it, and the charge was dismissed."

"What was his second offense?" I asked.

"About this time last year, Brock was arrested in Orlando with 25 grams of coke in his backpack, just below the threshold for trafficking," Bruno said. He glanced back over his shoulder and gave us a nod. "It appears his folks pulled some strings and Brock got off pretty light. Five years on probation and a stretch of community service, along with a $5,000 fine."

"Nothing since then?" I asked.

"We have no proof," Bruno said, "but we think Brock Attleman could now be on Eleuthera. We're running a check on his passport right now."

"Maybe he's rooming with Dabney," I said. "When we were in her house a few days ago, I spotted a man's shaving kit in the bathroom. And a sleeping bag on her porch."

"And that evening, we thought we saw Dabney take the dinghy to the yacht," Leslie said. "I suppose it could have been Brock who drove up in her car. It was dusk and neither of us got a good look."

"You're right," I said. "We spotted the pink Volkswagen and assumed it was Dabney."

We drove past the Governor's Harbor airport and watched a Bahamasair plane taxi toward the terminal. Staring at the aircraft, I wondered when Leslie and I would be able to fly back to Little Rock. And I wondered if we'd leave with good news or bad news about Jonah.

Bruno hit a pothole, bringing my short reverie to an abrupt end. Stroble's iPad flew from his lap but he grabbed it in midair.

"Any video transmissions regarding the world's most valuable birdhouse?" I asked as we passed the small road leading to Jonah's properties.

"Nothing at all except for your cameo appearance yesterday," Stroble said. "We hope that's a good sign."

"If you can get the weather on that thing," Leslie said, "let's check the current forecast."

Moments later Stroble snapped his fingers. "Excellent news! That tropical storm has stalled 500 miles southeast of here."

"Meaning we've been given another day or two to wrap this up," I said.

"I fear we'll need every hour of it," Leslie said, and she got no argument from any of us.

Stroble cleared his throat. "That it's stalled is the good news. The bad is that the storm is strengthening and has forecasters worried. Real worried."

A few minutes after passing the Barracuda Bay sign, we entered Governor's Harbor. I directed Bruno to the inn where Channing had rented a room and was surprised to see her Wrangler parked in the same place where we'd left it last night. After Bruno pulled in beside the Jeep, Leslie stepped from the car and went to knock on Channing's door. She returned seconds later, shaking her head.

"Let's drive to the harbor," Leslie said. "I'm sure she'll be somewhere nearby."

A couple of turns later and the dock came into view off to the right.

Bruno whistled when he saw the *Vulpecula*.

"Damn," said Stroble. "That is one big boat."

As we neared the Administration Building, a familiar Volkswagen caught my eye. "There's Dabney Attleman's car just ahead," I said. "The pink Beetle."

Leslie gasped. "Dabney's sitting on the bench—and talking to Channing!"

Leslie and I slumped down, bumping our heads in the process.

"No worries," said Bruno. "We'll drive on by. Stay out of sight."

"Which one is Channing?" Stroble asked.

"She's on the right," Leslie said. "The one wearing the orange cap."

"Take a left at the next street," I said, my face pressed against the floorboard. "Go about a block and you'll come to a cemetery. We can park there and figure out what to do next."

# ~ THIRTY-THREE ~

The car came to a stop and Bruno turned off the engine. "You two can surface," he said, peering into the backseat. "We've arrived at the cemetery and it's otherwise deserted. Perhaps we can go through the motions of a family paying its last respects to a distant relative."

I doubted if any of the locals would be fooled. But Leslie and I raised ourselves from the floorboard, climbed from the car, and followed the agents to a nearby gravesite. Piled high with conch shells, it was topped with a small Bahamian flag fluttering in the breeze.

"What do suppose Dabney Attleman and Channing Creekmore are discussing?" Stroble asked.

"That same question is all I've thought about for the last couple of minutes," Leslie said. "I was stunned to see them together and cannot imagine what they'd be talking about."

"Dabney is gregarious," I said. "Remember, she's in sales. Chances are she simply spotted Channing on the bench and went over and introduced herself." I noticed that no one bothered to second my theory.

The sound of an outboard motor echoed across the harbor. While my associates continued to debate the unexpected situation with Dabney and Channing, I slipped away and walked toward the spot where the women had been talking moments earlier. When I got to the corner, I peeked around the Administration Building.

Channing remained on the bench, book in hand, but Dabney had disappeared and her car was gone. I turned and faced the harbor and saw the dinghy at the dock, taking on provisions from a nearby pickup. A pair of men transferred a load of cardboard boxes from the truck to the small boat.

I whistled and got Channing's attention. After motioning for her to join me, I slipped behind the building. She arrived half a minute later.

"What's going on?" she asked. She carried a small pack over a shoulder and held a worn paperback in her hand. It was a copy of Ian Fleming's *Thunderball*.

I pointed to her book. "I wouldn't have pegged you for a James Bond fan."

"You'd be right," she said. "But this one's set in the Bahamas so I decided to give it a try. Research—of a sort."

"And?"

"Fleming is a misogynistic cad with a violent streak, but otherwise it's mildly entertaining."

I glanced over my shoulder and saw Leslie and the two federal agents gazing our way. Maybe it was time to end the literary chit-chat. "That's the DEA duo at the cemetery with Leslie gawking at us. They're eager to visit with you."

They continued to stare as we walked their way.

"So, I assume you recovered from your nasty case of hiccups?"

"Thanks for getting me to my room," Channing said. "It was a rough night, and I'm still paying for it. I walked over here, thinking the exercise might do me good. How's Leslie?"

"I'd rate hers as a class-five hangover. She did not, shall we say, awaken outgoing and ebullient."

When we reached the others, I introduced Channing to Stroble and Bruno. After they exchanged handshakes, she and Leslie hugged and commiserated for a bit about their recent alcoholic adventure and its related infirmities.

Agent Stroble examined his watch. "This day is almost half over. We need to have a serious talk."

"Why don't I grab a quick lunch for all of us and we can eat at the picnic table," Bruno said and pointed to a far corner of the cemetery. "I saw a sign for pizza as we drove into town."

Leslie and Channing opted out for food, but asked him to bring them colas. Bruno left for the lunch run and the rest of us strolled to the table.

"Channing, we noticed you and Dabney Attleman talking as we came into town and—"

"I couldn't believe it," Channing said, interrupting Leslie. "Especially after what you'd told me yesterday. I'd assumed my usual position on the bench, keeping a wary eye on the yacht, when she parked nearby, strolled over, and introduced herself. I told her I'd come to Eleuthera for a break following a family death. She seemed pleasant enough and invited me to visit her dress shop in Gregory Town."

"That was the extent of your conversation?" Stroble asked. "Nothing more?"

Channing thought for a moment. "Dabney said she'd driven into town to get a prescription. She also mentioned something about a big storm brewing somewhere out in the Atlantic and made a few passing references to the yacht, but that was about it. Why?"

"Given some new evidence, we now believe Ms. Attleman's brother may figure in with Mr. Jefferson's disappearance and the missing cocaine," Stroble said. "We're still trying to connect all the dots."

"She certainly seemed familiar with activities related to the yacht," Channing said. "Dabney stated the guys supplying it would continue their work through tomorrow morning. But she never tried to quiz me."

"As you can imagine," Stroble said, "we are quite interested in the *Vulpecula*. I understand you might be able to help us with information on its layout."

"That I can do." She reached into her daypack, extracted a thumb drive, and handed to the agent. "My brother-in-law went to a lot of trouble to acquire this," she said. "It's a complete set of the boat's plans, current through the latest overhaul."

"This may prove quite useful," he said. "In fact, I'll download this data and send it to a select group of colleagues right now."

Channing shook her head. "The file is huge. It'll take forever to transmit—if it's even possible."

"We have several advantages over the civilian population," Stroble said. "Not only do we have better apps, our electronic devices are the best available. I've yet to encounter a file too big to handle within a few minutes at most."

Stroble connected the flash drive to his iPad, fiddled with the tablet for a bit, and turned back to Channing. "What else can you tell me about your investigation?"

She was about a minute into her story when Stroble's computer chimed. He removed her flash drive and returned it to her with his thanks. For the next quarter hour, Channing shared the same story she'd told Leslie and me a day earlier, although Stroble's occasional question elicited additional details. When he asked her about the head man, as he put it, who was rumored to be living on the yacht, Channing hesitated.

"I'm not sure—"

Bruno appeared with a pizza box and a sack of drinks. He placed his purchases on the table and then stepped back, his face tense. He looked like eating lunch was the last thing on his mind.

"I heard some disturbing news at the pizza joint," he said. "The cashier and the customer ahead of me were discussing an incident that may have some relevance to our case."

"What's happened?" Stroble asked.

"A body's been discovered this morning several miles south of here," he said, "washed up on the shore on the Caribbean side of the island."

We all stared at Bruno, each lost in our own thoughts.

"I understand the Royal Bahamas Police Force is on the scene," Bruno said.

"The Governor's Harbor Station?" Stroble asked.

Bruno shook his head. "The Rock Sound Station is handling it."

There was another long pause.

"Any identification?" I asked.

"Not yet, at least not for public release. But they were told it was a male. An older white male."

Leslie and I made eye contact and mouthed the same word: Jonah.

# ~ THIRTY-FOUR ~

Stroble removed a cell phone from a leather case on his belt, referred to a business card he pulled from a shirt pocket, and tapped in a series of numbers. Placing the phone next to his ear, he stared at the ground for several seconds.

"Inspector Mumford?" There was a pause. "This is Agent Jack Stroble with the DEA. If you'll remember, we met earlier this week." After another moment's delay, he continued, "Very well, sir. However, I've just learned about a tragic incident in your district." He listened and nodded. "When you make a positive identification, will you give me a call? Thank you."

He placed the phone in its case and looked to us. "A local fisherman found the body after dawn this morning. Somewhere south of Rock Sound."

"Did he confirm the preliminary details?" I asked. "That the victim is an older white male?"

"That he did. A forensics team has been dispatched from Nassau and should arrive on the island soon."

"Any idea when an ID will be released?" Bruno asked.

Stroble shook his head. "Mumford said wave action had tossed the body against the rocky shore all night. His guess is that identification may take a while."

"Maybe longer," Bruno said. "Especially if they have to track down dental records."

"Don't forget that we're operating on island time," I said. "Things here move at a much slower pace." I figured we wouldn't get any news for a couple of days at the earliest.

Bruno opened the pizza box, and he, Stroble, and I each reached for a piece. I wasn't sure if they still suffered aftereffects from their hangovers or were bothered by thoughts of a dead man, but Leslie and Channing declined our invitations to dig in. The men occupied one side of the long, weathered table and the ladies sat opposite.

Stroble set his half-eaten slice to the side and turned his gaze to Channing. "Back to your suspected European kingpin. First, I realize that you've spent many months investigating this case and I respect your decision to keep the man's name to yourself. Besides, I'm not sure I have another option."

"Personally, I would have recommended a vigorous waterboarding session," Bruno said with a wink, "although Agent Stroble has the final say."

"Thanks." Channing seemed relieved. Somewhat.

"However, I have a compromise of sorts I'd like to put on the table," Stroble said.

The hint of a frown appeared on Channing's face, but she gave him a slight nod. "The least I can do is listen to your offer."

"Rather than asking you to divulge his identity, what if I give you a pair of initials and you can respond—if you so choose?" Before Channing had time to craft a reply, Stroble said, "Would the initials 'G D' mean anything to you?"

Channing didn't have to say a word. The slight intake of breath and the widening of her eyes gave Stroble an indirect answer. The subtle blush creeping up her neck and across her face then removed any doubts he might have had.

"It appears you're concentrating on the same guy," I said. "What's his name?"

"Grégoire Delisle," Stroble said.

"Grégoire Pierre Delisle," Channing said. "He's a Frenchman in his early forties. The only son of a prominent family. Charming and handsome. Well-educated. Bilingual. An ex-wife; no kids. A new young lover every three to six months. Delisle started out running a small import business bringing in high-end knockoff merchandise. Scarves and purses at first, then watches and athletic shoes. At some point, he progressed to his current specialty: the pharmaceutical trade."

"You can add ruthless to your description of Delisle," Bruno said. "And let's not forget vindictive."

"A multi-national counter-narcotics team based in The Hague provided the name," Stroble said. "They've had this particular individual under surveillance for months. Despite their best efforts, he managed to vanish a couple of weeks ago. They then discovered that one of his shell corporations had done something quite unusual—booked a six-week rental of a luxury yacht. A little more work and they determined the *Vulpecula* was headed toward the Bahamas. And here we are."

"That's consistent with what I've uncovered," Channing said. If Stroble's clever ploy bothered her, she didn't let on. "In addition, I'm told two of his chief lieutenants are onboard as well—along with a small entourage of nubile nymphs. I've seen the girls sunbathing on deck multiple times." She turned and looked at me and arched her eyebrows. "European style."

I was musing about that intriguing cultural difference when I felt the sharp toe of Leslie's sandal ricochet off my shin. When our eyes met, her captivating wink and warm smile gave me some comfort, although her uncanny ability to read my mind continued to both amaze and worry me.

"When Agent Bruno and I were in DC earlier this week, our superiors felt something significant was about to go down here on Eleuthera," Stroble said.

"Something significant," Leslie repeated. "That's pretty vague. Any details?"

"I wish," Stroble said. "There's nothing concrete, but some reliable indicators, such as cell phone chatter, seem to point to a major event on this island. Our bosses shared these concerns with their counterparts in Europe who'd also noticed similar signals."

"In addition, we checked out Nigel Watlington, the neighbor of Jonah you mentioned," Bruno said. "He's clean and those incidents involving his son, while embarrassing, were minor."

"But we made some telling discoveries regarding the French couple," Stroble said. "The Marchants."

"Let me guess," Leslie said. "The lovely Madame Marchant ran a posh finishing school for debutantes on the Champs-Élysées in Paris."

Agent Bruno grinned and shook his head. "We didn't find out much about her. It appears she served as a low-level municipal clerk or in similar posts for most of her adult life in France."

"That's scary," I said. "I cannot imagine her interacting with human customers. But what about her delightful husband?"

"Monsieur Marchant is far more fascinating," Stroble said. "Like our friend Jonah, he retired after working 20 years in law enforcement. But unlike Jonah's, his history in public service was not what you'd call distinguished. Checkered would be a very generous description."

"Was he corrupt?" Channing asked.

"If not, he came close," Stroble said. "It appears he discharged his duties as a foot patrolman, directing traffic and writing parking citations for the most part. He never advanced because of a series of setbacks over the course of his career. Marchant was accused of petty theft on at least one occasion, of under-reporting his taxes on another. Local scuttlebutt suggested his forte was providing fraudulent passports—for a substantial fee, of course."

"The final straw was an alleged shakedown of a local vendor," Bruno added. "Caught on video. Marchant's older brother, who was the longtime mayor, couldn't protect him anymore."

"Following that last incident," Bruno said, "Sergeant Marchant retired from the municipal police force in Gassin about five years ago."

"Did I hear you correctly?" Channing was on full alert. "Did you say the Marchants lived in Gassin?"

"It's a quaint village in southeastern France near Saint-Tropez," Bruno said. "Emmanuelle Béart, the actress, hails from the same community."

"It's also the hometown of Grégoire Delisle," Channing said, "although he now resides in Nice. His parents and younger sister still live in Gassin. Some 2,000 or so people reside in the town."

Things got very quiet at our impromptu picnic.

"That seems to be a strange coincidence," Leslie said. "Almost too strange."

As their expressions changed, I got the feeling Stroble and Bruno were entertaining similar thoughts.

"France has a reputation for generous pensions," I said, "but—given their backgrounds—I'm surprised the Marchants can afford to live on Eleuthera. You wouldn't think they'd be wealthy people."

"I picked up a handful of real estate brochures when we first arrived on Eleuthera," Leslie said. "Prime beachfront property like theirs is exorbitant. It's well beyond the reach of folks with modest incomes."

"Not to mention food, fuel, utilities, and all the other living expenses," I said. "The government's tariffs on most imports are substantial. Their Peugeot alone would cost a small fortune to bring in."

"Perhaps those two pensions don't provide their sole income," Channing said. "Maybe the Marchants have developed a supplemental source of revenue."

The glances exchanged by Stroble and Bruno indicated this was something they'd not considered.

The sudden chirping of Stroble's cell phone startled all of us. He brought the compact device to his face and said, "Hello." He then stood, extricated himself from the confines of the picnic table, and walked to the center of the cemetery. The four of us watched as he carried on a conversation out of earshot. Bruno and I put the time to good use and claimed the last two pieces of pizza. A few minutes later Stroble rejoined the group, his phone once again in its case.

"This situation continues to evolve," he said as he slid into his place at the table. "The call was from our DC colleagues. It seems another yacht of interest has entered the picture."

He saw most of us turn to face the harbor. "Not here, but in the Exumas—the chain of small Bahamian islands about 75 miles due west of us."

"If my math's accurate," Bruno said, "it's only about a half hour ride by helicopter."

Although Leslie and I hadn't visited the Exumas, we'd flown over the stretch of uninhabited cays days earlier and marveled at the brilliant turquoise waters spotted with reefs. I knew from guidebooks that the Exumas had long been a favorite with bareboaters searching for great diving, world-class bonefishing, and isolated beaches. Privateers such as Captain Kidd had flourished in the region three centuries earlier, and Sean Connery spent many weeks in the Exumas while filming *Thunderball*. In more recent years, Johnny Depp, Keira Knightley, and their *Pirates of the Caribbean* cohorts had navigated the same waters.

"This 'yacht of interest,' as you say... Did it also sail to the Bahamas from the Mediterranean?" I asked.

"Its point of origin is what makes this second ship so intriguing," Stroble said. "The boat departed from Cartagena, a port on Colombia's Caribbean coast, about ten days ago and anchored yesterday afternoon in a remote cove in the Exumas after an 1,100-mile journey."

"And Colombia, if my memory is correct, is among the world's largest producers and exporters of cocaine," Channing said.

"You are indeed correct," Stroble said. "A few days ago, Agent Bruno suggested that our intelligence team study recent satellite imagery to determine if anything unusual was going on. The analysts located this particular craft and, by using previous photos, backtracked it to a port on the Colombian coast. It's not every day that a mega-yacht sails from Cartagena to the Exumas." He gave Bruno a thumbs up.

"Is it as big as the *Vulpecula*?" Leslie asked.

"This yacht is named the *Rosalita*," Stroble said, "and I was told it's somewhat smaller than the boat anchored here at Governor's Harbor. But it's every bit as comfortable. And, as in the case of the *Vulpecula*, it also includes a landing platform for helicopters."

"Do you have any idea who's aboard?" I asked.

Stroble gave me a slight smile. "We know the *Rosalita* is owned by a formidable South American industrialist who, like the German proprietor of the *Vulpecula*, rents his yacht to well-heeled customers on occasion. That seems to be the case here. As for who's onboard, we have some ideas," he said. "But nothing's been confirmed. Yet."

"Let me get something straight," I said. "The European boat, that may or may not hold Grégoire Delisle, set sail for Eleuthera within the past two weeks. And the South American yacht, that may or may not house Alarico Villarreal, left port ten days ago."

It took a while, but I got nods from around the table.

"So, this apparent meeting or rendezvous, if you want to call it that, was arranged well before any problem with the drug drop."

"That's the way it seems," Stroble said. "The sack of cocaine went missing several days *after* both boats had headed this way."

"If they're not convening to resolve that matter, why are they getting together?" Leslie asked.

"The call I just received may shed some light," Stroble said after clearing his throat. "Members of our intelligence team have been struggling with that very same question. While they don't have a definitive answer, they've developed a provocative theory. The two suspected players—Delisle and Villarreal—share some remarkable similarities. They're both in their early forties and well-educated. They enjoy Sudoku, Cuban cigars, young models, high stakes poker, modern art, and fine wine. And, get this, they're both big fans of opera."

"I take it your experts feel this could be as much a social meeting as a business session," Leslie said.

"Strange as it may sound," Stroble said, "it appears they have a high regard for each other. In addition to having many common interests, they're more or less equals in an exceedingly small demographic group."

"Sort of like Bill Gates and Warren Buffett becoming best buddies," I said.

"Except for the color of their headgear," Bruno said. "These guys are the ones wearing black hats."

Great, I thought. A pair of world-class gangsters belonging to an exclusive mutual admiration society.

# ~ THIRTY-FIVE ~

We were quietly sitting around the picnic table, trying to absorb these latest revelations, when Stroble's phone rang again. He stepped aside to take the call. He nodded a few times and spoke only a few words before returning to our little gathering.

"That was Inspector Mumford again," Stroble said, "from the Rock Sound Station."

"No way they've already IDed that body," Bruno said. "Things don't move this fast even back in the States."

Stroble shook his head. "Not officially. But Mumford wanted to let me know that the driver's license found in the man's wallet matches the name of a cruise ship passenger who was reported to have fallen overboard the day before yesterday."

Leslie looked at me and shared a faint smile. The body recovered in the water was unlikely to be that of Jonah Jefferson.

"Mumford stated that dental records would arrive tomorrow morning, and a positive ID might be possible soon after," Stroble said. "He also informed me that they'd consulted with government oceanographers based in Nassau. These experts confirmed that, given the ship's route and local currents, the body's discovery was—quote—consistent with their mathematical models—unquote," he said, making quotation marks in the air with his fingers.

"What does that mean in everyday English?" Bruno asked. I was wondering the same thing.

"I believe the experts were telling Mumford that the body was found where they expected the body to be found," Stroble said.

Bruno and I made eye contact and exchanged shrugs.

"I don't know about you guys," Channing said, "but I'm going to take this as a positive development. At least as it impacts our situation."

But our good news meant a tragedy for another group of people, I thought.

"Excuse me for a moment," Bruno said. He reached into his pants pocket, removed a phone, and walked toward a far corner of the cemetery, talking as we went. Within a couple of minutes, he'd stepped back and approached his partner.

"That was my sister," he said. "There's been a family emergency and I really need to take off a few days." He paused and shook his head. "I know the timing couldn't be any worse."

"Not a problem," Stroble said, although he was clearly surprised by his partner's request. He returned to his place at the picnic table and ran a hand through his hair. "As you're well aware, the director has made it clear that family always comes first. And, as you know, we've got reinforcements heading this way. Go take care of things."

"Thank you, sir."

"I'll be glad to drop you off at the airport," Channing said to Bruno. "It won't be any trouble."

He turned to Stroble who gave him a nod.

"Sure," Stroble said. "That will be very helpful, Ms. Creekmore. Let's get Agent Bruno's duffel out of the back of our car and you can be on your way. I've got several other calls I need to make."

As the two agents walked to their car, I remembered that they'd driven Leslie and me into Governor's Harbor much earlier in the day. Our vehicle remained at our rental cottage.

I tapped Channing on the shoulder. "Any chance you could give us a ride, too?" I asked. "Our place isn't but a few miles beyond the airport, north toward Gregory Town."

"Certainly," she said. "To be honest, my mind's about to be overloaded with all this stuff going on. A relaxing drive up the Queen's Highway will do me plenty of good."

The DEA agents soon rejoined us. Stroble patted Bruno on the back and said, "Keep me posted on your family situation." A moment later Stroble's phone rang. He mouthed "Sorry," removed the phone from his belt, and gave Bruno a quick wave.

The four of us piled into Channing's Wrangler, Bruno riding shotgun with Leslie and me occupying the rear seats, and headed north out of town toward the airport. The windows were down, making for a noisy trip, and we didn't have much opportunity to talk. When we arrived at the airport, we each shook Bruno's hand and wished him the best. He thanked Channing for the lift, grabbed his duffel from the back of the Wrangler, and slipped into the small terminal.

Leslie scooted into the empty passenger seat and got Channing aimed in the right direction. After we left the airport, I suggested that we backtrack and take a detour to show Channing Jonah's property. She turned off the highway and pulled to a stop at the cottage Leslie and I'd rented days earlier.

"Let's walk from here to Jonah's house," I said. "It's only a short distance."

As we approached his home, Leslie pointed out the customized birdhouse containing the cache of cocaine.

"It's ingenious," Channing said. She took several photographs of it with her cell phone. "If I'm lucky, I'll write an award-winning article on this whole story, and this picture might get prominent play."

I hoped she'd indeed be lucky, sure that the rest of us—to include Jonah Jefferson—would share in her good fortune.

I next led Channing toward the garage and pointed out the hidden camera. "You might as well get a photo of this little gizmo, too," I said. "It may help us catch the bad guys." After Channing got her shot, we all posed and waved at the DEA device.

"Can we take a peek into Jonah's workshop?" Channing asked. "I'd like to see where he made that birdhouse."

We walked into the garage and over to Jonah's workbench. The place was still a mess.

"They really did a number on his workshop, didn't they?" Channing said. She took some photos of the destruction.

As we stepped from the garage, a deafening whump-whump-whump pounded our eardrums. A helicopter buzzed low overhead, surprising us. It hovered above Jonah's property for a few moments, then lifted up and sped away.

That was strange, I thought. Leslie stared at the chopper until it disappeared from sight, then turned to me, every bit as puzzled as I was.

"Did you happen to get a picture of that helicopter?" I asked, looking at Channing.

She shook her head. "Why? Was it important?"

"Probably not," I said. "But it would be nice to have a record of its registration number. I'm curious why anyone would be flying so low over Jonah's house right now."

"Maybe I'm imagining things," Leslie said, "but I got the feeling that it hurried off as soon as we came into view."

That same thought had occurred to me.

* * *

When we arrived at our rented cottage, Leslie escorted Channing inside for a quick tour. I slouched down in a lawn chair on the deck and gazed west, staring across the vast open waters of the Caribbean. A couple of miles or so offshore, a catamaran skimmed over the gentle swells, sailing toward the southern end of the island. As I stared at the waves breaking on the distant reefs, I tried to imagine the fury of a Category 4 hurricane hammering this small island. The storm surge, I realized, might well inundate the very deck I was on.

"Daydreaming again?" Leslie asked as they joined me.

"Hardly," I said. "I was trying to visualize what this spot might look like in another week if that storm comes this way."

"It's still stalled somewhere southeast of here," Channing said. "Hundreds of miles away."

"But gaining strength by the hour," Leslie said. "And headed this way."

I glanced at my watch, surprised by the lateness of the day.

Leslie must have read my mind. Again. "Shall we make plans for dinner?" she asked.

"I enjoyed yesterday's lunch," Channing said. "Are y'all up for another trip to Baby Sue's?"

Leslie and I climbed into our land yacht and followed Channing into Governor's Harbor where we had another delightful experience of good service and delicious food at the local diner. Channing then returned to her room at the nearby B & B and Leslie and I drove back to our place.

The moonlight reflecting off the Caribbean should have captured my thoughts, but my mind kept wandering back to Donnie Bruno and his sudden departure. Something about it just didn't ring true.

# ~ THIRTY-SIX ~

Leslie spent an hour on the phone the next morning talking first to her agent and then to a pair of photo editors. "Good news," she said as the last conversation ended. "When we get home, I have a couple of assignments in northwest Arkansas. One to shoot tailgating prior to the Arkansas/Alabama football game later this month in Fayetteville and the other to capture the Christmas pageantry in Eureka Springs. Would you have any interest in continuing your apprenticeship as a photographer's assistant?"

"What's in it for me?

"Your food, lodging, and transportation will be covered." Giving me a wink, she added, "And I suspect you'll get to sleep with the photographer."

"I'm in."

I then borrowed her cell and called the office. My news wasn't so good. One of our longtime clients, a local insurance agency, had been bought by a Texas outfit and the services of Lassiter & Associates would not be needed beyond the first of the year.

Mid-morning found us back at Governor's Harbor. We watched as several loads of supplies were brought to the pier, offloaded onto the dinghy, and then ferried out to the *Vulpecula*. I commented that the apparent lack of urgency surprised me.

"That yacht can easily outrun a hurricane," Leslie said.

"On another matter," I said, "did yesterday's abrupt departure of Donnie Bruno seem strange to you?"

"Now that you mention it, I was taken aback by his request," Leslie said. "I noticed that although Agent Stroble also appeared rather surprised by it, he recovered quite nicely. He implied that Bruno's absence wouldn't hamper DEA's plans."

"Even so, for Bruno to suddenly exit the scene while things appear to be coming to a head just doesn't feel right," I said, shaking my head.

"Randy Lassiter," Leslie said. "You're so old-school. Society is changing. Federal agencies are leading the way on expanded family leave and things like that."

"Maybe so, but doesn't his timing seem weird to you?"

"It's not like Stroble and Bruno are the only two DEA folks involved in this. Stroble himself has made references to other associates assigned to the case," Leslie said. "If you'll remember, they had one of their colleagues distract Nigel a couple of days ago when we inspected Jonah's birdhouse. For all we know, there may be another team of agents on Eleuthera right now, not to mention their coworkers working remotely from D.C."

When Channing joined us later in the afternoon, I asked about her reaction to Bruno's unexpected departure. It was similar to Leslie's. "It caught me a little off-guard," she said. "But I'm not alarmed if that's what you're asking."

I decided to drop the topic.

"But I do have a bit of news to report," Channing said. "One of my contacts in Paris said that rumors circulating on the street indicate a big shipment is heading their way. But everything was vague; no details at all."

As evening approached, things were quiet along the waterfront. The last fishing boats motored in as dusk settled, and Leslie, Channing, and I watched the stars little by little appear in the dark Caribbean sky. Every now and then a car drove past our bench near the Administration Building and, in the distance, we caught the faint beat of live music from the Jellyfish Lounge.

"What was that?" Leslie asked, her body stiffening. She stared toward the large yacht anchored several hundred yards away.

"It sounded like a distant splash," Channing said.

I hadn't heard a thing.

Leslie and Channing stood and walked to the edge of the seawall, gazing into the harbor. Two or three minutes passed.

"Over there!" Leslie pointed across the water. "Is that a dolphin?"

I got to my feet and joined them. I didn't see anything, but continued to search the harbor's dark surface. And then I spotted something breaking through the water with a regular pattern.

"That's not a dolphin," I said. "That's a person swimming. And he's heading our way."

"Something tells me this is not a recreational outing," Leslie said.

As the swimmer approached, we could tell he was struggling. I climbed over the wall and entered the water, pushing off toward him. Thirty yards or so later, I met an exhausted man who reached for my outstretched arm, and we slowly swam toward shore. Given the poor lighting and hectic circumstances, I wasn't sure but his face seemed familiar, thinking that he might be one of the young yachtsmen who'd befriended Leslie and Channing the previous evening.

"Thank you," he said as our feet touched bottom. He had a European accent.

Leslie and Channing met us as we emerged from the water. I noticed that he was wearing cargo shorts, a sleeveless tank top, running shoes, and a *Vulpecula* baseball cap.

"Anton?" Channing asked, placing her hands on his shoulders. "Are you okay?"

Breathing hard, he gave her a smile. "Yes," he said. "Can you help me?" He looked back at the yacht. "I have to leave. At once. You must help me."

"We can help," Leslie said, "but you must first explain what's going on."

Leaving a watery trail, we led him across the road to the bench that we'd occupied much of the evening.

"Please sit down," I said. "And catch your breath."

He took another furtive glance toward the yacht.

"I received a message that my dear mother is in a hospital in Paris," he said, his chest still heaving. "She is very ill. I am her sole child and must go see her."

My immediate thought was that he'd chosen an unusual option for the first leg of his journey. Leslie and Channing seemed to be equally confused. Anton noticed our puzzled expressions and shook his head. He then removed his cap and flung it to the ground.

"The uncaring captain," he said, pointing toward the boat, "is a monster." He kicked at the cap. "The bastard would not allow me to leave. I had no choice but to jump overboard, and here I am. I must get to Nassau for a flight to Paris. We must hurry." He patted a rear pocket. "I have money to pay you. Please help me."

I looked to Leslie and then to Channing. Both gave me subtle nods.

"Anton," I said. "These women are your friends, and they can drive you to Dunmore Town right away. First thing in the morning, you can take the ferry to the harbor in Nassau. From there, it's a short taxi ride to the airport."

"You will do this?" he asked, turning to Leslie and Channing.

"Come with us," Channing said. "My car's a few blocks away. There's a towel in the backseat." She and Anton began walking toward her Wrangler.

Leslie gave me a kiss and a hug. "You're soaking wet," she said.

"I'll drip dry."

"We'll be back in a couple of hours."

"I'll wait right here," I said. "Be careful."

"Same goes for you."

She turned and trotted away, catching up with Channing and Anton moments later. I watched as this unlikely trio disappeared into the darkness.

They were hardly out of sight when I heard the whine of an outboard engine. I saw a light bobbing across the water, heading toward the seawall. I assumed it was the dinghy, and I guessed the captain had discovered that one of his crew members had gone AWOL.

I had a decision to make. I could slip into the shadows and watch whatever happened from a safe distance. Or I could remain where I was and let things play out, perhaps adding to our limited understanding of this increasingly strange situation. I chose the latter, and watched the boat drew nearer. As it closed to within a 100 feet, I could make out the silhouettes of two sitting figures, one in the prow and the other in the stern controlling the motor. The engine died.

Soon after hearing the hull of the boat scrape against the rocky shore, I saw a pair of faces appear above the seawall, clambering up the same place where Anton and I had climbed out only minutes earlier. One of the men pointed to the wet spot on the pavement where we had paused to rest, creating a small pool of water. Once on the street, they looked up and down before following a series of wet footprints that led directly to me. I spotted Anton's cap on the ground at the base of the bench and grabbed it, unsure what to do with the damn thing. I leaned forward, slipped the cap under my butt, and then sat on it, averting a potential disaster. At least for the short term.

"Good evening," one of them said as they got within 20 feet. His jacket appeared way too warm for the balmy temperature. "It appears that a member of our crew fell overboard within the past hour." He pointed over his shoulder to the *Vulpecula*. "Have you seen anyone come ashore?"

Taking a deep breath, I shook my head. Despite my years of work in the advertising business, I've never been very good at stretching the truth. "Nope," I said, hoping my voice wouldn't crack.

"You're lying," the other said, moving a step closer. A large man with a shaven head, tats running up and down both arms, and muscles straining the seams of his t-shirt, he did not appear to be a friendly sort. "Someone came out of the water right in front of you." He pointed toward the puddle near the seawall.

Under normal circumstances, I would have taken offense at a stranger calling me a liar. But this wasn't a normal situation. Besides, they had me outnumbered two to one, and I had some concern about what might be hiding in the jacket pockets of the first man. And I had, as I reminded myself, just brazenly lied to both of them.

"Dat was me," I said, trying my best to sound a bit inebriated. "My clothes are still wet." I extended my arms to show them my damp shirt, making sure that they swayed a little. Unfortunately, I'd never been much of an actor either. My starring role in high school theater class had been set designer, and that had occurred a couple of decades ago.

"You picked a strange place for a swim," the first man said. "And a strange time to do it."

"Hear dat music?" I asked, giving my head an uneven jerk toward the Jellyfish Lounge. "Had too much fun over dere. Trying to sober up. Don't wanna get 'rested." I then resorted to a skill I'd learned back in my youth, the ability to belch at will, and emitted a loud burp. "Know whata mean?"

Cursing and giving me a dismissive wave, the men stalked off, one going in one direction and the other the opposite way. I stretched out on the bench and pretended to be sleeping when they returned about half an hour later. They got into their dinghy and headed across the harbor toward the yacht. As they puttered away, I tried to determine what valuable insights I'd picked up from our encounter. Nothing, I concluded. Not a damn thing. Except that I could still burp on command.

* * *

It was after 11:00 p.m. when Leslie and Channing returned. Not desiring to remain on the bench and in view of anyone on the yacht with binoculars, we climbed into Channing's Wrangler and drove around the corner, stopping in the empty parking lot of the BP station.

"What happened after we left?" Leslie asked. "Anything out of the ordinary?"

"An unsavory duo from the yacht showed up within minutes," I said. "Nothing came of it. But had I not sat on this," I said, holding up Anton's cap, "the conversation could have taken a different tone."

Channing gasped. "I'd forgotten about that."

"When they wanted an explanation about the wet pavement where Anton and I came ashore, I claimed that I'd gotten tipsy at the Jellyfish Lounge and took a dip to sober up."

"And they bought that story?" Leslie asked. She knew that I seldom drank more than two beers at one sitting. And that I wasn't a particularly good liar.

"That seems to be the case," I said. "They did a quick search of the area and then returned to the yacht."

Channing slipped Anton's hat onto her head. "I still prefer my Longhorn cap," she said, "but this'll be a nice souvenir."

"Now," I said, "tell me about your evening."

"There was very little traffic on the highway, and we made good time getting Anton to Dunmore Town," Channing said, adjusting her new headwear. "We left him at an all-night coffee shop. He was very appreciative for the assistance, and asked us to thank you again for your help. He tried to pay us, but we declined."

"I hope you won't mind," Leslie said, "but Anton's now wearing a pair of your gym shorts and the last of our *Arkansas the Natural State* T-shirts. We stopped at our place near Gregory Town to get him into dry clothes."

"As for the prisoner, we were right," Channing said. "There's definitely one aboard."

"Any details on this captive?" I asked.

"Only that it's a man," Leslie said. "Anton never saw him. But he gave us a detailed sketch of the yacht's floorplan, marking which room holds the prisoner."

"Our DEA contacts will be pleased to get that drawing," I said.

"And there's more," Channing said. "Anton claimed that the yacht was visited by an important guest earlier this afternoon, a man who arrived by helicopter. The captain was emphatic, ordering the crew 'to stay out of sight.'"

"The visitor must have gotten turned around, searching for the head. Anton inadvertently ran into him in a passageway," Leslie said. "The man tried to look away, but Anton got a good glimpse of him."

207

"Did he appear Hispanic?" I asked, instantly thinking of Alarico Villarreal, the Colombian drug lord on the DEA radar.

"Not at all, according to Anton," Channing said. "Medium height, sort of stocky, and not much of a neck. With dark, curly hair."

"But get this," Leslie said, her eyes wide. "When they met, the man raised his right fist to shield his face. Anton remembered that this prominent guest wore a large ring on his right hand."

A large ring on a man's right hand. I stared at Leslie, trying to decipher her message. Where had I seen such a ring? And then I recalled a certain conversation in a hotel room in Dunmore Town days earlier, and my chin dropped.

Channing caught my reaction. "What are you not telling me?" she asked.

# ~ THIRTY-SEVEN ~

"Donnie Bruno, the DEA agent, wears a large ring on his right hand," I said. "It's from Clemson University, his alma mater."

Channing stared at me, slowly nodding.

"He showed it to us when we first met him and Agent Stroble in Dunmore Town days ago," said Leslie. "Bruno claimed that he never would have received his degree without Jonah's help."

Channing shook her head. "I'm sorry, but I just don't get their connection. I know Jonah's a retired cop, and Bruno's with the DEA but—"

"I think we failed to tell you that Jonah Jefferson is Donnie Bruno's godfather," I said, interrupting. "We're not sure what happened to Bruno's biological father, but Jonah appears to have stepped in at some point as a surrogate dad."

Channing took her time absorbing this news. "But the ring that Anton spotted isn't necessarily Agent Bruno's, is it?" she asked. "After all, it could be nothing more than a coincidence."

"You're right," Leslie said. "However, I don't recall that many men wearing large rings on their right hands. It seems we should at least mention this to Agent Stroble."

"Didn't Anton's description of that mysterious visitor to the yacht bring Bruno to mind?" I asked. "Dark curly hair and no neck?"

"You're right; Anton was quite insistent about those characteristics," Channing said, "repeating them several times."

Leslie reached for her cell phone. "Let's give Stroble a ring." She searched through her directory and then placed the call. He must have answered at once. Leslie told him that we had an interesting development to share. She then listened, said "yes" a couple of times, and then thanked him before ending the conversation.

"He's staying about five minutes away," she said. "When I acknowledged that we were in Governor's Harbor, he suggested that we meet at our favorite picnic spot. I'm surprised that he didn't ask more questions."

Stroble's playing it safe, I thought. He didn't want Leslie to divulge any information over the phone.

We walked beneath the street lights and through the shadows to the dark and quiet cemetery. We'd been at the picnic table all of three minutes when headlights swept over the gravestones. Once he parked his car, Stroble trotted to us, carrying his attaché case, and took a seat next to me, opposite the women.

"What's this 'interesting development'?" he asked. "I believe those are the intriguing words that Ms. Carlisle used to arouse my curiosity at this god-forsaken hour."

"One of the young men working on the yacht jumped overboard," Leslie said. "Anton. We were there when he swam to shore earlier this evening. He immediately asked for our help, stating that he was desperate to get to Paris to see his hospitalized mother."

"Anton told us the captain refused his request for leave, giving him no choice but to abandon ship," Channing said.

"And you believed him?" Stroble asked.

"We had no reason not to," I said. "It wasn't an easy escape, plus he had no idea we'd be waiting near the seawall."

"Go on," Stroble said, nodding.

"Channing and I took Anton to Dunmore Town," Leslie said. "He plans to catch the inter-island ferry to Nassau in the morning and then fly straight to Paris."

"All this seems pretty far-fetched," Stroble said, his impatience showing. "An unlikely scenario."

"We also wondered about that," Channing said. "But he showed Leslie and me his passport. He had plenty of cash and tried to repay us for taking him to the far end of Eleuthera."

Stroble held up the palm of his hand. "Okay, let's say Anton's unusual departure is on the up-and-up. How does this shed any light on our situation?"

"Leslie and Channing had an hour to talk with Anton as they drove him to Dunmore Town," I said. "They can tell you what they learned."

"He confirmed that there's a prisoner onboard the *Vulpecula*," Leslie said. "And Anton—"

"This prisoner," Stroble said, interrupting. "Any details on him? Or her?"

"A man," Leslie said, "but nothing beyond that."

Channing removed a sheet of paper from her purse and handed it to Stroble. "Anton drew this sketch of the yacht's interior showing where the captive is held."

Using the flashlight on his cell phone, Stroble studied the drawing. "It'll be interesting to see how it matches up with the schematic that you gave us earlier," Stroble said. "Thank you." He slipped it inside his attaché case.

"There's more," Channing said. "Anton told us that the yacht hosted an important guest this afternoon. A man who arrived by helicopter."

"This visitor was stocky and had dark curly hair," Leslie added.

"When he tried to hide his face, Anton noticed that he wore a ring on his right hand," Channing said. "A very large ring."

I turned to look at Stroble, waiting for his reaction. It didn't take long.

Stroble's chin dropped and he shook his head. "You're not suggesting that Agent Donnie Bruno landed on that yacht, are you? That's preposterous."

"Maybe it is just a coincidence," I said. "But we wanted to play it safe and share this incident with you."

Stroble rubbed his face with his hands and then cocked his head back, gazing into the heavens. "Coincidences. When you've been in law enforcement as long as me, you start to question them." He sighed and then checked his watch. "It's nearly one o'clock. Way past my bedtime. Anything else?"

"We visited Jonah's house earlier this afternoon," Leslie said. "The birdhouse was still there."

"We all waved at your camera," Channing said. "Did you see us?"

"I haven't taken a look today," he said. Stroble removed the laptop from his briefcase. As he turned it on, Leslie and Channing left their seats and circled around the picnic table so they could gaze at the screen over Stroble's shoulder.

"Thank God Donnie Bruno is a whiz with this stuff," he said. He selected a program and we soon saw the outline of Jonah's house in the dark and the stark silhouettes of the birdhouses in his yard. "Let me go back and check the earlier footage," Stroble said. "About what time did you visit Mr. Jefferson's property?"

"It was before we had dinner," I said. "Around five o'clock, more or less."

Stroble scrolled back through the video feed, keeping an eye on the ever-changing time stamp appearing in the lower right corner of the screen. "We'll begin at 4:30," he said, "and will fast forward until we spot your smiling faces."

He advanced the footage through 5:30 p.m. We never appeared.

"That's strange," Stroble said. "Are you sure about the time?"

"Wait a second," I said. "Look closely at those birdhouses." Leslie, Channing, and Stroble all leaned forward.

"What's your point?" Stroble asked.

"That cannot be a recording of a live feed," I said. "There's no movement. No birds flying around. It's a static image."

Muttering under his breath, Stroble again scrolled back through the footage, stopping at noon. He then pressed another button and we saw Jonah's house and his assembly of birdhouses in the bright sunlight. Clouds eased across the top of the screen and birds flitted back and forth through the air, some landing on the houses and others flying off. Stroble fast-forwarded the video feed and all seemed well until he reached 4:00 p.m. From that point until the 6:00 p.m. time stamp, we observed the same identical image: no motion anywhere on the screen.

"There's a two-hour gap here," he said. "Exactly two hours." He squeezed the bridge of his nose. "I don't believe it's a glitch in the system."

"What do you mean?" Channing asked.

"I'm not certain, of course, but it appears that someone managed to override the protocols and insert that still shot."

"Who has access to your laptop?" I asked.

Stroble stared into the dark and ran a hand across his scalp and through his hair. "What's important right now is to determine what occurred during that two-hour window."

Leslie's subtle squeeze of my shoulder let me know she realized that Stroble had failed to address my question.

"Could this have something to do with that helicopter we saw flying low over Jonah's house?" Channing asked.

Stroble looked up from his laptop, his eyes wide. "What helicopter?" he asked.

"When we emerged from Jonah's garage, a chopper was hovering low over Jonah's property," Leslie said. "If the pilot hadn't spotted us, I'm convinced it would have landed in his front yard. It lifted and flew out of sight."

Stroble stared into the darkness, deep in thought. I then gave him another matter to consider.

"What about the tiny transponder that was placed in the bag of cocaine?" I asked. "Has it shown any sign of movement?"

Stroble typed in a few commands on his laptop and studied a chart that appeared on the monitor. A few more taps on the keyboard brought a different graphic to the display. "Nothing," he said. "Not a damn thing."

"What do you mean?" I asked.

"It's not transmitting," he said. "It appears to have been disabled."

Slamming the laptop shut, Stroble extricated himself from the picnic table. "I'll be back in touch," he said, shoving the computer into his attaché case. "My advice to you is to get some sleep."

We watched him jog to his car and drive off, his taillights disappearing into the darkness.

# ~ THIRTY-EIGHT ~

A loud and incessant knocking on the door of our rental cottage woke me from a troubled sleep. I glanced at my watch as Leslie stirred.

"What's going on?" she mumbled as the hammering continued.

"It's 6:15 and somebody's pounding on the front door." I slipped into my shorts and a t-shirt and stumbled from the bedroom, heading toward the racket. Through the picture window I saw Dabney Attleman's pink Volkswagen parked in the driveway. When I opened the door, she stood on the porch, looking stressed.

"We've got to talk," she said, darting into the living room. "Is Leslie here?"

"Yes," Leslie answered from the doorway to the bedroom. "Present and accounted for, but not yet fully awake. What's the matter?" She cinched the belt of her robe.

"It's my brother Brock," she said. Dabney must have realized that she'd never mentioned him during any of our conversations. "My younger—and only—sibling. He moved to Eleuthera a few months ago and has been staying with me, off and on."

"Is he okay?" I asked.

"I'm not sure."

"Would coffee be a good idea?" Leslie asked.

Following my eager nod and Dabney's emphatic "yes," Leslie wandered into the kitchen and began making a pot. Dabney followed, wringing her hands.

"This brother of yours," I said. "Is it something he's done?" I tried without much success to recall what the DEA agents had shared earlier about the young man. Maybe a stout cup of coffee would help my brain engage.

"Brock's been in trouble a time or two over the past couple of years," Dabney said. "Back in Florida. But he's always managed to skate away unharmed. This time, though, things are different."

"What can we do to help?" Leslie asked as she placed cups and saucers on the countertop.

"Right now, I need to vent, to have someone listen to me," Dabney said. She pulled a tissue from a pocket and dabbed her eyes.

We took our coffee cups into the living room and sat down, Leslie and I on the sofa and Dabney in a nearby side chair.

"I'm not sure where to begin," Dabney said. Avoiding any eye contact, she reached for her coffee and took a sip. "I've just learned about some things that put me in an awkward situation. Well beyond awkward, if you want to know the truth."

Knowing the truth would be a nice place to start, I thought. "Why don't you begin with your brother?" I asked.

Dabney inflated her cheeks and then slowly exhaled. "Brock knocked on my bedroom door late last night, asking if he could come in. He said we needed to talk."

"May we assume this has something to do with the disappearance of Jonah Jefferson?" Leslie asked.

"Very much so." She set her coffee cup aside, got to her feet, and began pacing back and forth across the room. "Ever since he was a kid, Brock has had trouble with his friends," she said. "He seems to have developed an uncanny ability to pick the wrong ones."

She then explained that Brock had been hanging around with Clivon Baines, a young man she knew by sight and reputation. Though his father, a retired customs agent, was held in high regard by the community, Clivon hadn't exactly developed into a role model for his peer group. According to Dabney, he'd become something of a resident poster boy for troubled youth. She stopped at her cup and took another sip of coffee.

"Wasn't Baines one of the names on Jonah's list of possible suspects?" Leslie asked.

"I should have taken Jonah's concern more seriously," Dabney said. "I didn't give it much credence."

"What kind of vehicle does this Clivon Barnes drive?" I asked. "Any chance it's an old white Chevrolet van?"

My question surprised Dabney. "I've seen his van a time or two," she said. "I'm not sure if it's a Chevrolet, but it's white. At least the portions that aren't rusty."

"Why don't you tell us a little more about this younger Baines character?" Leslie asked.

"I'm told he's had trouble holding a job," Dabney said. "Clivon's worked a little in construction, with a mechanic for a while, and similar work. And he's had a few brushes with the law. Accused of stealing a motorcycle, selling liquor to juveniles, that sort of thing." She paused and stared down at her feet.

"But something else has now come up, right?" I asked.

Dabney looked up and gave me a telling nod. "Yep. It seems that Clivon heard through the local grapevine that Jonah had come into possession of an extremely valuable bag of cocaine. He recruited Brock to participate in what was supposed to have been a simple 'grab and go' operation."

"'Grab and go'?" Leslie asked.

"Clivon figured that Jonah would take the coke to the authorities later that day, most likely Dunmore Town. So, he talked Brock into borrowing my VW," Dabney said. "When Brock got the call from Clivon that Jonah was heading toward the north end of the island, Brock would pretend to have mechanical problems on the Queen's Highway. Of course, Jonah stopped when he saw my car parked on the shoulder, thinking it was me. About that time, Clivon arrived with plans to steal the sack of coke. The old grab and go."

"But Jonah didn't have the coke?"

"That's right," Dabney said. "But Clivon was so hell-bent on cashing in his ticket to sudden wealth that he made another bad decision: kidnapping Jonah, again using my car. His idea was to force Jonah to hand over the coke."

"You learned all this last night from your brother?" Leslie asked.

"And more," Dabney said, shaking her head. "Not only did they fail to find the coke in Jonah's truck, they searched his house, his shed, and Jonah's cottage that you two had rented. As you know, they even ransacked my house."

Leslie brought the coffee pot into the living room and refilled our cups.

"This unfortunate story goes on and on," Dabney said. "Clivon's been known to do a little carpentry work in the area, and several years ago he helped with a remodeling project for the Marchants, that strange French couple living a short distance beyond Jonah's house."

"Let me guess," Leslie said. "Jonah was held captive in the Marchants' basement?"

Dabney's chin nearly bounced off her chest. "How did you know?"

"That doesn't matter," I said. "But Clivon must have some serious leverage over the Marchants to get them involved."

"Clivon confided to Brock that the Marchants do a rather brisk importing business on the side without paying duties to the commonwealth. Something that's been going on for several years now. Clivon threatened that he'd anonymously report them to the government authorities if they didn't let him hold Jonah captive in their basement for a few days."

"So," I said, "where's Jonah?"

"Brock told me that Jonah had been moved to a big yacht that's anchored in Governor's Harbor. In fact, he visited the boat earlier and says that Jonah's okay."

"Did Brock share anything about the people on the yacht?" Leslie asked. "Who they are, where they're from, and so on?"

Dabney shook her head. "Clivon told Brock to buy some new clothes for Jonah. He was led to Jonah's room on the yacht, delivered the package of clothing, and then sent back ashore. Brock never talked to anyone other than his escort."

Our disappointment must have shown.

"But he remembered hearing what appeared to be a party somewhere on the yacht," Dabney said. "Some loud music and lots of laughing. And what sounded like conversations in French. He also recalled the distinctive smell of cigars. He'd halfway expected to catch a whiff of marijuana when he boarded the yacht and was surprised by the strong aroma of cigars."

Leslie gave me a slight nod. She must have recalled the same conversation I remembered from the DEA agents: that two of the most notorious drug smugglers in the world shared a passion for fine stogies.

"Did Brock give any indication of what's next?" I asked.

"He feels that things are starting to move pretty fast," Dabney said. "Somehow, they discovered where Jonah had hidden the sack of cocaine. If they've not already retrieved it, they plan on getting it today."

I caught another subtle glance from Leslie. This couldn't be good news for Jonah.

"He also mentioned that his escort on the boat said something about getting out of Eleuthera soon. Hurricane Nikita is growing more intense and the storm is tracking this way. He thinks the yacht will sail once the last of the provisions are loaded."

"Any idea when that'll be?" Leslie asked.

"Very soon," Dabney said. "Later today was his guess."

"It's time we give Agent Stroble a call," I said.

Leslie reached for her phone and dialed his number.

"Brock's going to be in big trouble, isn't he?" Dabney asked.

It wasn't a matter of 'going to be,' I thought. Brock Attleman was already in plenty of hot water.

But was it too late to save Jonah?

## ~ THIRTY-NINE ~

Stroble didn't answer when Leslie dialed his number. She was leaving a message when his return call came back through.

"Sorry," he said. "I was on another call. You're up rather early, aren't you?"

"Dabney Attleman is here with Randy and me," Leslie said. "She has some things to share with you. I've got you on speaker phone."

"Good morning, Ms. Attleman," he said, "I'm Jack Stroble, special agent with the U.S. Drug Enforcement Administration. I don't believe we've met, but I'm eager for you to tell me what you might know about the disappearance of Jonah Jefferson."

"My brother—"

"That would be Brock Attleman, right?" Stroble asked. "Nineteen years old?"

Dabney was clearly surprised by Stroble's knowledge about her brother. "Yes," she stammered. "Brock told me late last night that he and one of his friends, a local man named Clivon Baines, tried to steal a sack of cocaine from Jonah. When that failed, they kidnapped him and held him hostage for several days."

"Do you know anything about Mr. Jefferson's safety? And his whereabouts?"

"According to Brock, Jonah is alive and being held on a big yacht that's anchored in Governor's Harbor," Dabney said.

"Has Brock himself observed Mr. Jefferson on that boat?"

"He saw Jonah when he delivered a change of clothes to him a couple of days ago."

"Thank you," Stroble said. "This is encouraging news."

"But there's some bad news, too," I said. "Dabney's brother told her that Jonah's hiding place for the cocaine is now known. And the bag of coke is going to be removed today, if they haven't already gotten it."

I expected a reaction from Stroble, but he remained silent.

"Can you update us on what's going on?" I asked.

"I'm not at liberty to—"

"And," Leslie said, interrupting Stroble, "give us an update, on the 'whereabouts,' to use one of your words, of Agent Bruno?"

Stroble cleared his throat. "A complete accounting will emerge in good time," he said. "I must go now. Thank you." The line went dead.

Leslie stared at her phone in disgust and then tossed it onto the couch. She wasn't used to people hanging up on her.

"What's next?" Dabney asked.

"I don't think we have any choice," I said. "We need to get down to Governor's Harbor."

"What's our plan?" Leslie asked.

"That's still to be determined," I said.

The three of us piled into our rental car, Leslie riding shotgun and Dabney struggling to get comfortable on the trio of milk crates that served as the back seat. As I pulled onto the Queen's Highway, Leslie fiddled with her phone.

"I'm calling Channing Creekmore," she said, and then turned to face Dabney. "She's the woman you recently met in Governor's Harbor."

"What does she have to do with this?" Dabney asked. "I thought she was just another tourist."

When Leslie looked to me for guidance, I gave her a shrug.

"Channing Creekmore is an investigative reporter," Leslie said, once again turning to face Dabney. "For months, she's been working on a story about a drug ring in France."

"And it's somehow tied into what's going on here in Eleuthera?" Dabney asked.

"That appears to be the case," I said. "And things seem to be coming to a head."

Leslie held up her hand, signaling that Channing had answered her phone.

"You're right," she said, speaking into the cell. "It's only 6:45, and way too early for a call. But something important's come up."

I glanced into the rearview mirror and saw Dabney's face. She stared out the window, gazing at the Caribbean and biting her lip. Her eyes had lost their usual sparkle. I wondered what she was thinking.

"What happened is that Dabney Attleman showed up at our place first thing this morning," Leslie said, the phone at her ear. "She'd learned from her brother that he and a local man had kidnapped Jonah. Dabney confirmed that Jonah's held captive on the *Vulpecula*."

I passed a delivery truck, the only other vehicle we'd seen on the deserted highway.

"Yes," Leslie said, giving her head a vigorous nod. "We shared this information with Agent Stroble moments ago. We're driving toward Governor's Harbor and should be there soon." She looked at me and raised her eyebrows.

I mouthed the word "ten" to her.

"Ten minutes," she said. "Take your time. We'll be at that bench overlooking the harbor." She signed off.

"We woke Channing," Leslie said, "but she'll get dressed and meet us as soon as she can."

When we passed the Governor's Harbor Airport, I noticed a Bahamasair plane parked on the tarmac and a few lights were on in the terminal. I thought back to the morning when Jonah Jefferson picked Leslie and me up at this place. Leslie must have been recalling that same experience; she gave me a slight smile and squeezed my knee.

As we approached the Barracuda Bay intersection, I slowed down.

"Something tells me we need to make a quick stop to check on things," I said, turning onto the rough road. "Channing will understand if we're running a few minutes late."

A few birds flitted back and forth in the dawn light as I parked next to Jonah's darkened home.

"Which one of his birdhouses holds that cache of coke?" Dabney asked.

I led her to it. She was inspecting the handsome addition when I spotted Leslie giving me a wave.

"Randy," Leslie said, a trace of tension in her voice. "Take a look at this." She gestured to something at her feet.

I trotted to her and stared at a pair of long parallel indentations in the grass for seconds before realizing what we were seeing. "A helicopter set down here," I said. "Those are the marks left by its landing skids."

We then turned and looked at the birdhouse above Dabney. She'd heard our comments.

"Somebody's been here," she said, pointing to the ground. "There are a lot of tracks in the dirt at the base of this pole."

Working together, the three of us managed to lift the birdhouse from the ground. It wasn't as heavy as it had been earlier. Not a good sign. After carrying it into Jonah's shed, we placed it on the workbench. Leslie switched on the light.

"They're ahead of schedule," I said, shaking my head. "They've already got the coke."

"How do you know?" Dabney asked.

I directed their attention to the bottom of the birdhouse's base. "Jonah used eight screws to secure this compartment, and we replaced all eight when we checked this out several days ago."

"And now?" Leslie asked.

"Only four."

We knew what we'd find when we removed the base, but we went through the motions anyway. The burlap bag and plastic garbage sack remained, but the cocaine was gone.

"Damn," Leslie muttered.

My thoughts exactly.

"They must have returned in that helicopter right after we left," I said. "They probably observed us leaving from a distance and then swooped in and removed the coke."

"There was still a good amount of time in that two-hour window of opportunity provided by the system override," Leslie said. "There won't be any video evidence on Agent Stroble's laptop."

"There's no need to mess with this," I said, gesturing toward the disassembled birdhouse. As we trotted to the car, Leslie dialed Stroble. When he failed to answer, she left a brief message summarizing our discovery. We then climbed into the car, and returned to the Queen's Highway, heading toward Governor's Harbor.

Leslie phoned Channing to explain our delay. After she'd told her about the birdhouse, Leslie asked for an update.

"What?" she asked. "You've got to be kidding!"

I glanced at Leslie. Her eyes were wide.

"We'll be there soon," she said, ending the call.

"What's going on?" Dabney asked.

"Channing's at the harbor," Leslie said. "There's a lot of frantic activity involving the *Vulpecula*. It looks like the yacht will be sailing within the hour."

# ~ FORTY ~

We pulled in and parked behind Channing's Jeep Wrangler near the Administration Building. She was sitting on a now-familiar bench, binoculars at her face, watching the activity on the pier. Dabney, Leslie, and I walked toward her.

The dinghy pushed away from the dock and began motoring toward the *Vulpecula*. A man standing next to a pickup waved at the departing boat. He then closed the tailgate, climbed into the cab, and drove off, nodding to our group as he passed.

"I'm told that's the last load of provisions," Channing said, lowering the binoculars as we approached. "The captain fired up the engine of the yacht about 15 minutes ago. Once those supplies are off-loaded and the dinghy's hoisted back into place, they'll be ready to go."

"I can't believe these guys are about to sail away, free as can be," I said.

"They're not."

We all turned around to see Agent Jack Stroble standing behind us. Without his DEA windbreaker and wearing khaki shorts, a deep green knit shirt, and sandals, he could have passed for the standard, all purpose male tourist. He pointed out to the open sea beyond the harbor.

"Look closely on the horizon and you'll find another boat out there."

I squinted toward the area Stroble indicated, but saw nothing. Channing aimed her binoculars in that direction and slowly moved them back and forth. Her movements stopped and I watched as she adjusted the focus.

"I see it," she said. "It looks big, like something from a navy." She pivoted to face Stroble again, awaiting some elaboration.

"What Ms. Creekmore has spotted is the *Valiant*, a U.S. Coast Guard Cutter stationed out of Jacksonville, Florida," Stroble said.

"You mean the military is helping out?" Leslie asked.

Stroble gave her a faint smile. "You might be surprised by the collaboration that occurs when your U.S. government takes on the international drug traffic."

"What happens next?" I asked.

"The *Valiant* will intercept the *Vulpecula* in the next half hour or so, dropping a team of commandos along with a handful of our agents on board via helicopter to secure the boat and its contents. Senior officials from the Royal Bahamas Police Force will also participate in the search."

"And then?" Leslie asked.

"If they find what we expect, certain individuals will be detained. And the yacht will be seized."

"Seized," I said, "like in confiscated?"

Stroble nodded. "And perhaps sold via a federal government auction, depending on how months and months of litigation play out."

I realized that Agent Stroble and Dabney had not met, so I introduced them.

"How much trouble is my brother in?" Dabney asked.

"I'm not an attorney and am unfamiliar with the laws of the Commonwealth," Stroble said. "But if Brock's guilty of criminal acts here in the Bahamas, I would encourage him to be forthcoming with the local authorities. I've found them to be good people."

Given her reaction, his words did little to reassure Dabney.

"Should we read anything into the absence of Agent Donnie Bruno?" Channing asked. "I don't believe we've seen him today."

Stroble ran a hand over his face and grimaced. "Can we go off-the-record?" he asked.

She thought about it for a moment and then bobbed her head. "Deal."

"It appears that Agent Bruno's claim of a family illness was without basis," he said.

"Is that a polite way of saying he lied to you?" Leslie asked.

"Let's just say that specific aspects of our investigation seem to have been compromised by my former colleague," Stroble said.

His use of the word "former" did not go unnoticed.

"May we assume that Bruno reprogrammed your laptop to—"

Shaking his head, Stroble placed his open palm above the extended fingers of his other hand, giving me the traditional signal for a time-out. "Let's dispense with questions for the present," he said. "Additional details on this operation will be available as the day progresses."

Across the harbor, the crew on the yacht winched the dinghy from the water and swung it into its place near the stern of the larger boat. As a pair of crew members secured the dinghy, the yacht began slowly moving toward the harbor's entrance, startling us all with a blast from its horn.

"I think the captain of the *Vulpecula* is in for a big surprise," Stroble said. "His boat may be fast, but it's not going to outrun a cutter of the U.S. Coast Guard. And most assuredly not its helicopters. And, now, if you'll excuse me for a moment, I need to make a call."

Stroble rejoined us a few minutes later. "The *Vulpecula*'s departure signaled the beginning of the second phase of our day's activities," he said. "At this time, another U.S. Coast Guard ship has intercepted the *Rosalita*, the yacht that sailed from Colombia days ago."

"Is it still anchored somewhere in the Exumas?" Leslie asked.

"That's correct," Stroble answered. "Personnel representing our joint task force have boarded that vessel and are now conducting a systematic search." His phone beeped and he started walking away. "Thanks for your earlier message about Jonah's special birdhouse," he said, looking over his shoulder. "We expected as much." He then disappeared behind the Administration Building, the phone at his ear.

\* \* \*

A little before ten o'clock, Leslie and I drove to the nearest C-store to buy bottled water and snacks for our foursome.

"Did you notice that Stroble has said nothing about Jonah?" she said. "Not a word."

"I'm going to assume that no news is good news," I said. "As you know, I'm an unrepentant optimist."

"Isn't that required of anybody in the advertising business?" Leslie asked, giving me a wink.

She had a point.

We returned and shared our sack of purchases with Dabney and Channing.

"Any news from our DEA guy?" I asked.

They both shook their heads.

"He's not reappeared," Channing said. "And outside of a fishing boat or two heading out, things have been quiet in the harbor."

Dabney looked at her phone. "That may not be the case for long," she said. "Hurricane Nikita is moving again. Gaining strength and speed and heading this way."

A little after noon, the four of us walked to Baby Sue's for lunch where we had the place to ourselves. While the ladies opted for conch salad, I ordered grilled red snapper with rice and pigeon peas. As before, we got delightful service from the young lady with a shy smile. Little conversation occurred as we ate, and most of it revolved around the tasty dishes. We all seemed preoccupied with our own private thoughts, no doubt most revolving around Jonah's fate.

Agent Jack Stroble rose from the bench as we neared him following our lunch break and gave us a friendly wave.

"I have good news," he said. "The captain of the *Vulpecula* obeyed orders from the *Valiant* and dropped anchor at once. Our crew then conducted a thorough search of the entire vessel."

We all stared at Stroble, waiting for him to continue.

"And…," Leslie said, almost begging him for an answer.

"A total of nine large bags of the highest-quality cocaine were discovered in the kitchen of the yacht," Stroble said, "hidden in the deep recesses of the walk-in freezer. All of them wrapped in very distinct packaging."

"What about Jonah?" I asked.

Stroble shook his head. "Mr. Jefferson was not found on the *Vulpecula*," he said. "Nor was he located on the *Rosalita* when it was searched earlier today."

"Where could he be?" Dabney asked, her eyes wide. "Surely they didn't—"

Leslie reached out and patted Dabney on her back. "He's going to be okay," she said.

"Our team is now interrogating people from both boats," Stroble said. "I expect to have an answer soon."

"What about the crew members and passengers on the boats?" Channing asked.

"Our officers are still trying to sort everything out," Stroble said. "The captain of the *Vulpecula* and his crew are insisting they're innocent, that they knew nothing about the cocaine. Likewise, the passengers are claiming they're blameless, unaware of the drugs, and throwing the crew under the bus. Or under the yacht, in this case."

"Is Grégoire Delisle among those detained?" Channing asked.

Stroble removed a sheet of paper from a pocket and studied it for a moment. "That name is among the list of those now in custody." He managed to hide most of a smile. "I'm told Mr. Delisle is clamoring for an attorney."

"What can you tell us about the *Rosalita*?" Leslie asked.

"An exhaustive search of that yacht yielded no contraband," Stroble said. "Our team thanked the captain and his passengers for their full cooperation and allowed it to sail. Given the situation with Hurricane Nikita, I believe the *Rosalita* is now heading back to port in Colombia."

"Did the passengers include a certain Alarico Villarreal?" I asked.

"An individual by that name was on the boat," Stroble said, "but we had no legal grounds to hold him."

Stroble's cell phone beeped and he once again disappeared behind the Administration Building.

*  *  *

When Agent Stroble returned late in the afternoon, he seemed to have a bounce in his step. I started to ask him about it when a distant whump/whump/whump diverted my attention. I glanced over my shoulder, past the harbor, and saw a helicopter approaching against the setting sun. I looked back to Stroble.

"What's going on?" I asked.

He gave me an innocent shrug and then waved a hand to get Channing's attention. "Ms. Creekmore," he said, "you might want to get your camera ready."

The huge chopper, making an incredible racket, circled the harbor and then gently descended, landing in the middle of the pier. Bright red, it had US Coast Guard stenciled in white paint on the fuselage behind the doors. We crossed the street and trotted after Stroble, stopping well short of the big machine until the main rotors came to a full stop. A helicopter door swung open, and Jonah Jefferson stepped out.

# ~ FORTY-ONE ~

"Jonah!"

Channing snapped her picture, and Leslie then took off for him on a dead run with Dabney not far behind. After Leslie whispered something to him, Jonah stepped back, extended his arms, and placed his hands on her shoulders, staring at my bride. His face then lit up as he shook his head back and forth. Beaming as if he'd just won the latest Powerball jackpot, he had one arm wrapped around Leslie and another around Dabney when Channing, Stroble, and I reached them.

"I cannot believe this," Jonah said. "I've never had more dedicated guests." After examining my face, he gave me a firm handshake. "And to be sure, none who've transformed their appearances like you and your lovely wife."

"Jonah Jefferson," I said, motioning for Channing and Agent Stroble to step forward. "I'd like you to meet Ms. Channing Creekmore, a free-lance investigative journalist, and Agent Jack Stroble with the U.S. Drug Enforcement Administration."

"My pleasure," Jonah said as he exchanged handshakes with them. "I understand you two get a lot of credit for putting an end to this nonsense."

I noticed that Jonah looked like he'd lost a few pounds. And, strangely enough, his face and head appeared to be a bit sunburned.

"Seems to me a celebration is in order," I said. "I'll spring for pizza and drinks if Jonah's game."

"That sounds like the perfect end to a memorable day," he said. "But first, I must thank these amazing guys for rescuing me." He turned and stepped back into the Coast Guard chopper.

Leslie volunteered to lead our small group to what we now viewed as our personal picnic table in the nearby cemetery while I bought food and drinks. Jonah was still thanking his squad of liberators when I hurried off to get dinner. Minutes later, while I paid for three pizzas and two six-packs of beverages, I heard the helicopter lift up and fly away.

When I rejoined this merry band, Channing was telling Jonah about her months of background research in Europe and how she came to be on Eleuthera. As I passed the pizza boxes around, Stroble rapped his knuckles against the table.

"Tonight's going to be an atypical evening for me," he said. "Normally, I'm isolated in an out-of-the-way place interviewing a suspect or, as in this case, a victim. But given the tensions of the past few days, I think we should take a little time to relax. I'll get with Mr. Jefferson first thing tomorrow morning for his official statement." Turning to Channing, he said, "And any remarks I make to this group are off-the-record. You and I can visit privately should you have specific questions for me."

Raising her beer, Channing gave him a knowing nod.

For the next hour, Jonah told us about the attempted robbery, his kidnapping, and subsequent imprisonments, first in the Marchant's house and later on the *Vulpecula*.

"To be honest, I never felt that my life was in danger," he said. "The two young men who planned to rob me were rank amateurs. As my daddy might have said, 'They weren't the sharpest hooks in the tackle box.'"

"You've got that right," Dabney said, rolling her eyes.

"I never saw the Marchants," Jonah said. "Somebody corralled their dog and I was led downstairs to a basement. I didn't even know their house had a basement. And the room was weird, like something out of a torture chamber."

I caught Leslie giving me a sly wink.

We congratulated Jonah on his inspired decision to hide the bag of cocaine in the birdhouse.

"Frankly, I was worried that news about the cocaine might be circulating after Nigel and the two boys spotted the bag. I didn't want to take it with me to Dunmore Town, and was desperate for a solution. That particular birdhouse was already 90 percent done," he said. "All I had to do was devise a larger base."

"I guess you know they did a number on your truck," Leslie said.

Jonah nodded. "I can borrow that Wrangler that you and Randy were using."

"We left it at the airport," I said.

Jonah looked at Stroble. "I'm afraid to ask about Agent Bruno," he said. "From things I overheard, I…uh…fear that he may have yielded to temptation. Switched over to the wrong team."

Maintaining eye contact with Jonah, Stroble displayed no visible reaction to his damning allegation. "Departmental policy prevents me from saying anything," he said, "other than Agent Donnie Bruno is on administrative leave pending results of an internal investigation. As for his present location, that's something we're still trying to ascertain."

Jonah sniffed and wiped at his eyes. "This whole situation is so damn tragic… My own godson…" A tear trickled down his cheek. "I only learned in recent weeks that Donnie had developed a terrible gambling problem, accumulating a tremendous debt with some very bad dudes. His soon-to-be ex-wife shared a pretty grim future, struggling to raise two small children without a partner."

Life is so strange, I thought. Bruno served on the front lines fighting one form of addiction, yet had himself succumbed to an altogether different kind of uncontrollable craving.

"How did you wind up on the *Vulpecula?*" Leslie asked.

"Through the local grapevine, the French guy, Delisle, had heard about that one sack of cocaine coming into my possession and my subsequent kidnapping," Jonah said. "He then arranged for me to be brought to his boat from the Marchant's house late one night."

"What kind of host was Delisle?" Channing asked. "If host is even the right word."

"I can tell you he was a no-nonsense kind of guy," Jonah said. "He asked if I was familiar with the term 'hum chum.' I told him I wasn't."

"Hum chum," I said. "What's that?"

"Delisle took great delight in explaining it," Jonah said, "claiming that he originated the phrase. Evidently some of his associates had spent a good deal of time in a nearby cove known to be infested with bull and tiger sharks. They'd been regularly feeding these enormous beasts with barrels of fish scraps, causing a feeding frenzy." He paused. "Delisle said if I didn't tell him the location of that last bag of coke, I'd be tossed into the water at the next feeding. That I'd be a fine example of human chum, or, to use his wording, hum chum."

We all stared at Jonah, shaking our heads.

"He actually showed me the stinking barrels of fish heads, skins, and guts they'd set aside for my upcoming swim with the sharks. Delisle told me he'd taken his new business associate from Colombia to the site for a personal inspection, stating that the sharks put on a spectacular show."

I thought back to the shark that Leslie and I'd encountered during our snorkeling excursion days earlier. One shark in retreat was scary enough. I couldn't imagine dealing with dozens crazed by gallon upon gallon of fish blood and parts.

"But somehow Delisle got a tip about the location of the coke," Jonah said, looking at Stroble, "and I was spared the hum chum experience."

Stroble didn't acknowledge Jonah's comment and glanced at his watch.

"Agent Stroble told us you weren't found on either of the yachts," Channing said, changing the subject. "Where were you?"

"Two nights ago, I was flown by helicopter from the *Vulpecula* to the *Rosalita* somewhere west of here," Jonah said. "And then yesterday morning, I was transported by dinghy to one of the uninhabited islands in the Exumas. They gave me a sleeping bag and enough food and water for two weeks." He ran a hand over his sun-burned head. "Unfortunately, I had no cap."

Leslie gave me a slight smile, apparently remembering our unusual discovery under the stairs leading to the basement of the Marchant's house.

"They chose not to kill me, and I must give credit to Donnie Bruno for that," he said. "They knew that I was an ex-cop and had lived in Miami. Donnie told them how a trio of my fellow officers had tried to frame some Cuban refugees on trumped-up drug charges, and that I'd exposed the scheme, ultimately sending the dirty cops to prison."

"That was you?" Stroble asked. "I always thought that would've made a great movie."

"Maybe we can get Ms. Creekmore to draft a script," Jonah said. "Anyway, my assumption is they felt that abandoning me on that remote island would buy them a considerable head start. I'd already crafted a 'HELP' message on the beach using palm fronds. But given the area's popularity with bare-boaters, I told myself it would just be a matter of time—certainly less than two weeks—before somebody found me."

"Another couple of days," Dabney said, "and Hurricane Nikita might well inundate that island."

"Nikita?" Jonah asked. "I haven't heard about this one. Is it heading our way?"

"We'll know more in about 36 hours," Dabney said. "But things could get bad."

"On that note," Stroble said, "this boy's going to turn in. I've had a long day." He scooted out from the table and got to his feet.

"What's going to happen to those people who've been detained?" I asked.

"They'll be taken to Nassau tomorrow and formally arraigned," he said. "Afterwards, we'll hold a news conference with the Bahamian authorities to announce today's seizure." With that, he waved good-bye and disappeared down the street.

Channing departed moments later, promising that we'd hear from her soon. Dabney, Leslie, Jonah and I then climbed into our rental car for the short drive to Jonah's home.

"Where did you get this thing?" Jonah asked as he tried to get situated on one of the milk crates. "A car similar to this was assigned to me back when I was on the force in Miami."

"It's a long story," I said.

As we drove toward Jonah's home, Leslie warned him about how his place had been turned upside-down. We spent a full hour helping him sort through the mess and get his bedroom back in order. Afterwards, we adjourned to the deck.

"I owe both you and Leslie an apology," I said to Jonah. "I should've minded my own business and left that damn bag in the sand."

Jonah shook his head. "You did the right thing, Randy. Thanks to you and Leslie, one of the world's leading scumbags should soon be in prison for what we can hope will be a lengthy stay."

"But we caused you so much harm and danger," Leslie said.

Jonah shrugged. "I have no real complaint. They fed me well and even brought me a change of clothes. But my big problem is this: I have no idea how the Dolphins are doing!"

Jonah gave Dabney and Leslie hugs and I got a handshake, and we then left, heading up the Queen's Highway toward Gregory Town. When we pulled in at our rental cottage, Dabney gave Leslie a kiss to the cheek and then did the same to me, much to my surprise, before stepping into her VW.

"I've got a large group from Club Med arriving first thing in the morning," she said, "and have lots of restocking to do. Please return to Eleuthera sometime soon!"

We waved as she backed down the driveway and then pulled onto the highway.

"I'll meet you in the hot tub in five minutes," Leslie said.

It was an offer I couldn't refuse. My beautiful bride soon returned with two cocktail glasses and a bottle of our Bahamian rum. The tasty drink was even better than I remembered. And the jets of hot water did wonders for my tension. So did Leslie's interest in some physical release.

# ~ FORTY-TWO ~

We were awakened by the ringing of Leslie's phone at 6:30.

After her sleepy "hello," she looked to me and mouthed "Stroble."

I climbed out of bed, stumbled into the kitchen, and got the coffee underway while she continued the conversation. She walked in as I scrambled eggs for breakfast.

"Agent Stroble called with an interesting proposition," she said. "It would mean a change in our travel plans, but I found certain aspects of it moderately intriguing."

"I trust this doesn't include getting grilled by a team of aggressive federal government attorneys."

"He's invited us to attend a news conference this afternoon in Nassau," she said. "The 'multi-national task force,' to use his words, will provide details about the capture of a major drug trafficker."

"And you found that intriguing?"

"That was just the first part of his proposal." She cocked her head and gave me a clever little smile.

"And the second?" I asked, handing her a plate of bacon, eggs, and toast.

"A small crew from the Coast Guard will sail the *Vulpecula* to Miami afterwards. We've been invited to travel back to the States aboard that luxury yacht."

"That could be interesting," I said.

"He promised us the master suite."

Over breakfast, we decided to accept Stroble's unexpected offer. As I washed, dried, and stored dishes, Leslie called him, confirmed our interest, and jotted down details. We packed in record time, loaded the car, and left the cottage key under the conch shell where we'd found it. By 8:00, we were headed north on the Queen's Highway toward Dunmore Town. About halfway there, we drove past Vernita's Beauty Shop, the place where Leslie and I both got our new hairstyles a few days ago. Vernita was sitting on the steps of her shop and returned our waves.

Leslie chuckled and shook her head. "I'd like to see the expressions on the staff at Lassiter and Associates when you walk into your office," she said. "Nobody's going to know who you are."

"That reminds me," I said. "I need to check in again later this morning."

After returning the rental car, we caught a water taxi across the harbor to the pier where the ferry to Nassau was berthed. While Leslie bought tickets for the next departure, I borrowed her cell and phoned my office.

"How go things in Little Rock?" Leslie asked after I ended the call.

"The agency won half a dozen ADDY awards for a couple of our clients, to include the coveted 'Best of Show' recognition," I said. "And a long-delinquent account is now paid in full."

"Maybe you should leave more often," Leslie said.

"Strange that you should mention that," I said. "Those were almost the exact words I heard from my assistant."

An hour later we were on the fast ferry, skimming across the shimmering Caribbean. As we enjoyed a light lunch on the top deck, we spotted a massive cruise ship in the distance. Once we docked at Nassau, we made a hurried trip to the airport by taxi, retrieved the luggage and Leslie's photography gear that we'd stored in the locker days earlier, and then returned to the harbor for the big news event. We spotted the *Vulpecula* at once. It was easily the largest vessel on the water.

"There's Agent Stroble," Leslie said, pointing down the pier. Channing Creekmore stood behind him. They waved when they saw us, motioning for us to join them. Stroble glanced at his watch as we neared them.

"Glad you could make it," he said. "The media event is scheduled to begin in 15 minutes."

He then led us down the dock, pausing as we neared the *Vulpecula*. A table stood in front of a podium, with flags of the Commonwealth of the Bahamas and the United States posted on either side. Escorted by a pair of Royal Bahamas Police Force cruisers, a black SUV, its deeply tinted windows hiding any occupants, came to a stop within 20 feet of the podium. Four armed police officers emerged from the police cars and took conspicuous positions near the table, two on each side. Several more official vehicles arrived, and men in suits and uniforms began gathering behind the table. Stroble excused himself and joined the throng of dignitaries.

Channing, Leslie, and I watched as teams of reporters erected tripods and secured cameras, checking their light-balance and audio. A small crowd of spectators began assembling behind us.

Channing looked over all the activity before locking her gaze onto the huge yacht that provided an impressive backdrop for the forthcoming news conference.

"I still cannot believe this strange chapter of my life is coming to a close," she said. "That I'll soon write the final paragraphs in a months-long story."

"What's next on your agenda?" Leslie asked.

"A real vacation," Channing said, giving us a grin. "Somewhere up in the mountains."

A woman wearing a Royal Bahamas Police Force uniform walked past, distributing media kits to the journalists. Channing got her attention and asked for one. I watched over Channing's shoulder as she opened the folder and examined its contents, first removing an official news release followed by several 8 x 10 photographs of the confiscated drugs. The last photograph was a shot of the *Vulpecula* tied to the *Valiant*, the Coast Guard cutter.

Channing withdrew a piece of paper from the folder and, after studying it for a moment, handed it to me. It was a program for the news conference. I noticed that Agent Jack Stroble was slated to speak.

"Testing one, two, three. Testing."

I looked up to see a senior officer with the Royal Bahamas Police Force standing behind the podium, backing off from the microphone. After he nodded toward the SUV, the doors opened, and two men carried a plastic crate to the table and removed its contents. They arranged nine sacks of cocaine with the Robin Hood motif on the table and then stepped away, blending into the crowd. Channing, I noticed, took a series of shots as the drugs were displayed.

According to the program, the man at the podium was Jarrette Adderley, the Commissioner of the Royal Bahamas Police Force. Maybe that explained the array of medals on his handsome uniform. He introduced members of the task force, all of whom stepped forward one at a time. Commissioner Adderley then announced that as a result of a collaborative effort between the Commonwealth of the Bahamas and the United States of America, one of the world's leading drug lords, Grégoire Pierre Delisle of France, had been taken into custody the previous day along with a substantial quantity of narcotics.

He next asked Jack Stroble, special agent with the U.S. Drug Enforcement Administration, to come forward and share details of the joint operation.

Stroble stepped to the podium, shaking hands with the Bahamian Police Commissioner as they passed.

"Thank you, Commissioner Adderley," Stroble said. "I'm pleased to report that the U.S. Drug Enforcement Administration, working in close cooperation with the Royal Bahamas Police Force and the U.S Coast Guard, intercepted a significant shipment of cocaine yesterday morning bound for France."

Stroble gestured down to the table below him. "Our multinational task force confiscated 41 kilos of highly refined cocaine yesterday off the coast of Eleuthera. The estimated street value of what you see on the table in front of me is $4.1 million."

He slowly swung around and pointed to the yacht behind him. "The cocaine was discovered in the freezer compartment of the *Vulpecula*, a boat that had been chartered in France several weeks ago by Mr. Grégoire Delisle. Mr. Delisle and two of his associates have been detained and will be formally charged with drug trafficking. As for the *Vulpecula*, it has been confiscated by the government of the United States. Are there any questions?"

A hand waved in front of us, and Stroble gave the young woman a nod.

"Have you been able to determine the source of these drugs?" she asked.

"We have good reason to believe this shipment originated in South America," he said, "but we've been unable to confirm that." He gazed over the crowd. "Other questions?"

Channing raised her hand. "Were members of the yacht's crew charged?" she asked.

Stroble shook his head. "Members of the crew along with three passengers have already been flown back to France." He again surveyed the crowd and asked if there were any additional questions.

"Can you give us any idea how this shipment came to your attention?" The question came from a young man standing beside Channing.

"As you might expect," Stroble said, "we cannot divulge much, given the sensitive nature of our investigation. But I can tell you that this intervention would not have been possible without the help of two American tourists who brought some rather unusual events to our attention."

Leslie edged closer and gave my hand a squeeze.

Stroble turned and looked back at Commissioner Adderley. "Start to finish, this operation was an outstanding success. On behalf of the government of the United States, I'd like to thank Commissioner Adderley and his colleagues in the Royal Bahamas Police Force for their exceptional help and cooperation."

As Stroble stepped aside, Commissioner Adderley returned to the podium. "This concludes today's press conference. I must ask that everyone remain in place as our officers collect the evidence and secure it in a safe location."

Reappearing with their plastic crate, the two men quickly collected the nine sacks of cocaine, climbed into their SUV, and sped off, accompanied by the pair of police cruisers.

Channing glanced at her watch. "I'm booked on a red-eye flight to Paris later this evening," she said. "I hope you two will plan on visiting me one of these days."

She embraced Leslie with a nice hug, and then had one for me, too.

"You can count on it," Leslie said. "And when you schedule a trip back to the States, please come see us in Little Rock."

I handed Channing one of my business cards. "Make sure to send us a link to that story you write. We're eager to get the full details."

"You're not fooling me," she said, giving me a big grin. "You want to make certain I get the spelling of your name right."

With a final wave, our new friend—and Leslie's one-time "unsub"—hailed a cab and left for the airport.

# ~ FORTY-THREE ~

I felt a hand on my shoulder. It was DEA Agent Jack Stroble. Leslie and I turned to face him.

"I hope you and the task force associates are pleased," Leslie said. "Things seemed to go well. Not counting Channing Creekmore, you had at least three teams of reporters covering the media event."

"We'll consider it a success if one of the major national networks picks up the story," he said. "It's nice to hit a home run every now and then."

"Jonah Jefferson is safe and Grégoire Delisle is in custody," I said. "What more could you want?"

"To tell you the truth, I can think of two things," Stroble said. "It would be icing on the cake to have nabbed Alarico Villarreal along with Delisle. But what I really wish is that I had my partner back." He sighed and shook his head. "Donnie Bruno screwed up big time. Not only did he squander a promising career, he destroyed his marriage and a young family. And odds are he's going to face some serious time in one of those lovely gated communities known as a federal correctional institution. How much is anybody's guess."

"Is Agent Bruno in custody?" I asked.

Stroble shook his head. "Not yet, but it's only a matter of time before he's found. I suspect he's trying to maintain a low profile somewhere on Eleuthera."

"Jonah seemed devastated," Leslie said. "He and Agent Bruno had a long history."

"I debriefed Mr. Jefferson earlier this morning," Stroble said. "And you're right; Bruno was much more than a godson to him. He teared up while talking about Donnie's fall. As you might expect, he's also very worried about Donnie's two young kids. And, get this. The boy's named Jonah."

A blast from the horn of the *Vulpecula* startled us.

"It appears the boat's ready to depart for Miami," Stroble said. "Is this all of your gear?" He nodded toward the collection of bags at our feet.

Stroble grabbed Leslie's tripod and she and I got the rest. We followed him 100 feet or so down the dock to a gangplank that led to the *Vulpecula* and then onto the yacht. Once we stepped on the deck, I realized it was even larger than it looked from shore. Much larger.

A handsome young man wearing a Coast Guard uniform met us.

"Welcome aboard!" he said, sharing a nice grin.

"This is Ensign Charlie Powers," Stroble said, introducing us. "He'll show you to your quarters."

Powers took the bags from Leslie's hands.

"But before I go," Stroble said, "let me thank you both for all you've done."

He shook hands with us, first with Leslie and then with me.

"I suspect I also owe Randy an apology for my less-than-cordial reception when he first approached me in that restaurant days ago in Dunmore Town," Stroble said. "If my memory's correct, I was rather skeptical when Randy claimed you two had witnessed a drug drop."

"You had a right to be testy," I said. "I interrupted a fine lobster dinner."

"I cannot tell you how much I appreciate your help in bringing a bad actor to justice," he said. "You have done a great service for the Drug Enforcement Administration. Best wishes for an enjoyable trip to Florida and then on home to Arkansas."

Stroble gave us a nod, turned away, and began walking toward the gangplank. Halfway there, he stopped and faced us. "One other thing. You'll find a small surprise in your suite from my head boss at DEA." After a final wave, he trotted down the gangplank and gestured for a taxi.

"Please follow me," Ensign Powers said. "After we stow your gear, I'll give you a tour of this fine vessel. We'll go the back way, using the crew's corridor." He opened what looked like a closet door and led us into a narrow hallway.

"Crew's corridor?" I asked.

"This is an exceptionally outfitted yacht," he said. "Members of the crew can go about their business without interrupting the guests and their activities. We were told that the ultra-rich insist on privacy, often preferring not to mingle with the common folks."

We emerged in an attractive foyer lined with abstract oil paintings. Originals, I noticed. Not prints.

"These first two doors open onto guest cabins," Powers said. "The last one leads to your quarters."

The word "quarters" didn't do our suite justice. It was huge with floor-to-ceiling windows overlooking a private deck. There was a mini-kitchen with a fully-stocked wet bar, a loveseat conveniently situated in front of a wood-burning fireplace, and a state-of-the-art entertainment nook. One corner of the suite served as a compact office with a computer and printer/scanner arranged on an antique desk. The enormous bathroom included a bidet, heated towel racks, and a walk-in shower for two outfitted with an array of nozzles mounted on the walls.

"Randy," Leslie said. "Come here and check out the bedroom."

I stood beside Leslie at the door and gazed into the room. The first thing I noticed was an inviting hot tub. And then my eyes settled on a bed large enough to accommodate a serious orgy, complete with a mirrored headboard. I spotted a white envelope atop the pile of pillows on the bed.

Ensign Powers walked up behind us. "That letter on the pillows is the item Agent Stroble mentioned earlier. He asked that we leave it for you."

Leslie walked across the room and picked it up. She opened the envelope, removed a sheet of paper, and began reading. She then looked to me, her mouth open.

"You won't believe this," she said, giving me the letter. Her hand seemed to be shaking.

"Is everything okay?" Powers asked.

"Yes, things are fine," Leslie said. "They couldn't be better, in fact. His...uh...thank you note caught me...off-guard."

As I read Stroble's missive, I soon had the same reaction. Typed on official U.S. Drug Enforcement Administration stationery, it read:

*Dear Ms. Carlisle and Mr. Lassiter:*

*Under authority granted to the U.S Drug Enforcement Administration by the Congress of the United States, the agency is pleased to award you a total of $100,000 for your invaluable assistance in the apprehension of a notorious international drug trafficker. An amount equal to this sum will be deposited into your joint checking account within the next 30 days.*

*America continues to make progress in its never-ending war against the illicit drug trade. On behalf of the 9,500 dedicated employees of DEA, I'm pleased to express our sincere appreciation for your vital help in these important efforts.*

It was signed by the agency's director.

After replacing the letter in the envelope and tossing it back onto the bed, I took Leslie's hand and led her from the bedroom. We'd talk later.

"Shall we continue the tour?" I asked, looking to Ensign Powers.

We left the master suit and walked back into the foyer.

Powers pointed to the door of one of the guest rooms. "This is where Mr. Jefferson was held captive for a time."

247

We peeked into the suite and saw nothing that indicated our friend was once imprisoned here. Although not as impressive as the master suite, it was certainly more charming than the little dungeon in the Marchants' basement.

Powers then led us into a room that was a combination theater/library. Next on our journey through the *Vulpecula* was a modern dining room, accented with a dazzling crystal chandelier, that could seat a dozen guests. From there, we entered what Powers called "the commons," a spacious area with a comfortable assortment of couches, chairs, and tables.

"Through that door," Powers said, pointing to an entrance on the far wall, "is the yacht's wine cellar. We're told that its collection is worth a little north of one million dollars."

When we stopped out onto the deck, we were once again startled by the *Vulpecula*'s horn. I felt a subtle movement of the boat.

"We're getting underway," Powers said. "Let's make a quick trip to the bridge."

He took us past the helicopter landing pad to stairs leading to the top deck. We then entered a small room surrounded by windows where he introduced us to two of his Coast Guard colleagues. The first, standing at the helm, was Commander Randolph Nelson, and the second, stationed in front of a bank of instruments, was Lieutenant Michelle O'Connell.

"Welcome to our sunset cruise," Nelson said, giving us a warm smile. "We're 177 nautical miles due east of Miami. We'll take our time crossing the Gulf Stream, arriving a little after sunrise tomorrow."

"We've got a real pro in Commander Nelson," Powers said. "He's retiring at the end of this month following 30 years of active service. This will be his last voyage."

"I'm accustomed to larger vessels and bigger crews," he said. "But this is not a bad way to go out, eh?"

"As long as you can keep us out of the path of that hurricane," Leslie said. "Should we be worried about it?"

O'Connell tapped a couple of keys on her computer and studied the screen. "Hurricane Nikita continues to gain strength, now registering as a Category 4 storm with top winds in excess of 150 miles per hour," she said. "Our latest model calls for it to track south of the Bahamas and Florida. It now looks to be heading toward the Dominican Republic and Haiti, and then on to Cuba. Wherever it makes landfall, Nikita is going to wreak havoc."

Powers glanced at his watch. "Dinner will be served in the dining room at 18:30 sharp," he said. "I'll escort you to your quarters now."

We thanked his colleagues on the bridge and backtracked down into the interior of the *Vulpecula*. Powers left us at the door to our suite, saying, "We'll see you in 45 minutes."

As we unpacked our luggage, I noticed something I hadn't seen earlier—a shiny metal pole positioned near the base of the bed. It extended from the ceiling to the floor.

"What's this doing here?" I asked. "It looks like an unusual place for a support."

Leslie shook her head and snickered. "I believe that's a little bonus for guests who enjoy a rather specific...uh...shall we say, athletic activity."

"I have no idea what you're talking about."

"Pole dancing."

I stared at my bride. How did Leslie know such things?

She gave me a clever little grin. "You'd be surprised at what a girl can learn from the articles in *Cosmopolitan*."

That explanation struck me as one that I'd heard before. "Have you—?"

"No," she said, interrupting me. "I've had absolutely no experience as a pole dancer. None whatsoever." She paused and then winked. "But I'd be willing to give it a try if you're interested."

"Perhaps we should wait until after dinner?"

"Perhaps."

When we resumed unpacking, Leslie found that cute sundress she'd bought in Dabney Attleman's shop days ago. "A little touch-up with an iron and this'll be ready to wear."

"While you do that, I'm going to hit the shower," I said.

249

I was rinsing my hair when I felt a gentle pat on my butt. "Mind if I join you?" Leslie asked. The over-sized shower proved to be an excellent amenity.

Leslie looked gorgeous in her colorful dress as we strolled into the dining room. Commander Nelson joined us promptly at the appointed hour, explaining that the remainder of the crew was occupied. Lieutenant O'Connell was at the helm with Ensign Powers at her side. Two men were assigned to the engine room and another pair worked in the kitchen.

The meal was delicious. Following a salad, we enjoyed prime rib with asparagus, glazed carrots, and scalloped potatoes, with chocolate crème brûlée for dessert. Leslie and I consumed two fine bottles of French Cabernet Sauvignon over the course of the dinner, but Commander Nelson passed on the vino. Thanking us for our companionship, he excused himself, stating that he'd nap for a couple of hours before resuming his duties on the bridge.

Leslie and I returned to our suite following the meal. Within minutes we were up to our necks in the hot tub, enjoying a bottle of Dom Pérignon Champagne I'd discovered in the mini-refrigerator.

"Can you believe it?" Leslie asked. "A $100,000 windfall."

"I've been giving that some thought," I said, "and have come up with a few ideas."

"Me, too," she said. "But you go first."

"What would you think about setting aside half the money for college scholarships for Donnie Bruno's two children?"

"I was going to suggest the same thing!"

"I'm sure Jonah can put us in contact with their mother. One of the local banks should be willing to hold the funds in trust until they reach college age."

"Let's make that a priority once we return to Little Rock," Leslie said.

"What about the rest of that award? The other $50,000?"

"I have an idea for that, too," Leslie said as she leaned over and gave me a kiss.

"Let's hear it."

"I don't want you to take this wrong," she began. "I love our historic home and its high ceilings, hardwood floors, wraparound porch, and curb appeal."

After our engagement and before our recent marriage, Leslie had moved in with me into my circa-1895 house in Little Rock's Quapaw Quarter District. For the most part, we'd successfully melded the two households. I'd given her the two largest closets in the house. And I'd donated my ping pong table along with my priceless collection of Dallas Cowboys memorabilia to the Boys & Girls Club.

"But?" I asked, raising my eyebrows.

"I think it's time for us to upgrade the bath. Maybe even to add a new master bathroom."

Leslie was right; our shared bath was small and antiquated by today's standards. After mulling over her suggestion for several seconds, I asked, "Would you consider including a shower for two in the plans?"

Leslie gave me one of her beguiling smiles.

"I believe I'd be good with that."

We finished the Champagne, stepped from the hot tub, and dried ourselves with the most luxurious bath towels I'd ever experienced. Still wrapped in the thick towels, Leslie reached for my hand, led me to the massive bed, and gently pushed me onto the mattress. Spellbound, I watched as she loosened her towel. It slowly slid off her exquisite body, catching on her hips for a moment before tumbling to the floor. Leslie then grabbed the metal pole with her right hand, placed her left foot at its base, and hooked her right leg around the pole.

"Are you ready for my initial dance?" she asked, wearing nothing but a captivating grin.

It was a silly question.

# ~ FORTY-FOUR ~

We made the transition from island time to our Little Rock routines easier than I'd expected, but my radically revised physical appearance caused more than a few heads to turn when I showed up in the office. Fortunately, I had ditched the stud from my right ear before anyone had a chance to comment. Meanwhile, Leslie's friends seemed to approve her new look although I noticed she chose to wear a ball cap when she ventured outside on her photo assignments. She assured me that, in time, her hair would grow back to its earlier color and length.

A week or so after we'd returned, the *New York Times* ran Channing Creekmore's extensive story on the arrest of Grégoire Delisle, the seizure of the *Vulpecula*, and the busting of one of Europe's major drug rings. Thankfully, neither Leslie nor I were identified in her front-page piece, showing up only as an unidentified couple from the South who'd brought an unusual incident to the attention of Drug Enforcement Administration officials.

An e-mail from DEA Agent Jack Stroble informed us that the Bahamian authorities had arrested the Marchants on a variety of tax-evasion charges. He also shared news that Brock Attleman had been cooperating with the Royal Bahamas Police Force and might escape a prison sentence.

A day or so later we got a postcard from Jonah Jefferson, inviting us to plan a return visit to his rental cottage on Eleuthera for our first anniversary. "I've already reserved it in your names for a full week. My treat! I'll expect a positive reply." While we hadn't yet responded, we both seemed to be leaning in favor of it. I, for one, hadn't gotten my fill of snorkeling. And Leslie admitted to a craving for a plate of conch fritters.

We'd been back in Little Rock about ten days when Leslie's cell phone rang during the dinner hour, one of her pet peeves. She glanced at the screen and I expected her to ignore the call. But she then looked back to me, her eyes wide. "It's Agent Jack Stroble."

"Good evening, sir," she said, answering the call. "This is an unexpected pleasure." After a pause, she added. "Of course. I'll place you on speaker phone at once."

She pressed a button on the phone and set it on the kitchen counter between us.

"Agent Stroble," I said. "This is Randy. Our letter thanking the DEA for its generous gift went out in yesterday's mail."

"Using those funds, we've already hired an architect," Leslie said. "We hope to begin a major home renovation project within the next few months."

"I heard from Mrs. Bruno that you set aside half your reward money for the Bruno youngsters for their college expenses," Stroble said. "What a wonderful act on your part. I cannot tell you how much that meant to me. Needless to say, she's very appreciative."

"Is there any word yet on your former colleague?" I asked. The last we'd heard was that Agent Donnie Bruno had evidently gone into hiding. While it seemed clear that it was Bruno who'd removed the sack of cocaine from Jonah's birdhouse and delivered it to Delisle, there'd been no reports of seeing him since the day he asked Stroble for some time to deal with his alleged family emergency.

"Yes," Stroble said, "at long last we have news about Agent Bruno." There was a long pause. "But it's not good. He's...he's dead."

"I'm so sorry to hear that," Leslie said, as her mouth dropped open. "He was such a young and talented man."

Stroble cleared his throat. "Yes, truly one of life's terrible tragedies."

"What happened?" I asked.

"As you know, Donnie had developed a terrible gambling addiction. He ran up a considerable debt with an illicit syndicate out of southern Florida," Stroble said. "To no one's surprise, there's a lot of overlap between the gambling organizations and the drug-trafficking outfits. They tend, shall we say, to look out for each other's interests."

I didn't like where this conversation seemed to be headed.

"It appears that Donnie's accumulated gambling debts were even far greater than any of us could have ever imagined. Time and again, he'd been warned that repayments were due and there'd be consequences—serious consequences—if he failed to meet his obligations," Stroble said. "But he ignored those warnings and then foolishly piled up even bigger losses."

"It appears you're saying that Donnie Bruno saved Jonah Jefferson's life, but was unable to save his own," I said.

"That's correct," Stroble said. "You may remember in our informal debriefing around the picnic table with Mr. Jefferson that he brought up the term 'hum chum.'"

"Yes," Leslie said, nodding at the phone. "That was Grégoire Delisle's disgusting shorthand for 'human chum.'"

Stroble again cleared his throat. "You may also recall Mr. Jefferson's mention that Delisle had arranged for a demonstration of the 'hum chum' technique to his new friend from Colombia, Mr. Alarico Villarreal."

I suddenly felt sick to my stomach.

"Surely, you're not telling us that's how Donnie Bruno died?" asked Leslie.

"I'm afraid that's exactly how he was killed," Stroble said. "One of Delisle's men has copped a plea, directly implicating his boss in the execution of DEA Agent Bruno. While Alarico Villarreal watched, Grégoire Pierre Delisle fed Donnie Bruno to sharks in the Exumas. Formal charges of first-degree murder will be filed tomorrow."

"So, will it be one man's statement against another's?" I asked.

There was another long pause. "No," Stroble finally said. "The murder indictment issued against Grégoire Delisle is based on much more than a written statement. We have obtained a series of disturbing photos from the cell phone of Delisle's chief lieutenant. Included in the mix is a graphic 20-second video clip."

Following a long, awkward silence, Stroble told us his next conversation would be to pass this distressing news along to Channing Creekmore. After once more thanking us for our help in Eleuthera, Stroble ended the call.

"I'm stunned," I said, gazing at Leslie. "I cannot believe what we just heard."

Leslie leaned forward, her elbows on the countertop and her head in her hands. When her face appeared seconds later, tears trickled down her cheeks.

"I can think of one thing that might be appropriate," Leslie said, sniffing. She wiped her face, walked across the kitchen, and opened the door to our liquor cabinet.

"What's that?"

Leslie removed the small bottle containing the last of the Bahamian rum we'd brought back with us and poured two shots, emptying the flask.

"To Donnie Bruno," she offered, raising her drink.

"To Donnie Bruno," I replied. We clinked our shot glasses together.

*The End*

# About the Author

A former partner in a canoe outfitting business on the Buffalo River, Joe David Rice spent a good deal of time roaming the Ozarks during his younger days. And, as Arkansas's tourism director for over 30 years, he gained an unequaled familiarity with the state, its people, and Arkansas's intriguing nuances. A prize-winner in the Ozark Creative Writers Conference, he's also the author of the two-volume *Arkansas Backstories: Quirks, Characters, and Curiosities of the Natural State*. He and his wife Tracey enjoy their cabin in Newton County which backs up to the Buffalo National River's Ponca Wilderness.

*A Piece of Paradise* is the third novel in the Randy Lassiter/Leslie Carlisle series. They meet in the first book, *An Undercurrent of Murder*. Randy and Dr. Gib Yarberry, his brother-in-law, are on a hiking getaway in the Buffalo River country and stumble into Leslie, a professional photographer in the area on an assignment, during their October trek. A chance encounter with a group of desperate drug-runners soon has them fleeing for their lives, battling both Mother Nature and some very bad dudes.

The second book in the trilogy, *A Nasty Way to Die*, finds Leslie and Randy searching for Dr. J.J. Newell, Randy's close friend and soon-to-be best man. Newell, a professor at the local university, has strangely vanished. The hunt for their missing friend leads to something far beyond what they could have imagined.

Made in the USA
Middletown, DE
09 December 2022